RAIN DANCE

RAIN DANCE

Joy DeKok

Mill City Press, Inc.

I dedicate this book to my Redeemer–He lives!
And to Jon–the love of my life

Ezekiel 36:25-26
I will sprinkle clean water on you, and you will be clean; I will cleanse you from all your impurities and from all your idols. I will give you a new heart and put a new spirit in you; I will remove from you your heart of stone and give you a heart of flesh.

CHAPTER 1

Jonica

Life as I knew it ended.

In the waiting room I sat in the front row, hoping the chair next to me would remain empty. A year ago, when we first came to the clinic, hope ruled. The receptionists smiled and welcomed me with friendly small talk.

It didn't bother me that the infertility department was in the same section of the clinic as OB/GYN. I loved watching new moms cradle their little ones wrapped in soft blankets, toddlers by their sides.

Once, while a woman nursed her fussy newborn daughter, I sat on the floor and played Hot Wheels with her three-year-old son. When the nurse called his mom, he grinned at me and said, "Tanks!" as we collected his cars from the floor and put them in his bag. He grabbed his mom's outstretched hand, curling his fingers around two of hers. The reach pulled up his red Pooh T-shirt and his little belly button peeked out. I yearned to feel my child's hand hold fast to mine.

Painful tests, frequent invasive exams, nauseating drugs, terrible periods, and embarrassing questions became my reality.

The gals at the desk no longer chatted-they accepted my appointment card and directed me to sit down. The air filled with baby sounds and smells now made me sick. Bile burned in my aching throat.

I clenched my jaws and begged the Almighty silently, *Please don't let anyone ask, "How far along are you?" I'm tired of telling women with swollen stomachs that I'm here for infertility testing.*

I buried my nose in a magazine that Ben, my husband, had received in the mail and wanted me to read. As I browsed the first few pages, my mind wandered.

I'd made this appointment to tell Dr. Steele we no longer wanted medical intervention to help us conceive. It cost too much in every way. Our health insurance didn't cover any of the testing and we'd paid more than ten thousand dollars with no end in sight. Putting a dollar amount on the changes inside our marriage proved impossible. Our intimate life revolved around my temperature. Charts and a thermometer took the place of candles on the nightstand.

Each month when my flow started, our failure to conceive was once more confirmed. Every cramp slammed the truth home. No success again. *Why have you betrayed me again?* I accused my body. I chastised myself, *you keep messing up.* I defended myself to my internal tormentor, *it isn't my fault.*

Then the cycle started again with the silent hope...*maybe next month...* easing its way back into position.

I didn't want to disappoint Dr. Steele. His raw passion for the work inspired respect and his stern demeanor intimidated me. I longed to be one of his success stories instead of admitting defeat. A high voltage man specializing in invitro fertilization, he focused his energy on finding an answer-he didn't consider quitting an option.

I lifted a silent cry to God. *Infertility is harsh and relentless. Where are You in all of this?* I stiffened my spine and tried to swallow the lump in my throat. I ordered my tears to stay put. This wasn't the time or the place.

I regretted not calling his assistant and leaving a message. Why did I have to see his furrowed brow and hear his certain criticism?

A still small voice said, *"Do not be afraid, but speak, and do not keep silent; for I am with you."*

I knew the Voice but was in the mood to argue. I was so fragile and broken I was sure that nothing I said could possibly help anyone. *Pick someone else!* My heart screamed.

He didn't.

A couple of chairs down, two women talking interrupted my internal babbling. "This blotchy upholstery makes me dizzy. Of course, it could be the morning sickness."

The other huffed as she pushed on her side. "This one won't keep his foot out from under my ribs!"

When a nurse called the woman with the rib tickler, she stood up with a soft grunt and followed the nurse, one hand on her back, the other resting on the mound of unborn baby under her maternity top.

I had dressed in comfortable clothes for the appointment: jeans and my favorite soft pink sweatshirt. The loose fit sometimes hid my flat stomach. In this room I was an oddity-a true outsider.

In a flurry of color and energy, a woman stood in front of the chair next to me. Shiny, jaw-length, layered jet-black hair and jade green eyes sparkled in the clinic lights. Her flat stomach caught my attention and I wondered if she was like me.

"Hi, is anyone sitting here?"

"No."

She sat down and crossed her jeans-clad legs. Her purple silk blouse and short, clear-lacquered nails glistened. The scent of jasmine swirled by then seemed to waft back to her as if unable to bear the separation.

She pushed her hair behind her ears, and silver dangly earrings twinkled. "Hi, I'm Stacie."

"Hello, my name's Jonica."

"Pretty name."

"Thanks."

She pulled a book out of her bag and asked, "So, how far along are you?"

I gave my new answer, "I can't have children."

The statement sounded clipped and whiny, so I added, "We've been coming to the infertility clinic for months, but now I'm here to terminate medical intervention." Instead of confident, the words sounded defensive.

"Can't, but still want to-huh?"

"Yes. But not this way."

She raised a sculpted eyebrow and said, "I'm here to terminate something too-a pregnancy."

She rushed on. "I'm new in a local law practice. My goal is to be a partner one day, representing women and children damaged or wronged by men. A pregnancy right now could hold me back or even halt the process. I need to establish myself first. There's time for a family later-much later. I'm glad we can choose when and if to complete a pregnancy."

She took a deep breath and exhaled, then tightened her lips and turned to her book flipping it open. The light danced off a silver-trimmed boot as her foot began to swing slightly.

Tingles of shock pricked my fingertips and toes. My lips went numb, and my throat constricted. I took a deep breath, and looked down. Her offensive made me want to defend life, but I didn't have the strength. I needed to conserve my energy for my meeting with Dr. Steele.

I flipped a page in my magazine and stopped. Every muscle in my already stressed body tensed. The photo in front of me showed the tiny hand of a pre-born baby resting on a surgeon's finger. The doctor had performed corrective surgery invitro when pre-natal tests confirmed spina bifida.

God, give me the courage to show this to Stacie.

The nurse stepped up to the microphone and called my name. I closed the magazine, offered it to Stacie and said, "I'm done with this, you might find it interesting."

She looked up briefly, took the magazine and tucked it into the outside pocket of her purse.

"Thanks. Nice to meet you."

"Same here."

I followed the nurse down the hall, watching her waist-length auburn braid swish against her straight back, thinking I'd just lied. It wasn't nice to meet her. I could have lived my whole life never having heard her pro-abortion dissertation.

"Dr. Steele will be right in for your consultation. Just have a seat on the couch," the nurse said.

As I waited for the doctor, my dread increased. Dr. Steele was confident we could conceive with a little help from a friend-him. Photographs and thank you letters lined the walls. Smiling parents held babies, celebrated birthday parties, and faces beamed from family pictures.

I remembered the questionnaires we had filled out about our health, motives, and ability to pay. The doctor invited us to add a page about anything we wanted. Ben and I wrote about our faith.

Dr. Steele read it and commented, "I feel much like a creator myself."

Ben said, "We believe in only one Creator."

Our physician shrugged his shoulders and diverted our attention to the first test. He kept all conversations professional from then on despite the intimacy involved in our circumstances, even when disappointment moved me to tears in front of him. I guess that made it easier for all of us.

My damp, cold hands gripped each other in my lap, and my thoughts tip-toed back to the woman in the waiting room. I decided it was time for a brief pity-party.

How could this happen today of all days? I'm saying good bye to a dream and she sits next to me? There's nothing wrong with her goals. All the things she wants to do are good, but she is willingly sacrificing her baby on the altar of achievement. Does she think because abortion is legal all women agree with her? Who was she trying to convince-herself or me? It's not fair. Why can she conceive and I can't?

Before I could battle the subject out further, the door swung open on silent hinges and Dr. Steele entered. His short, bristly gray hair stood straight up. Hazel eyes with amber flecks smiled from behind gold-framed glasses. His yellow smiley-face tie softened his starched shirt, creased trousers, and shiny shoes. A stethoscope hung from his neck.

"Hello, Jonica."

We shook hands, and he sat in his desk chair.

"Where's Ben?" he asked, as he slid a brochure on in vitro fertilization toward me. His chair creaked when he leaned forward. He paused for a moment anticipating an affirmative answer. "We can start anytime you're ready."

A Godzilla-sized cramp squeezed my stomach.

I heard myself say, "Ben and I are done. Our insurance doesn't cover the financial end of it and the emotional costs are far too expensive. We don't want to face the moral and ethical dilemmas that heroic medical methods involve."

All my practice in front of the mirror at home hadn't improved my verbal delivery here either.

He snapped his chair into the upright position. His eyes lit with a golden fire and his lips drew a straight line across his face. He ran his hand through his hair, and let out a loud, slow breath.

"I can't believe an educated and intelligent couple like you and Ben can't see the future in medical science. Why let some outdated religious beliefs keep you from realizing your dreams?"

"God is the Creator of science. He knew you before your conception and gave you life as well as your incredible abilities as a doctor.
He is the One who leads Ben and me in all areas of our lives. We're
uncomfortable with frozen sperm, harvested eggs, and test-tube
babies. We don't want to deal with three to six microscopic
embryos- which we believe are human beings-inserted into my body
and possibly losing them all. Each time we lost even one, we'd grieve.
We've decided to focus our love on the children already in our lives."

"That's quite a sermon."

Suddenly short of breath, I couldn't get a single word out. Cool air
crossed over my tongue so I knew my mouth was open. The sensation
caused a reflex action and I pressed my lips shut.

"I'm sorry you feel this way. My confidence is in human abilities
and science. Many Christian couples come to me for help and are
grateful for our methods." He flipped my file shut and continued,
"What makes you superior to them?"

"We're not better than anyone else-and if it works for others
without guilt, I'm happy for them. It just isn't right for us. I'm sorry I
sounded so defensive. I hate it when I get that way. We made this a
prayerful decision. I hoped you'd accept our choice," I said. "I didn't
want it to end this way."

"This is good-bye then. I wish you the best in your life." He said,
rising to leave.

"Do you ever wonder if you're wrong and God is real?" I asked, also
standing.

He held the door open for me. "I don't need to hear about your
beliefs. I read your forms, and other Christians come here. I've heard
it all before."

I reached into my purse. "I'd like to give you a small gift as my
thanks for your effort to help us."

"Clinic policy doesn't allow us to accept gifts from patients."

"Maybe you'd like to borrow this book from me then?" I handed
him *The Case for Christ*.

"This is a new one!" he muttered, glancing at the back cover.

"I know you're disappointed and so are we. Please know we appreciate your knowledge and the time you spent with us. I'd love to be
able to send you a photo of a little girl that looks like me or a little boy
that looks like Ben celebrating a birthday or Christmas. Without

divine intervention, that's not going to happen." The lump in my throat warned me I was close to tears but I managed to say, "Goodbye Dr. Steele."

The golden flames in his eyes receded. "Good-bye."

I watched him walk away. For all his gruffness and disbelief, I would miss him. He wanted to help us conceive and couldn't. In a way, we'd both just lost. I walked down the hallway in the opposite direction. It was over.

In the waiting room I heard the receptionist call, "Stacie Cutter." She got up and disappeared down the other hall.

I wanted to run, and considered finding the stairs. Instead, I paced while the elevator made a slow climb to my floor. A man on crutches and a woman in a wheelchair shared my descent and got off on different floors along the way down. I dug the keys out of my purse while I speed-walked to the parking ramp. Shaking, I missed the lock on my car door and the key scratched the paint.

Yanking on my seatbelt, I grabbed my payment stub from behind the visor. The tires squealed as I took the tight ramp corners a little faster than usual. *Hold on until you get home*, I commanded my tears.

I paid the smiling man at the booth then, three red lights and two stop signs later, pulled into our driveway. I ran up the sidewalk, unlocked the back door, and threw my purse on the counter.

I stood in the middle of the kitchen floor with both fists clenched so tight my fingernails gouged my palms. My mind registered the pain and then I pressed harder.

I sobbed out loud, "Lord, I'm angry! Why us? We waited for intimacy until marriage; we did what You asked. We love children. We tithe, we pray, we go to church. We believe in You and we always will. Please tell me why You give children to women who will throw them away. Father, I feel so empty!"

Only the ticking clock answered my cry.

God said no. Our dream died, and Ben would always come home to only me.

Stacie

I wanted it to be over.

At the clinic I sat in the gaudy chair next to a natural beauty with just the right amount of shine. The woman's long hair hung in soft, thick waves below her shoulders. Light lemon highlights shimmered among darker blonde tresses. She wore only a clear coat of polish on her rounded nails and sat with her slender legs crossed at the knee. She flipped through a business magazine. We talked for a while. When she told me about her infertility, I blurted out my reason for coming. She stared at me for a moment, eyes opened wide as if in shock, then returned to her magazine.

What in the world is wrong with you? I chided myself. *Why did I tell a complete stranger my life story? What if she's one of those religious anti-abortionists?*

The woman seemed sweet, but tense. She wanted children and couldn't have them. I was pregnant and didn't want to be. Reality as I saw it went this way: when life handed us challenges, we needed a plan and the guts to work it.

As a part-time research assistant I believed my career would soon advance. A little pink on a home pregnancy test didn't change anything.

Mike was out of town on a business trip, but I knew he agreed with my goals. Starting a family right now didn't fit our plan. We wanted a bigger house, nicer cars, and money to travel-freedom.

Hunger for success gnawed at my insides. A law degree and passing the bar exam had begun the process. I wanted to give the abused a voice. I sometimes wondered why I resented men. The guys in my life treated me with love and kindness. I pushed back the question and told myself, *Who cares. Women need you.*

As I waited to be called, my annoyance grew. Sitting idle was never one of my strengths. Even as a kid I hated to wait my turn. I preferred action and if it didn't come my way, I found creative ways to start arguments and if given enough time, fist fights.

What a hassle. Dr. Steele had better know someone who performed abortions and soon. Waiting meant time to think and I'd done enough of that.

I shoved away my niggling nerves and calmed myself with the

reasoning I had learned in health classes at school and at home all my life: "It's your body; your choice. The world is full of unwanted and unloved children. Complete a pregnancy only when the time is right for you. Besides, the world is overpopulated anyway."

The words helped-sort of like a religious mantra, except I didn't believe in God. No church or guilt feelings were going to get in my way. The only creed I knew Eve, my mother, had instilled in me long ago. It involved believing in her, in the superior abilities of women and in my rights. I struggled with the me part. If she was never satisfied with me how could I be? The men in my life adored me. Why wasn't that enough?

Although grudgingly Eve admitted I was beautiful, but even that didn't garner her approval. I could still hear her telling me on my tenth birthday, "Stacie, your beauty can be a handicap or a powerful tool. Men will see you as someone to control and often make their choices based on your appearance. Use your looks to get to the door of success then knock it down with your brain. You must always be in control of your body, mind, and destiny. Reproductive choices belong to you."

The fire in her heart flashed into her jade eyes when she shared the importance of women's rights. Eve's passion. A childish desire bothered the edges of my mind. I longed to be the one she fought for, stood with, and held close. I wanted to be her passion. I didn't even come in second.

She molded me from a distance but with determination. She regarded any and all resistance as rebellion. No free-thinking was allowed. She badgered me with her beliefs as if I were someone to be converted to her cause at all costs. I questioned her only in my mind.

Her strong voice echoed in my memory, "I sacrifice any kind of personal life to make the world a better place for you and all women. As a senator I can stop men from holding women back."

Sometimes I believed her. Most of the time, I just missed her.

I heard the woman next to me breathe in sharply. I thought she was going to say something to me but the nurse called, "Jonica Johnson."

She stood, took a step, then turned back, and offered me her magazine.

My mind wandered again to Eve. Although we enjoyed different styles of clothes and decorating, in the mirror I was her reflection. I hoped when she saw herself in me it helped. I wanted her love, but more than anything I yearned for her to be proud of me. College graduation and passing the bar had worked for a while. But Mike and marriage came between us.

He made enough money as an architect and encouraged me to follow my dreams. Eve insisted that he had a hidden agenda that translated into me to becoming a dependent wife.

"He will insist his ways are your ways," she warned.

Dad enjoyed watching me fall for Mike and get married. He believed our relationship energized me. He was right.

My father allowed Eve to follow her dreams, standing beside her when she asked and apart from her when she didn't. He understood that her job demanded times of separation.

Eve considered my love for Mike a weakness. She didn't want me to need anyone-especially a man. The independence she wanted for me required complete acceptance of her ideology. No wavering or defining my own way - that had been done by the feminists who had gone before me.

In my first big act of rebellion, I planned the wedding. My dad wrote the checks and celebrated my excitement. Eve made an appearance and only enjoyed the day when the press arrived. While she posed and postured, I danced and fantasized about my honeymoon.

I considered telling her about the pregnancy. I knew it would displease her. I could feel her disdain over what she would assume was my lack of physical restraint and my misuse of birth-control. I couldn't tell her we'd used so many products I had no idea how one tiny cell from Mike connected with one from me. She'd take that as a lie and question my intelligence yet again.

Time to talk to her later, after I made the reproductive choice she'd fought so hard for. I wanted to tell Dad, but couldn't stand the possibility he might be happy to be a grandparent. Mother's philosophy drove me on.

I'd craved Eve's acceptance for as long as I could remember. Moving ahead of my class in elementary school and graduating from high school and college early weren't enough. None of my accomplishments satisfied her. She continued to push me on to yet bigger things.

I looked at the time on the watch Eve had given me for college graduation. The silver scales-of-justice charm twinkled in the artificial light. After not reading a single word in my book, I closed it. Jonica came around the corner, clutching her purse as if holding on for dear life. She hesitated as if unsure which direction to go.

The nurse called out, "Stacie Cutter."

I rose and followed her down the hallway, glad for the sterile environment. The room's vinyl couch and medical instruments provided a sense of cold detachment. It was all business here. These things worked for me.

After a brief wait, Dr. Steele entered. "Good morning, Mrs. Cutter."

"Stacie please, Doctor."

He smiled. "What can I do for you today?"

"I'm pregnant and want an abortion."

He asked a few medical questions then, "How far along do you think you are?"

"About eight weeks. I just missed my second period."

He handed me a gown. "Please go into the dressing room and put this on."

Following a short exam, and discussion about my home pregnancy test, he washed his hands and after thoroughly drying them, helped me off the examination table.

"Get dressed, and I'll give you a recommendation."

I put my clothes on and returned to the vinyl couch, its coolness reaching through my jeans.

Dr. Steele handed me a business card. Printed in raised black letters were a doctor's name and the address of a women's clinic.

"Dr. Adams is professional and thorough. I've known her for years."

"Where is this clinic?"

Opening the blind, he pointed. "Right there."

The small brick building across the street had only the number 123 on the solid door. "Why no sign?"

"To try and keep radical pro-lifers from bombing the place. They always seem to find us."

"Has the clinic been threatened?"

"No."

I'd never understood what Eve and others in the pro-choice movement feared. Abortion was legal and although a couple of twisted radicals had attacked clinics, Eve's team seemed to enjoy lumping all their opposition into the same category. It made no sense to me.

On the sidewalk outside the building stood an older couple holding hands, their gray heads bowed.

"Those two are there Monday through Friday."

"They don't look much like mad bombers."

"Beware of wolves in sheep's clothing. Just because it hasn't happened here yet doesn't mean it won't." He snapped the blind shut.

Handing me a booklet, he said, "Here's some information you'll need to prepare for the procedure."

"Thanks."

He opened the door and followed me into the hallway. "Have a nice day, Stacie."

"Thanks. I will. You too." I walked to the elevators, reaching into my purse for my phone. I punched the speed dial number for my office.

"Hi, Monica. I'm on my way in."

Walking up to my navy blue Taurus, I remembered the red Mercedes I had taken for a test drive the week before. "Someday!" I declared as I pressed the unlock button. Shutting the door, I reached for the business card in the side pocket of my purse and dialed again.

While the phone rang, a tiny nagging doubt assailed me and instinct suggested, *maybe you should talk to Mike.*

The receptionist answered. "First Avenue Women's Clinic."

"Hi, this is Stacie Cutter. I need an appointment with Dr. Adams."

"Yes, Stacie, I just spoke with Dr. Steele. We can set up your appointment for Friday morning at nine. Will that work for you?" The voice of doubt silenced.

"Nine on Friday works for me. Will it be done then or later?"

"Dr. Steele will send your records over so the ultrasound and procedure will be done when you get here. Read the materials he gave you, get plenty of rest, and come with an empty stomach. Do you have any other questions?"

"Will I be able to work later on Friday?"

"Most women prefer to take the day off. The decision is up to you. We recommend you don't drive."

As I pulled out of the parking ramp, I recognized the perfect timing-Mike would come home on Saturday to only me.

CHAPTER 2

Jonica

Grieving is hard work.

I wandered around the house for a few days after my appointment with Dr. Steele, unable to think about anything but my sorrow. My body was a restless mass of pins and needles yet I didn't want to go anywhere. Every step felt like I was slogging through mud bogs. While tiredness overwhelmed my mind, sleep evaded me.

Friday I decided to get back into my routine. When the alarm rang, I got out of bed instead of pulling the covers over my head. Ben and I munched on toasted English muffins with peanut butter, and drank hot coffee. We laughed and shared nutty-flavored kisses.

After a long hug, Ben left for work. He popped his head back in for a moment, "I missed you, Joni."

I gave him another kiss-the kind with a promise attached. "Hurry home, Ben."

He winked and shut the door.

Doing dishes, I listened to the radio and splashed water on the floor while lip-syncing to "I Am Woman." When I wiped up the slippery tiles, the song on the radio changed to "Pretty Woman."

What kind of woman was I anyway? Pretty empty. I couldn't even be fruitful and multiply. The familiar heaviness settled in my chest. I heard my voice say, "What a waste of womanhood!"

I poured another cup of coffee and headed for the window seat in our living room. With my legs stretched out and crossed at my ankles I settled in for a sympathy shower in honor of me. On the way I'd gotten a glimpse of myself in a mirror. I couldn't miss the dark circles of sadness resting under my swollen eyes

A Bible verse sparked in my soul. "*You are fearfully and wonderfully made... I knew you before you were formed in your mother's womb.*"

Immediate anger rose in my heart. "So, You knew ahead of time I wasn't going to be able to get pregnant? Why God? Why am I so flawed?"

"*I have a purpose for you. My plans are for you to succeed.*"

"How?"

"*Blessed are those who morn, for they will find comfort.*"

I resisted His invitation to solace. "I am not there yet, Lord. The loss is big and so deep. Accepting the death of my dream as Your plan for me is going to take a supernatural act on Your part. I can't do it."

Tired of thinking about my loss, I got up and dumped out my now cold coffee. Upstairs in my office an unfinished book manuscript waited for me. Perhaps putting some words on paper might help.

Instead, I threw a load of laundry in the dryer, watered the Boston fern on the stair landing, and cleaned the master bathroom. The grandfather clock chimed noon, so I made a tuna sandwich with lots of dill pickles, poured another cup of coffee, and grabbed two chocolate chip cookies.

Setting the lunch tray on the desk, I fired up my computer, read e-mail messages and devoured my sandwich. Munching on a cookie, I looked around the room. Sunshine danced on the sage green walls and rested on my favorite sculpture. A group of pre-school aged children in bronze, holding hands ran together as if celebrating life. I could almost hear their laughter. I hoped the kids who read my books would race head long into each day believing it was meant to be enjoyed. I'd been like that. I missed her - the little girl who skipped and twirled through her days, dreamed big, and giggled out loud. Lately a silent smirk was the best I had to offer.

Then, I thought about her. Stacie. Her face and words hovered in my thoughts.

"God, we are so different."

I pictured us on two sides of the Grand Canyon. A Voice inside me urged, "*Bridge the gap.*"

"Oh for crying out loud! Me? How? Why can't I just spend some time letting my own wound heal? I'm struggling with the fact that everyone will know we can't have children. It hurts and I'm embarrassed. Your Word says children are a blessing from You. Why don't we get blessed? God I'm sick to death of this!"

The words to a childhood jingle skipped across my mind.*Same song...same verse...a little bit louder and a little bit worse.*

A single beam of sunshine settled on the cross hanging on the wall. I contemplated Jesus. Beaten and ridiculed in public, He carried His cross in front of the crowds. People stood around and watched Him die. Some loved Him and others were there to hurl ridicule at Him. He suffered, and everyone knew. So much for thinking I deserved a private time to grieve.

Another Bible verse spoke to me: *"Whatever you do, do it heartily as to the Lord, and not to men, knowing you will receive the reward of the inheritance, for you serve the Lord Christ."*

I tried to resist the conviction of those gentle words but I just couldn't.

"I want to serve You, Lord, even while I'm grieving. Help me care about other people right now when my own circumstances threaten to take over my life."

"Let your gentleness be evident to all. The Lord is near. Do not be anxious about anything, but in everything, by prayer and petition, with thanksgiving, present your requests to God. And the peace of God, which transcends all under-standing, will guard your hearts and your minds in Christ Jesus."

"Thankful for infertility? Are You kidding me?" The sound of my own voice smashed through the stillness and seemed to bounce back at me, the sharp edges piercing my conscience.

I knew obedience was a choice and I wanted to choose rebellion but I was already finding the price too high.

I walked down the hall to our bedroom and knelt at the foot of the bed. As I rested my head on the comforter, an even deeper pain came over me-bigger than my sorrow.

Urgency filled my heart for Stacie, and I prayed, "Please bridge the gap between us. I can't reach out to her on my own, but I can do all things through Christ who strengthens me. I don't know where Stacie is right now Lord, or what she is facing, but I know You do. Please be with her."

I wondered about the little one in her womb and distress flooded my soul. Tears once again overflowed. Would they ever stop?

Stacie

No one warned me about the grief.

Wednesday and Thursday I worked overtime and finished the research on my pending projects. Evenings I walked around the house, listless. Unable to get much rest, I outlined the next week's work.

After tossing and turning most of the night, I got up early on Friday and went for a run. Normally I found each stride exhilarating. The exercise had always cleared my brain, and I loved the feeling of my body moving to its own internal rhythm. Today, instead of feeling energized, my body shook and my stomach rolled. I moved like a robot with metal joints. The ground before me was flat and the air was still. By the time I reached home sweat was pouring down my face, yet I was cold all over. I undressed and turned the shower faucet to hot. I lathered, then rinsed in cold water, hoping the shock would shake loose the weird lethargy taking over my limbs and mind.

I pulled on my jeans and one of Mike's old college sweatshirts then glanced at the information on my reproductive rights and the instructions given me by Dr. Steele. Skipping over the fine print, I regretted not telling anyone about my decision. I brushed my hair and called a cab.

I hurried to a corner several blocks away, where I had asked the dispatcher to send the taxi. I didn't want the doorman to wonder or speculate with the building personnel why I didn't drive myself wherever I was going.

The yellow and black cab pulled up, and I jumped in. Slamming the door, I told the driver the address. He punched down the meter handle, and we pulled out. I wished for tinted windows.

"Five fifty," the cabbie muttered as he wiped some jelly from his donut off the corner of his mouth.

I handed him a ten and said, "Keep the change."

On the sidewalk stood the old couple I had seen from Dr. Steele's office. They smiled at me and then bowed their heads. Angered by their presence, I hurried into the building. "Who do they think they are?" I mumbled not quite to myself.

In the foyer, I let the quiet envelop me before I walked into the waiting room. I was bewildered by my presence there. I'd always pictured clinics like this one full of teenagers who were sexually active too soon, had been careless, and were way too young to parent a child. I didn't see married women who'd taken extra precautions to prevent pregnancy needing these services. Yet, here I was. I realized that abortion had become my newest form of birth control. While I found it offensive, I also accepted it as my truth. I concluded that part of being pro-choice meant always having a way out.

The inner door opened, and a pale young woman exited alone. She walked outside toward the still praying couple. She said something to them and they looked up. I saw her shoulders heave as they took her into their arms. I assumed she had changed her mind. Certainly those two wouldn't welcome anyone with open arms who chose an abortion.

I grabbed the door handle and pulled. It opened with a gentle whoosh. Warm air washed across my face but my heart seemed to stand frozen in my chest. My breaths were shallow and choppy. I worried I might hyperventilate so I took a few deep breaths as I walked to the desk.

The room was empty except for the receptionist, who looked up and said, "Good morning!"

"Hello, I'm Stacie Cutter."

Her nametag, in black capital letters, read "Sandy." She handed me some papers.

"You'll need to sign and return them to me right away."

I skimmed the pages and I signed the forms-even the one agreeing that I'd been offered other options. No one had bothered to explain any alternatives, and I also chose to ignore the part about possible risks. I agreed that I had followed the written instructions given to me, even though I hadn't read them.

Accepting the clipboard back, Sandy asked, "Do you want us to bill your insurance company, or would you rather write a check?"

"A check is fine." The last thing I needed was an insurance claim. The only people I wanted to know were Mike and the doctors involved.

As I paid for the procedure, an image of the woman at the clinic who couldn't get pregnant flitted across my mind, but I forced thoughts of her away. I would never see her again- that situation wasn't my problem.

Sandy thanked me and slid a brochure across the counter. "This contains the recovery information."

I stuffed it into my purse. "How long will it be?"

"The exam and procedure are usually completed in under an hour."

"No, I meant how long will I be waiting?"

A door beside her desk opened and a nurse in teal scrubs asked, "Are you Stacie?"

"I am."

"Come this way, please." Her nametag read "Darla."

I followed her down a narrow hall. Her soft-soled shoes squeaked on the old gray linoleum. Pro-choice posters lined the walls. Propaganda! flitted into my nervous brain. No way! the next thought countered.

We entered a small room with an exam table and two sheet-covered machines near the stirrups.

Darla handed me a gown. "Undress from the waist down, tie this in the back, and take a seat on the table. I'll return in a few minutes."

There was no dressing room so I hurried to change. I could not look at the machines. Instead, I sat on the edge of the exam table and counted floor tiles.

The nurse entered with the doctor. Small and wiry, Dr. Adams shook my hand and told me to lie back.

She lifted my gown and warned, "This gel is cold."

I jumped in spite of her warning.

She rubbed an instrument gently across my abdomen.

Moments later Darla wiped my belly clean, and Dr. Adams said, "We're ready to begin."

"Will I be getting any anesthetic?" I didn't want to feel anything - anywhere.

"You aren't far enough along to need it," the doctor said. "During the procedure, I will dilate your cervix. Then you will hear a loud noise and feel some mild cramping."

She said to the nurse, "Let's get started." Darla helped me scoot to the end of the table and guided my feet into the stirrups. Then she covered my knees with a sheet.

The metal speculum was cold and I stiffened from my toes to my clenched eyes.

The doctor patted my knees and said, "Relax. This part is no different than a normal exam."

I willed my muscles to relax. One by one they obeyed.

"You're going to hear some strange noises right now. It's nothing to be concerned about," the doctor explained when she finished the brief check on me.

As the machine invaded my innermost parts, hot tears slid down my face into my ears and hair. I asked myself silently, *Why do my mother's ways have to be my ways?*

Searing pain and sudden spasms coincided with the whir of the second machine. My whole body shuddered. It hurt. Bad.

"Please-no!" I heard myself cry out.

Darla bent down and whispered in my ear, "It's too late."

The machine whined as it stopped, reminding me of a vacuum cleaner shutting down.

My problem was permanently eliminated. I silently asked no one, *Where is the relief? Why do I feel so alone all of a sudden? Where did this emptiness come from?*

The doctor washed her hands and said, "You may experience some minor cramping and spotting for the next few days. It shouldn't be any worse than your period. Whatever you use for menstrual discomfort will work. If you experience any excessive bleeding or pain, call us." With those words, she left.

The nurse helped me sit up and offered me time to rest in the recovery area.

"I just want to go home, but can you please give me something for the pain?" I asked.

"Take some Tylenol and rest when you get home," she answered. "Here's a pad. You will most likely have some discharge for the next few hours. Get dressed, and you can leave." The door sighed shut behind her.

As I got off the table, some blood dribbled down my leg. A wave of dizziness and nausea assaulted me. On the wall beside the sink was a paper towel holder. I grabbed several of the rough sheets and turned on the cold water. I pressed the damp paper between my legs with one hand hoping I was cleaning up excess fluid from the procedure and not a fresh flow. I held on to the sink with the other hand as blood soaked the wet towels. I hoped this much bleeding was normal.

My reflection in the mirror above the sink stole my breath. *Who is this sad woman?*

I dressed, hoping the pad the nurse had left me wouldn't overflow before I got home. To my relief numbness settled over me as I prepared to leave. I stepped into the empty hall and followed the exit signs. When I reached the front desk I asked Sandy to call me a cab.

I waited in the entryway between the two doors looking out a side window. The old couple stood out there like silent sentries.

The cab pulled up, and I walked past them holding my head up.

I gave the cabbie my address. I could not walk several blocks- I no longer cared what the doorman or anyone else knew. More cramps stabbed my abdomen, and I reassured myself, *You are a woman-you just took advantage of your reproductive rights.*

The driver turned up the sound on his radio. Roy Orbison sang, *"Pretty woman walking down the street . . ."* The emptiness stretched its tentacles from my belly and twisted its way into the core of my being.

I heard my first grade teacher's voice say, "Pretty is as pretty does."

"There is nothing pretty in what I did today!" I whispered to myself.

I handed the cabbie another ten-dollar bill and pushed open my door. A rush of blood exited my body as I stood up. Dizzy and nauseated, I made it through my front door and stumbled past the kitchen to the bathroom, where I attempted to throw up. Dry heaves filled the room. I had fasted yesterday and today. As I stood up a warm liquid ran down my leg.

After replacing the old pad with a fresh one I called the clinic.

"This is Stacie Cutter. May I speak to Dr. Adams, please?"

"Dr. Adams is with another patient. How may I help you?" Sandy asked.

"I'm nauseated and bleeding pretty heavy."

"This sometimes happens. Try lying down with your feet up for a while. If you are still filling a pad every fifteen minutes or less, go to the emergency room."

I rested on the floor with my feet on the couch. Ten minutes later the warm liquid crossed over the barrier. I grabbed the phone and punched in number two on the speed dial.

"Dad?"

"Stacie! What's wrong?"

"This morning a doctor performed an abortion on me. Now, I'm hemorrhaging-can you come right away?"

"Where's Mike?"

"Chicago."

"I'll call an ambulance."

"No. Please, just come."

"I'll be right there."

"Dad? Please don't tell Eve."

I couldn't even get an abortion right-my mother's scorn was the last thing I needed right then.

"I won't."

In the emergency room, a female doctor examined me.

She concluded, "There is no sign of perforation, and the bleeding has stopped. If there is any spotting between now and your next period, see your regular gynecologist. If you start to hemorrhage again, come right back in. Here is a prescription for a stronger painkiller. Get some extra rest the next couple of days, and keep your feet up as much as possible."

A nurse helped me off the gurney. "Your dad is getting the car. When you're dressed, I'll walk you out to the entry."

Dad waited in my living room while I changed into soft gray sweats.

"I'm so tired."

"Where's your quilt?"

"On the top shelf of the front closet."

He brought the stitched blanket and a pillow to the couch. Tucking me in he said, "I love you, Stacie."

"I love you too, Daddy." The little-girl term of endearment felt right. I breathed deep of his cologne as he brushed my forehead with a kiss. As rich as he was, he still wore English Leather. Somehow it came to represent his steadfast spirit.

"Does Mike know about the abortion?"

"No."

"Are you sure that was a good idea?"

"He'll be fine with it."

"I hope you're right. I don't want to leave you alone, but I need to go pick up your mother. Do you want me to stop back later?"

"No need. After some sleep I'll be good as new."

He closed the door.

I asked an empty room, "Why don't they tell you getting an abortion is hard? That you might change your mind too late? That it hurts in more ways than one? And why, if it's legal, do I feel so awful? I don't do guilt!"

I wanted to cry but couldn't. The desire for tears scared me and the emotional pain confused me far more than the physical experience.

I begged the misery to stop its relentless invasion.

It didn't.

CHAPTER 3

Jonica

Sleep eluded me on Monday morning so I got up.

I wondered about Stacie again and wished she'd stay out of my mind. As I cleaned the house, I wanted to pray but questions distracted me.

Did she get the abortion? Did she throw her baby away?

She was just one big interruption.

My stomach burned as anger worked its way deeper and I started flinging the same old questions at God. Since He hadn't answered I decided I'd keep asking.

"Why do You give some people children who don't want them and withhold the blessing from us? It's not fair!"

"I rain on the just and the unjust."

I'd heard sermons on the subject and didn't want to continue this discourse with the Divine.

The phone rang, and the old cliché saved by the bell rang true in my life - or so I thought. The caller ID showed Ben's sisters, number.

"Hello, Natalie."

"Well?" her voice demanded.

"Well what?"

"Come on, Jonica-how did it go with Dr. Steele?"

"You know Ben and I decided not to pursue any more testing or heroic methods." I wanted to go back to bed-no one asked me questions there.

"That's ridiculous! A couple in our church conceived and delivered two beautiful children because of the new conception methods.

What's wrong with you?"

I clenched my free hand into a tight fist and my nails pressed into my already bruised palm. I couldn't seem to release my digits enough to get relief.

"Remember, Ben and I agreed on this before we started infertility testing."

"If God gave humans this knowledge, He must expect us to take advantage of it."

"There are too many moral questions we are uncomfortable with." Glad for cordless phones, I paced from room to room while we talked.

"Like what?"

I fought anger and the temptation to hang up.

"We've talked about this before. If three fertilized eggs are placed in my womb and two don't attach, they die right?"

"You think too much."

"These kinds of decisions require thought. We're accountable for our choices. Besides, we can love and spoil your boys even more."

I expected this comment to move us in another, more positive direction. Natalie and Dave often shared their family times as well as the joys and challenges of parenthood with us.

"That really bugs me. You cannot think for one minute that caring for my kids will make up for not having your own. They may look a lot like Ben, but they are not your kids."

"Natalie, please. You know we love being aunt and uncle to your boys. We don't ever cross the line of even pretending for a moment they are more to us or we to them. Don't choose to misunderstand."

Then she hit me with, "Are you sure this is what my brother wants? He loves kids and would be a great dad. Why aren't you willing to give him this when you know how much it means to him?"

"You know Ben and I are in agreement on this . . ." The words came out in a hiss as I tried to keep from saying what I was thinking. The fact she thought I'd intentionally hurt Ben this way almost justified the verbal return attack waiting to slip off the tip of my tongue. Before I could give the words their marching orders, she continued her assault.

"Yeah well 'Miss I Get Whatever I Want,' I'm not so sure about that. He'd do and say anything to please you."

Had she missed the fact that I'd never get the one thing I wanted more than anything - Ben's babies?

"Wait a minute..."

Her slams continued as if I'd said nothing. "Besides, I'm not sure if I can even trust you with our boys anymore."

All the air rushed out of my lungs and I couldn't catch a new breath. The sensation reminded me of the day in second grade when I fell off the swing and landed flat on my back. Unable to get up, I stayed on the ground gasping for air sure I was going to die.

"Why?" I whispered as a tiny amount of oxygen entered my lungs.

"You are not a mother-you won't understand their needs. And besides, I don't want you acting like a second mother to them. They have a mother-me!"

I exhaled as the ache sweeping across my heart plunged its way into my stomach. My body shook in an avalanche of anger.

"I need to go, Natalie. We'll talk later."

I threw the phone on the bed, stomped to my dresser sobbing, and started sorting socks and refolding T-shirts, thankful for the mindless task. "Who is she to judge me?" I growled out loud. "God, I'm tired of focusing on getting pregnant. I'm sick of waiting for the perfect day when kids will make us a real family. A man and woman are a family."

"...*from the beginning I created them to complete each other.*"

Anger drained out of me as if someone had pulled the plug in a full sink. God agreed with me.

I looked at the paraphernalia on my nightstand. I gathered up the thermometer and graphs we had faithfully used to determine the right time to get pregnant. We're finished. Relief surged though my body as I threw them away. I blew my nose and washed my face. Exhaustion replaced all emotion. The clock read ten o'clock-too early for a nap-but I crawled under the quilt on our bed anyway.

"Please give me rest," I begged.

"Joni?" Ben's deep voice reached into my sleep. "Honey-it's noon. Are you hungry?"

"Do I smell pizza or am I dreaming?"

"I picked up your favorite on the way home-beef with green olives and extra cheese."

"What's up? You don't come home for lunch. If I'd known, I could have fixed us something."

"Natalie emailed me at the office and told me about your discussion. I tried to call, but you didn't answer. I thought you might have gone for a walk."

I threw back the comforter and stomped downstairs, not bothering to straighten up the bed. Slamming paper plates and napkins on the table, I said, "Ben, I cannot talk to you about your sister right now. What do you want to drink?"

Watching the cola foam over the ice, I felt Ben's arms reach around my waist from behind me.

"Honey, I not only brought you food, I bring you my love. We made a very personal decision after a lot of prayer and soul searching. We knew not everyone would understand. Remember? The most important thing is we know we are doing what's right for us - we made a choice we can live with."

I turned and rested my head on his shoulder. His words washed over me like a healing balm.

He continued, "I'm offended too, but Natalie's biggest personal fear right now is of getting pregnant again. She can't understand because we're different than what she defines as normal. Our struggle frightens her - she can't wrap her head around it. In ignorance, she said things no one has a right to. And she may be a little threatened by your relationship with the boys. They adore you. I don't expect you to talk to her if you don't want to. I made sure she's very aware that when she hurts you she hurts me. I love my sister, and I know she reacts to fear by getting angry. Joni, you and I can't control her response to our choice or let her cruel comments steal our peace."

"Ben, I'm afraid."

"Of what?"

"People will think you should have married someone else-a woman who could give you sons and daughters."

Holding me back and looking into my eyes, Ben said, "Jonica, don't you think I fear the same thing? We didn't get conclusive answers. Is there something wrong with me-some genetic flaw? I hate the thought. Then I pray it is me-so you don't carry any guilt or shame. I sometimes wonder if you'd be happier with another man-one who could give you the children you long for."

"No, Ben! You are the love of my life. The man God blessed me with. Please know that our marriage is His greatest gift to me after my salvation."

"I feel the same way about you. I promise to chase the doubts away when they sneak in and threaten my joy. Will you do the same?"

"I'm glad I get to be your wife," I muttered into his shoulder.

"Me too but, Sweetheart, I'm hungry," he whispered into my hair as his stomach grumbled.

The pizza tasted good. I watched Ben eat and drink with enthusiasm as he does all things. He smiled at me over his fourth piece of Italian pie.

I knew I was blessed. My body no longer shook in anger. Now my insides quivered with desire.

"It's time to get back to work. Will you be all right?" Ben asked.

I tried to calm my passion but promised myself, "Later he is so mine!" Out loud I said what he needed to hear at that moment. "Yes. I'll clean up here and get some writing done."

As I did our lunch dishes by stuffing them in the wastebasket, the doorbell rang. My mind raced when I looked through the window and saw her face, still beautiful, but marred by a flood of tears. She turned to leave.

"No, Stacie! Please!" I cried yanking the door open.

I grabbed her arm and pulled her into the house. I kicked the door shut and turned to her.

She sobbed. "I made a mistake. I don't want to be here."

"Why did you come?"

A sudden fire ignited deep emerald flecks in her eyes and she said, "How could you? What kind of person are you? Who gave you the right to push your beliefs in my face?"

"I don't know what you're talking about."

"The magazine article . . . and now my husband left me."

Her knees gave way and she melted to the floor. Kneeling beside her, I took her into my arms. Her strength gone, she leaned in.

"I know why I came here but I don't know what I'm doing here. Everything is so different now."

"You are always welcome in my home," I promised, sure it was the right answer.

"I went ahead with the abortion. Am I still welcome?"

Her words jangled my nerves. I held her away from me for a moment and saw her eyes flash a challenge at me.

My soul cried out, No! yet I heard my voice say, "You are still welcome. I didn't give you the magazine to torment you. I hoped it might change your mind before you went through with an abortion. I don't know how to help you, but I'm going to pray for both of us right now.

"Dear Father, we are confused and hurting. Our hearts are filled with grieving and at this moment, we are both childless . . ."

Stacie

Still tucked in but not able to sleep, I practiced out loud what I'd say to Mike when he got home. I knew he wasn't going to like that I had made this decision without him. I focused on the lessons from my mother. She taught me that abortion was a simple removal of tissue-nothing more or less. A woman's right to choose belonged to her and no one else.

I asked aloud, "With such a strong mother, how did I get to be such a wimp?"

My brain refused to think anymore and I gave in to the exhaustion. I welcomed the opportunity to shut down, and I surrendered as sleep over took me.

"Stacie?"

"Mike. Are you home or am I dreaming?"

"I'm here. What's wrong?"

"I'm not feeling good."

"The flu?"

"No. Not exactly." I watched his eyebrows raise.

"Your cheeks are flushed. Do you have a fever?"

"I'm fine. I just had an abortion."

I waited for him to hold me close. Instead, he moved away.

"When?"

I sat up. His terse response sent tingles of shock through my body.

"Yesterday I think. Yeah. Friday. Since you're home, I guess I slept all night and most of today."

"Why didn't you wait for me?"

"I made a reproductive decision. It's no big deal. We aren't ready for a family. There are so many things we want to do before we're committed to caring for children and investing in their future. Besides, it's my body and my choice!"

The reasonable discussion I'd hoped we'd have never got started. My tirade went too fast and I'd given him no warning. Why? Something in our marriage altered. My life spiraled out of control with the speed of a tornado, leaving piles of emotional debris in its wake. My verbal defense left me breathless.

"Why are you still resting?"

"I needed to go to the emergency room."

"How serious are your complications?"

"There aren't any. I bled a little and need some extra rest is all."

"Did you consider all the risks, Stacie?"

"Risks? It's a simple procedure."

"What about the possibility of infertility and increased risk of breast cancer?"

"When did you start listening to anti-abortion propaganda?"

"Those are facts. And because of the increase in malpractice suits, many doctors are no longer willing to perform abortions."

"So! You're one of them now?"

"I don't know what I am. Confused for sure. You were pregnant. It's your body, but it was our child. I feel left out of one of the most important choices you will ever make. Marriage is a partnership and for it to succeed, we need to make decisions together. I'm sorry you aren't feeling good. I'm even more sorry you didn't trust me enough to share this with me."

"A partnership. Just like your parents right?"

"Yeah. They talk. About everything. They make decisions together, and they trust each other. I know you see them as old-fashioned-even laughable. But they are solid, and their marriage is vital." He paused and pushed his hands through his thick brown hair. "Are you sure you're going to be okay?"

He stood and backed away, keeping his eyes focused on the floor.

"I'm fine. Where are you going?"

"To work."

I watched him pick up his suitcase and stand in the doorway. Fear skipped across my insides.

"You need your clothes at the office?"

"I need time to think. Until this moment I had no idea I felt this way about abortion. Other than watching your dad for years, I had no clue a man could feel so left out of his wife's life."

I let my growing panic dissolve into anger. "Leave my parents out of this."

"Like you left me out of your decision?"

"I made the right choice for me."

"What about us?"

"How can there be an 'us' if you run away?"

His eyes met mine. Anger and mistrust mingled with something even more frightening-hurt. Everything I saw there scared me.

"I'll get a room and call you later. You have my cell phone number if you need anything."

My heart pounded so loud I didn't hear the front door close. I shouted to an empty room, "Who are you to judge me?"

For the next two days, anger propelled me. Nights with him gone bothered me more than I expected. Mike sent an email letting me know where he was staying, asking me to call if I needed him. Instead, I sat by the phone waiting for him to call admitting he was wrong and asking when he could come back to me.

The phone didn't ring.

Monday morning I planned to work at home. I pulled the research briefs from my purse and a magazine fell to the floor. The address label read Ben Johnson. The woman beside me at the clinic had given me this.

I poured a cup of coffee and stood at the kitchen counter thumbing through the colorful pages. There wasn't anything but old news until I saw the picture.

Out of an incision in a woman's belly a baby's minute hand rested on a surgeon's gloved hand. Pain stabbed the tips of my fingers and toes. I slumped on a stool and read the article. An ultrasound and tests had shown the presence of a birth defect which the doctor attempted to correct invitro. Anesthetized with his mother, he could not reach out to touch the doctor, so the doctor gently reached in and brought out his hand for the photographer. Five perfect fingers branded themselves on my brain.

A longing for the fetus now gone flooded my body and soul. I threw the magazine across the room and raged, "How dare she? Who does she think she is anyway? These anti-abortionists will use anything to get in our way. Abortion is legal. It is my right to choose. Just my luck to meet up with a radical, right-wing fanatic."

Fury turned to cold malice. For the next few seconds I found some creative verbal ways to condemn all religious know-it-alls who didn't know anything. I had marched against them with my mother as a little girl outside the White House and met the national leaders of the pro-choice movement. I decided to face this woman in person and let her know that her prejudice and judgment were not welcome in my life.

I tore the label off the magazine and grabbed my purse. Every light between my house and hers turned red making my mood even worse. I pounded the steering wheel and exceeded the speed limit. I didn't realize I was crying until I punched her doorbell button. Embarrassed by my tears, I turned away, wondering if I'd completely lost my mind.

Her hands gently pulled me in and my rage again found its voice. I don't remember all I said, but I felt the words leave my mouth like tiny bullets intended to inflict maximum injury. I wanted to wound her; to smear my anguish all over her.

I believed I was slinging the ultimate challenge at her. Her rejection would prove I was right about her kind.

Her welcome startled me. So did her next move. The truth cleared my mind as she prayed.

My childlessness became real.

CHAPTER 4

Jonica

Stacie's sobbing slowed to gulps. On her gray sweatshirt I saw a damp circle of my tears. On my shoulder a wet spot cooled the skin under my blouse.

"Let me get a box of tissues," I said.

Walking into the kitchen, butterflies danced in my stomach. What's up here?

We blew our noses and then just looked at each other. It's funny the details you notice in a moment of silence. She'd rolled up the sleeves of her huge sweatshirt and I watched her yank up her over-sized jeans. It looked like she'd lost weight in the few days since we'd met. Without makeup, her eyes and nose red, her hair uncombed, she still looked beautiful. She stuffed the used tissue into her pocket and I noticed her hands. It looked like she'd picked the polish off.

"Now what?" she asked.

"Would you like a tour of the house?"

"Sure."

Moving was better than standing and staring at each other. When we walked through the living room and into the dining room she stopped in front of my new shadow box.

"What's all this silverware mean?" she asked.

"It's sort of a family tree. The top group belonged to my great-grandparents. These were a wedding present to my grandparents. The next set belonged to my folks and these to Ben's. We were given these as a wedding present."

She studied the utensils for a moment longer, shoving her hands back in her pockets as if unsure what else to do with them.

"Let's go upstairs and I'll show you my office. I don't think I told you-I'm a writer."

"That's nice but what do you do career-wise?"

"I write." I sighed to myself as we climbed the stairs. Her response was the norm. Writing is often seen as a hobby. I hoped she'd see a professional when she looked into my office.

She asked about the big scrapbooks stacked on the floor. I explained how I sometimes worked with troubled kids in schools and churches and led them into writing as a way to help express their struggles. Often the kids stayed in touch. Sometimes they sent me notes or copies of essays they'd written. I kept them because every time I read them, they taught me something.

Then she noticed the frames.

"Book covers."

"Yeah. I let them motivate me when I'm stuck, discouraged, or getting rejected."

"These are the covers of your books."

"They take my breath away every day I walk in here. Kids all over are enjoying the stories I write. It's both wonderful and weird. You work hard and the dream comes true but you can't believe your words reach into so many lives."

We continued the tour.

I chattered and she nodded, her eyes moving over each room taking in details as fast as she could. I tried to shut the door to the little room next to our bedroom but she caught my hand.

"Who sleeps here?" she asked, stepping into the taupe and white room.

"It was going to be the nursery. I was so sure." Shame washed over me again for jumping so far ahead and decorating for a baby I'd never have.

She lingered in the room of dead dreams while I stood in the hallway. When she stepped out, I shut the door. The quiet click reminded me this chapter of my life was finished.

For a moment we didn't speak. There aren't words for that kind of pain. Relief washed over me as we started downstairs. How could she possibly understand my hopelessness? At least she knew she could conceive.

In the kitchen I offered, "How about a fresh cup of coffee?"

"Sounds good."

"Feel free to make yourself at home."

As I ground hazelnut-flavored beans and poured water into the coffeemaker, she wandered into the dining room again. I pulled out oversized plum-colored mugs, sugar, cream and put a few homemade cookies on a plate.

I jumped when I heard her voice behind me. She held her arms crossed as far around herself as they'd reach. "I'm cold."

For the first time I noticed her feet-bare inside damp, paint-spattered sneakers.

"Wait here-I'll get you a pair of socks."

A blush rose in her cheeks and she looked down. "I don't think I've ever gone out of the house looking like this."

"Stacie, you look sensational-even ratty."

I heard her choke out what sounded like it might be a giggle as I ran upstairs.

I found her in the living room holding my Amish quilt.

"Who made this?"

"I bought it from a Mennonite woman. She lives just east of here and her name is Jenny. Her signature is on the reverse side."

"I know her. She's my aunt. I have one like it."

"No way!"

"Yeah."

"Is this cool or what?"

"Or what."

She set the quilt down and took the socks. I noticed she'd slipped off her shoes and put them by the door. Her toenails shimmered with burgundy polish. What would she think if she knew I wore Crimson Rose on mine?

I hurried to the kitchen when I heard the coffeemaker gurgle at the end of its brewing cycle. "I'll be right back."

In the kitchen I picked up my silent dialogue with God again. *What can I say to her?*

Let Your light shine.

My shine feels a little tarnished. Please let her see You in spite of me.

"I hope you like double chocolate chip cookies." I said.

She grinned, flashed her hand at me so that a large marquis-cut diamond caught the light, and said, "Next to diamonds-chocolate is a girl's best friend."

"A woman after my own heart."

We both yummed in delight as the hot coffee melted the chocolate in our mouths then peeked over our steaming mugs at each other.

"You got books!" She smirked and pointed at my overflowing bookcases.

"I do," I admitted looking at the collection that displayed my love of words. I don't watch much TV. I prefer reading books and watching old movies."

"Me too. I collect the oldies-Roman Holiday, The Bishop's Wife, and White Christmas . . ."

"The African Queen, The King and I . . . next time you come, let's plan a movie marathon!"

"With buttered popcorn."

"You're on."

We sipped our coffee in silence for a moment. It wasn't comfortable or uncomfortable-it just was.

"Do I see Koontz and Grisham on that shelf?"

"You do."

"I like them too but I assumed you'd be more into religious books."

"I read books on faith, but I also enjoy being scared spit-less by Koontz now and then."

I was amused by the unspoken questions I knew danced in her curious thoughts. In her mind, she had put me in a box I didn't fit into.

"So have you read the latest Grisham?" she asked.

"Yes. Have you?"

"No, but it's waiting for me at home under a pile of paperwork."

We shared another quiet moment before she set her mug down. "Speaking of home, I'd better go."

"Do you think we could meet for lunch soon?" *For Pete's sake - why did I say that?*

"Sure. When and where?"

Her answer zinged through me and her eyes looked as startled as I felt.

"Do you like Chinese or Italian, and how about Tuesday?"

"One o'clock at Wong's sound good?"

"Works for me."

"All right then."

She walked across the room and slid her feet into her shoes. "I'll return the socks Tuesday."

I opened the door and there sat her car with its front tire up on the curb. I giggled. "In a hurry to get here, huh?"

She blushed. "See ya, Jonica."

"Bye."

I shut the door after watching her pull away. Our differences stood between us like silent sentinels, but our similarities shimmered like stars on a country sky-they were everywhere.

I couldn't wait to tell Ben.

Stacie

The tears I couldn't release at home poured out of me like flood-waters over a broken dam.

Jonica held me in a gentle hug and I found myself wondering how a stranger's embrace could be comforting. I'd have lingered but, my nose started to run and I needed something besides her shoulder to wipe it on.

I realized no one had touched me since my dad brought me home from the ER. I decided it was not time to go there in my mind, so I turned my attention to her living room.

Sunshine danced off the polished wood floor-just right for little stockinged feet to slide across. Multi-colored braided rugs and a bright quilt added color. Mission furniture with dark green leather cushions sat at friendly angles, inviting conversation, and a fire burned in the fireplace. She handed me the tissue box and we blew our noses in unison.

Where did my anger go? It evaporated like the morning fog as the sun burned it away.

She asked if I wanted to see the house. I did. I knew each room would reveal to me a little bit more about this woman.

Ivory doilies and vases full of silk sunflowers, blue delphinium, pink roses, and white daisies softened the masculine furniture. Sage green candles that smelled like men's aftershave, the gentle gong of the grandfather clock, and the faint smell of pizza all made it feel like a home. In the dining room the story of the shadow box full of silverware intrigued me.

I didn't expect her to have a real office. In the short trip upstairs I'd envisioned a hobby room. Instead a built-in desk wrapped its way around two of the walls and held a pc with a large flat screen. On the counter above several lengths of file drawers sat a fax machine and a copier. I noticed her date book was full of highlighting and post-it-notes. A large whiteboard covered one side of the room. Here she was planning the timeline for a book.

The other wall held her framed book covers. I was a little embarrassed when I discovered she was a published author but let myself off the hook. After all, I didn't do the children's section of the bookstore.

The only other artwork was a large bronze statue of some children. The woman loved kids. Of course there was a cross - not really art - but a silent symbol of her faith. There it hung; empty, wooden, haunting, and somehow beautiful. That and her open Bible confirmed my suspicions. A Christian. Most likely a God-lover and an abortion-hater.

She led me through each room, talking as we went. She noticed my raised eyebrows when I saw a room with twin beds and racecar comforters.

"This is where our nephews sleep when they come for overnighters."

The other guest room bid me welcome. A chair nestled into the corner where an antique end table held a lamp. Another quilt covered the queen-sized bed, and white walls made the room both light and bright with sunshine filtering in through the lace curtains.

I liked the master bedroom best. Deep plum, soft tangerine, and sage green velvet blended in a soft swirl in the comforter. A painting of a man's hand placing a wedding band on a woman's finger hung above the bed. A sculpture of two hands entwined was more sensual than the most blatant art I'd ever appreciated. This room was about a whole lot more than pro-creating. Everything in this space said: lovers.

A bow window matched the one in the living room directly below us. Two overstuffed chairs filled the space, one a deep plum leather wingback, the other a match for the comforter. The cushions in both were slightly indented and appeared to be saving the sitters' places. A stack of books sat beside each one. Even here, in this cozy setting, romance resided.

She tried to hide the little room from me. I didn't let her. For some reason I needed to know everything I could about her. Stepping inside almost undid me. A room sat ready for a child who would never come. Pictures of Jesus with little children around Him hung on the walls. The colors were warm and neutral - unlike any I'd normally attach to a nursery, and yet they were perfect. A shadow of her grief walked over my heart. *Why did her situation bother me so much?* Before my feelings slipped again, we left the sunny room and hurried down the stairs.

I wandered into the dining room while Jonica fixed coffee. I stood again in front of the shadow box and shivered. It ends here.

Goose bumps stood at attention on my skin. Between the cold and my nerves I felt my teeth start to chatter. I went to the kitchen and told Jonica about my chilly condition. She got me a warm pair of athletic socks. I had forgotten my coat and wore only my old deck shoes. Splotches of teal, purple, gold, and black paint stained the once white canvas, evidence of the time we redid our bedroom and bathroom. I was pretty sure I looked like a street person. For a moment I worried what Eve would say if I ran into her. I decided that would be no problem. She'd never recognize me.

Jonica said I looked beautiful and meant it. What did she see I couldn't?

We ate homemade cookies, drank coffee, and talked. I sat there thinking about my misplaced mission. I'd come with one goal - to cause her harm. Then it dawned on me. After days of feeling lousy, I felt safe.

This is supposed to be the enemy's camp-I should flee before I'm taken prisoner of war. Yet my own home offered me none of the comfort I found here.

Although her house was full of beautiful things, I knew it wasn't her stuff. Whatever I was feeling reflected in her home, came from deep inside her and the confidence she had in her marriage.

In that moment the truth nearly crushed my already shattered heart. If Mike never came back to me, I'd never be at home again.

After discussing movies and books, then making a date for lunch, it was time for me to leave. As she opened the door, I heard her giggle at my parked car-a glaring testimony to my anger.

Glancing back at her standing in the doorway, as I turned my key in the ignition, I wondered, *How can we be so vastly different and yet so surprisingly similar?* I wanted to call Mike, and the anger at Jonica flared once more. I knew it wasn't her fault, and just knowing that made me angrier. Someone had to be to blame for my loneliness.

I had no one to tell.

CHAPTER 5

Jonica

"Joni, you look like a cocoon wrapped up in there."

I woke up to Ben tugging the blanket away from my body.

"Let me stay until I'm a butterfly then," I mumbled, pulling back.

"Nope. It's time for our walk."

"Ben, it's still dark out! Why can't we go when the sun comes up?"

"I have a breakfast appointment, and isn't this your day for lunch with Stacie?"

This was the day. Adrenaline rushed my veins and my hit feet the floor. Pulling on my socks and sweats, I sang, "Jeremiah was a bull-frog..." After brushing my hair into a ponytail I announced, "I'm ready."

I chattered during the whole walk. Ben agreed or squeezed my hand at the right times. The hope of sharing my faith with Stacie sent ripples of hyperenergy through my body. We finished our walk earlier than normal.

While Ben showered and dressed, I dusted the furniture on the main level, singing along to a Rich Mullins CD, and sliding on our wood floors in my stocking feet from tables to shelves.

"Joni, I'm leaving."

I glided into Ben's arms for a kiss. Holding me close, he nuzzled my neck and whispered, "I love you and will keep your time with Stacie in my prayers."

As soon as the door shut behind him I ate a bowl of Grape Nuts then raced upstairs. After making the bed and dusting the second floor furniture, I showered then French braided my hair and applied my makeup with extra care. I put on pressed black jeans and a teal silk blouse. Dressed and ready to go, I checked the time. Ten o'clock. Shoot. I liked to be early but this neared ridiculous.

I curled up in my chair in our room, snuggling into its oversized comfort. I picked up my Bible and study book. The truth in first Corinthians 15:58 tap-danced across my mind: "Therefore, my beloved brethren, be steadfast, immovable, always abounding in the work of the Lord, knowing that your labor is not in vain in the Lord."

Relief flooded my soul. If I remained true to God and did what I knew He'd called me to do, the effort wouldn't be wasted.

I wandered into my office. Firing up my computer and printer, I sat at my desk and set the timer. Getting lost in my work was easy and I didn't want to miss this lunch date.

When the alarm went off, I slipped on my shoes, shrugged into my black blazer, and grabbed my purse. On the way to the restaurant, I wondered for the first time if she would come. *Oh Lord, please!*

I fed the meter and turned to walk the block to the restaurant. There she was, coming from the opposite direction. I knew I'd looked forward to seeing her but the love-fest taking place in my heart made even me uncomfortable.

"I'm so glad to see you!" I said.

I saw her body stiffen and knew my enthusiasm had put her off. I vowed to be more careful.

The hostess led us to a corner booth before Stacie could say anything.

After we ordered, I asked, "How are you?"

I'd expected opposition to my pro-life stand but not my belief system. She let me know she believed Christians were always looking for an opportunity to "preach" and that we were mostly a bunch of hypocrites. I hated the defensive answers that rose to my mind. They were too clichéd. Besides, she wasn't wrong.

"Sometimes we all do things contrary to our core beliefs." I said.

"Perhaps, but I think Christians should live to a higher standard."

"You're right. But how do you know I'm a Christian?"

"It shows."

Our egg rolls arrived and we poured apricot sauce over them in silence. I thought about her saying, "It shows" and a smirk tugged at one corner of my mouth.

"What?" she asked.

"Does it show like a pimple on my face?"

"No. It's like all around you but not visible. It's in you but it shows in your eyes. And I saw the cross in your office and your open Bible."

"Huh. Now, how are you?" I'd ponder her opinion of Christians later.

"You mean the abortion thing?" She asked putting her fork down and tapping her fingernails on the table.

"No. Well, maybe. Just how are you?"

"Okay."

"Okay is good right?" I asked.

"No. Okay is okay."

Our meals arrived and our waitress refilled our coffee cups. I knew I'd crushed a few of the egg shells I was walking on.

"Tell me about your work." I said.

I watched a light go on in her eyes. "Are you sure? This is one thing I can talk about for hours."

Looking at my watch I said, "Ready, set, go!"

And she did. Her zeal for helping women and especially children ran deep. How could a woman who loved them this much get an abortion? Her passion was so evident that, like me, she could not hold it in.

She closed with, "I'm building relationships with counselors, doctors, psychologists, social workers, and advocates. Right now I'm not doing any courtroom work. I'm little more than a highly educated assistant in a firm specializing in corporate law. I do their research. But someday I will be in there fighting and will have a team of experts behind me. I will be unbeatable!"

She took a deep breath and sat back. My plate was clean and hers was barely touched.

"Your turn," she said.

"You know I write."

"Another warm up?" the waitress asked, proffering the coffee pot.

"Yes," we replied in unison.

"What does that mean-you write? What does it feel like to be published?"

Now I was off and running. I talked about ideas, rough drafts, and rejections through three more cups of coffee. When Stacie pushed away her empty plate, I took a breath. The waitress brought our bill and I insisted on paying.

"It was my idea."

All right, but next time, it's mine."

I hoped there would be a next time.

"What are you doing with the rest of your day?" I asked.

Looking at her watch she said, "I'm glad I took the afternoon off. Do you realize we've sat here for two hours?"

"Time flies. Are you up to risking a caffeine-high?"

"What do you have in mind?"

"I'm in need of a new book to read, and Barnes and Noble is just down the street, and they have a Starbucks."

"You're on!"

We walked to the bookstore window shopping along the way. In Barnes & Noble we browsed, visited, and drank coffee for another two hours. She liked vanilla cream and I ordered a mocha latte.

When we parted, Stacie held her arms open and hugged me briefly. I returned the embrace as if her action hadn't shocked me, then handed her my business card and asked for hers.

"Call me," Stacie said.

"You too."

Could this be the start of something beyond a mere acquaintance - maybe a friendship? Or was she just offering the standard response?

As I drove away, a deep sadness engulfed me. Not once had I shared my faith with her.

Stacie

Getting out of bed all I could think of was, *"There is no way I'm going to waste an hour having lunch with her."*

I'd made the same promise to myself every day and wrote on a post-it note, "Call Jonica and cancel." I didn't. Instead I moved the yellow sticky from one page to another in my date book. I ran different excuses through my mind but they all sounded so chicken-hearted.

Walking to the restaurant, I hoped something had come up in her life and she wouldn't show. But no, there she was walking toward me from the other direction.

She seemed so glad to see me I was sure she was going to hug me. That was not on my agenda for the day. I couldn't figure out why was she so happy to see me unless she didn't want to miss a chance to evangelize me. I stiffened and took a slight step to the side.

We were saved by an efficient hostess who greeted and seated us, then showed Jonica recent photos of her new grandbaby.

"Linda, she's beautiful."

"Do you know her well?" I asked as Linda walked away and the waitress came to the table. "No. We just visit when I come in for lunch."

"Hi, Jonica. Do you want your usual?"

"Hi, Mo. Sounds great."

"What will you have?" Mo asked me.

"An egg roll with extra plum sauce and the Chicken Subgum Combination Plate."

Turning toward the kitchen she said, "It makes it easy for me when you order the same thing. I'll bring your egg rolls right out."

I felt my eyebrows rising as I asked, "You ordered the same thing?"

"Isn't that interesting?" She smiled as if truly delighted.

"More like strange."

"I guess it is."

Her grin seemed a little sly and I knew she was having a great time.

Then she asked how I was.

Her question made me angry. *How am I supposed to be?* I silently charged. My defenses rose. "Do you *really* want to know?" I demanded.

She did and I let her know I wasn't sure about seeing her again.

"Why?"

"I guess I'm wondering when the sermon starts."

"I didn't prepare one."

"I thought your kind was always ready with one."

"What kind?"

"You're religious and pro-life."

"How do you know these things? We've never discussed them."

"I guess part of it is this peace, love, and joy thing you've got going on."

"I'm not sure what you mean because my life is a mess right now. So if you see anything Christian in me - it's God. I'm too worn out to be of any good on my own."

Her answer punctured my anger bubble.

I was no where near okay but I decided it wasn't wrong to lie to her. However, when she accepted it as my answer I regretted it a little. I could have used some sympathy or a brisk debate. I was also relieved. We'd gotten personal so fast I wondered if she could be as safe as she seemed. How could I hold her at a distance when she already knew so much of my story?

I wanted to keep the focus of our discussion on the hypocrisy of the church, but my own stood front and center in my mind demanding an answer to the question, *"How could a legal medical procedure to remove a piece of unviable human tissue depress me?"* There was no escaping it. I missed that piece of tissue and I hated that truth.

Then she asked about my work. Her diversion proved effective.

I talked and let my passion show. I didn't expect her to be genuinely interested, but she gave me her full attention which involved her ears, eyes, and a few perfectly timed nods of her head. She asked intelligent questions, which bewildered me. I'd always considered religious people uneducated- almost feeble minded.

I remember saying, "Wow, you're a good audience."

She said, "You're a captivating speaker."

It was her turn. She told me about the myth of inspiration, the discipline it took to put her seat in the chair, the joy of a completed manuscript, the disappointment and doubt that rejections brought, and her journey to publication.

When lunch was over, we went to the bookstore. We talked and laughed like we'd known each other a long time, which was unlike me. I don't have old friends because I'd built no time in my life to communicate with people on a personal level. Time was to be invested, not wasted. I had contacts, not relationships. Until this day I did it on purpose. *How does she do this?*

We browsed separately and bought our books before meeting back at the comfy chairs in the store. While we sipped our coffee, Jonica pulled two books out of her shopping bag, one about helicopters, the other on guitars.

"It's Ben's dream to build and pilot his own helicopter someday," she said.

"Cool, what does he drive?" It didn't fit with flying, but I asked anyway.

"In the winter his Tahoe, and in the summer his Honda Gold Wing."

"No way. A Christian biker?"

Jonica laughed out loud.

I didn't see the humor. Besides, the sound of her laughter threw me. It was like hearing a new song and someone had turned up the volume. People in the store looked toward us and smiled as if hoping to enjoy the joke with us. Religious nuts were supposed to be boring. Stoic. Living by rigid rules and expecting everyone else to do the same.

Here she was, a published author, her husband rode a cycle, and she could laugh - from her gut - without embarrassment. It gushed out with unfettered joy from deep inside her soul. This woman and her husband did not fit my vision of right-wingers.

"Does he go to any wild biker rallies like Sturgis?"

"He threatens." Then she shocked me again when she said, "I ride with him most of the time."

"So what do you wear?"

"I have a full set of ..."

"Leather?" I interrupted.

"Black."

"Chaps and fringe and boots?"

She nodded while a big smile stretched across her lovely face.

My mind brought up a visual of this woman in a leather jacket and chaps with fringe and I realized my former theories about religious women were falling away. The Christian zealots in my mind covered everything from just below their chin to their ankles in loose, shapeless, prairie dresses. Not only was this one attractive, she was sexy.

"So, you're a 'motorcycle mama?'"

Sadness flickered across her face for just an instant. I hadn't intended to jab her or bring her infertility into the conversation, but I had.

"No but I am a biker babe." She saved the moment with a sassy wink and a kind answer instead of a payback.

It was way too much for my mind to comprehend, so I changed the subject before my prejudice could show any more.

"What does Ben do for a living?"

"He's an insurance agent."

"For real?"

"What did you expect?"

"I don't know. A preacher?"

"Nope. Not his calling."

She opened the book on guitars. Pictures of Jimmy Hendrix, Eric Clapton, and Chet Atkins splashed across the collage-style cover.

"Who's that for?" I asked.

"Ben. He plays the electric guitar in our church band."

"Cool." I muttered. Where did I get the idea Christians were no fun? Maybe the rest of them weren't. I decided she was probably the odd one and it was time to quit trying to figure her out.

I preferred it when the liberals I knew stayed within predictable boundaries. I especially wanted Jonica to color inside the lines...to stay in the mental box I'd built for her.

This chick destroyed my view of conservatives. A woman like her could be dangerous to all Eve lived for. I liked her a little bit more for that.

We drank and read in comfortable silence and watched people. Then walked back to where her car was parked.

I found myself offering her a hug. No one was more stunned than me. Could this woman I once considered a foe become my friend? Or had she already? And if she was, this friendship thing was sneakier than I'd imagined.

We did the socially acceptable thing, and exchanged cards and promises to call. You don't have to mean it, but it sounds good.

When I got back in my car, I saw her socks sat on the front seat, clean and ready to return. Here was a good reason to contact her and maybe see her again.

Driving away, relief washed over me. She had not tried to convert me.

CHAPTER 6

Jonica

Is Della right? Am I harboring a sin and is it hindering me from conceiving?

Sitting in the window seat, I hugged a pillow to my chest, trying to hold in the pain. It didn't work.

Her words echoed through my mind and my stomach somersaulted in response. Until that morning, I'd enjoyed helping clean up the coffee and rolls from the fellowship between Sunday school and the church service. Then Della clobbered me with her cruel message.

"Jonica, the Lord has a message for you and I am compelled to deliver it. God revealed to me there is a sin in your life hindering you from conceiving. When you repent, He will reward you. Children are a blessing from Him. Something in your life is holding Him back."

"No!" I raised my hand like a crossing guard with a stop sign, hoping to hold back her words, as tears filled my eyes.

"Jonica, denial will not help you. Mark my words."

As she opened the door to leave, I watched her floral dress float around her slender legs. She said to Ben who waited for me in the hallway, "You two better hurry or you will be late for church."

"Joni, what's wrong?" Ben asked.

"Can we please go home?"

Without any questions, he took my hand and led me outside. He pressed the unlock button on his key ring and opened the passenger door for me.

"Jonica, you need to tell me what's wrong."

Silent tears rolled down my face and cooled on my collarbone.

"Not here. Please."

I heard the click of my seatbelt locking into place, felt the leather seats warmed by the sunshine, and shuddered as a deep sadness settled into my soul.

As we pulled into our driveway, the tears became sobs. Ben got me inside and steered me toward the couch, sitting beside me. Then the sobs became dry gasps for air. I heard Ben getting me a glass of water. The sound of the ice clinking and water pouring over it calmed me.

"Here, Joni, take a drink."

I took a few slow sips, hoping I wouldn't choke. The heaving in my chest slowed and stopped. Ben handed me a tissue and said, "Blow."

I obeyed. His simple directions beckoned me out of my shock and grief.

Ben sat beside me, took my hands, and said, "Tell me when you're ready."

As I repeated Della's words, my eyes released another wave of hot tears. Ben got up and paced. I watched a quiet anger build in him. His neck turned red and his left eyebrow crooked up. He bit the inside of his mouth, and his normally gentle hands clenched into fists lined with white knuckles.

"Jonica, I can deal with almost anything-except when someone is intentionally cruel to you. Not being able to have kids it isn't about our sin-it is about God's will for us. I don't know how to prove that to you but I have to believe it or my faith will be crushed. I can accept infertility and the pain that goes along with it until a person causes you to suffer more or gives you a message that is contrary to the God I love. I'm angry. I'd fix this if I could. Please Joni, tell me how."

We were helpless, vulnerable, and singed by the fires of disappointment. We looked nothing like the bold and courageous Christian's we'd once thought we were.

Then something ugly turned in my gut. The ache morphed into a deep anger. The tears stopped and a searing energy flowed into my veins. Pulling my shoulders back, I clenched a wet tissue in my hand.

"You know what? Right now I'm angry too." It felt better than the pain and I decided to hang onto it for a while.

"Let's change our clothes and eat."

Upstairs, I put on my jeans and one of Ben's old flannel shirts.

"Why don't you throw this old thing away?" he asked, fingering the faded black and blue plaid.

"It smells like you and feels like one continuous hug when I wear it."

Downstairs again, I heated up dinner rolls and poured chilled raspberry juice and ginger ale into crystal goblets. The smell of baked chicken and rice beckoned. In the freezer, a chocolate almond ice cream pie waited. We loaded our plates and for the first time in our marriage, neither of us wanted to pray.

After a moment of silence, Ben bowed his head. "Lord, thank You for this food. Amen."

We tried to eat but spent more time pushing our food around on the plates. Both of us passed on dessert. While I cleared the table, Ben ran the pie to our neighbors. We knew seven-year-old Brady next door loved chocolate.

Ben let the kitchen door slam and took off his shoes. "Brady says 'Thanks.'" He grinned and added, "I think he has a crush on you."

"He's a sweet boy."

"What are your plans for now?"

I shrugged. "Read for a while I think."

"I guess I'll watch the races."

Curled up in the living room with a new book and my goblet of bubbly juice, I heard Ben turn on the big screen television in our basement. Racing was meant to be experienced in surround sound with the volume turned up.

I got up and put an instrumental CD on hoping the simple music might revive my parched soul.

Lord, I know Your Word says we are all sinners and fall short of Your glory. But where does it say You punish sin this way? What about the millions of babies aborted each year? Isn't there sin in their mothers' lives? Many of them get to conceive again later. What about the mothers who abuse their children? They still get to have them. Even good mothers sin - don't they?

God remained quiet. No verses of wisdom or comfort eased across my mind.

Outside the window, I watched the wind move a single oak leaf hanging onto its branch. The others had fallen when the frost loosened their grip or the snow weighed them down. My conversation with God changed directions. *I'm going to hang on to You the way this leaf is hanging on this branch. I don't understand but I refuse to let go of You.*

Monday morning I woke up angry again and decided to clean house. I spared no room, drawer, cupboard, or closet. Sweating, I turned off the furnace and cracked a few windows open. On the CD player, Charlie Daniels sang about redemption. His passionate, Cajun Christian country struck a tender chord in my heart and started to thaw the icy edges.

"Shoot!" I murmured. I'd wanted to stay angry a little bit longer.

I walked through the house later, admiring the shining furniture, polished wood floors, and sanitized bathrooms. I took a deep breath. Lemon wax, scrubbing bubbles, tropical breeze cleanser, and vinegar glass cleaner mingled with the cool air from outside. I enjoyed the smell of a clean house almost as much a dozen roses or fresh brewed coffee. As I poured myself a hot cup of Colombian roast, I thought, *two out of three ain't bad.* Then, the doorbell rang, and a delivery guy dropped off a dozen yellow roses. The card read, *Just because. Love, Ben.* Some days you just can't lose.

My peace was short-lived.

Tuesday morning I went to Bible study even though I knew Della would be there. Every week I hesitated about going. The women in the study were either young mothers or older women-mothers of adults and grandmothers. All of them had delivery room war stories. The whole group relived them every time someone else got pregnant. Even though I dreaded these announcements, I wanted to connect, and so I went.

Our pastor's wife, Janice, led the study, and her wisdom and gift of teaching made it worth the effort.

Life blind-sided me on that gray and blustery day. I entered the library, jiggled loose a Styrofoam cup, and poured myself some coffee. I settled in at the long table we used and watched rain spatter the window. Della and her best friend, Bernice, walked in and went to the coffee table.

"I think you might be right, Della. Although I wonder . . . maybe the Lord knows Jonica wouldn't be a good mother so He is withholding a child from her."

Things moved in slow motion for a moment. Raw, untamed, and unfamiliar emotions swept through me. I wanted to hit something - or someone. Instead, I gripped my cup, crumpling it. Hot coffee and tears hit my skin at the same time. I jumped up, staring at the spill.

I heard Bernice say, "Jonica, we didn't see you."

Looking at the two of them I wanted to hurl swear words at them. A few choice ones crossed my now not so pure thoughts. A rumble followed by a blinding shaft of light at that moment would have been nice. I'd have enjoyed seeing the ladies cringe when God chose not to accept their judgment of me. Although the rain continued outside, no thunder rolled and no lightened bolted.

I hoped I could keep my mouth shut. They didn't need anything else to use against me in their court of condemnation.

Neither one was even embarrassed that I'd heard them gossiping about me.

I grabbed my purse, walked past them and toward the door, my lips pressed tightly shut.

As the door swung shut behind me I heard Della say, "Well! At least she could clean up her mess."

Again I fled my church crippled by the verbal blast of a woman honored in the congregation. A strange homesickness flooded my soul. I knew it would be awhile before I came back - if I ever did. I started my car and stared at the building where I loved to worship the God I believed in with all my heart. "This is sad God. And wrong."

As I pulled out of the parking lot, the anger settled in as if making itself at home - again. I knew it was the dangerous kind of anger - the kind that breeds bitterness - by the awful taste in my mouth.

I wanted God to answer my internal shouts. *Is this how your people are supposed to behave? Isn't Your house to be called a house of prayer? A place of refuge? Right now, it feels like the residence of betrayal and rejection.*

Instead of going home, I went to the park. Its only inhabitants were the giant Canada geese. I bought some corn from a bin and sat under my umbrella on a bench. The sound of the metal door of the corn dispenser slamming shut had alerted the geese to a treat and the loud, pushy birds soon surrounded me.

I watched them shove and bite each other over the kernels I spread before them. If it looked like another goose was getting a nugget more, the jealous birds honked and pulled out a feather or two from the competitor. When the cup was empty, they turned and waddled away.

"At least I know what to expect from you," I commented to their feathery behinds. "You take and leave. You don't act holy, and then turn on me."

My discussion turned into a prayer.

"I expect compassion and mercy from believers. I don't need more pain heaped on me by Christians. In spite of everything, I know You're walking through this barren place with me. You never leave or forsake me. But why do you allow us to hurt each other? We are a family- bound by the sacrifice of Jesus. This is the blood that should be thicker than water. What did I ever do to these women? Do I deserve this punishment? If Stacie had been with me, this would have turned her away from You for good. She already sees most of us as self-righteous, harsh, judging hypocrites. And You know what? I'm not sorry yet for those nasty names I wanted to call them earlier."

My growling stomach interrupted my talk with the Lord. I looked around the park, glad I was still the only one there. All I needed was for someone to see me there, alone, talking out loud. I already been labeled a sinner in denial-I didn't need to add "crazy" to my list of titles.

I drove through Juan's and picked up some lunch-a crunchy taco, a bowl of beans, and a large cola. A blue car with an Eve Dunbar bumper sticker headed out of the drive-thru ahead of me. I wondered where Stacie was and hoped her day was going better than mine.

Eating my lunch in the parking lot, a deep loneliness settled into my soul.

Stacie

Is she right? Am I out of control? Weak?

My mother, Senator Eve Dunbar, was in town for a couple of days. Before she flew back to D.C., we met at the country club for lunch.

In the dining room, seated by the bay window overlooking the pond, I took a moment to appreciate the way the soft candlelight danced off the delicate crystal goblets and the soft ivory china bowl with pink roses arranged in a small, elegant mound.

"Isn't it pretty, Mother - I mean Eve?"

I didn't usually slip. My memory of her voice the day she requested I use her first name stood out. "I prefer you call me Eve at all times now, Stacie. Then you won't slip in professional situations." I was twelve at the time.

She chose to overlook my mistake but I couldn't miss the sarcastic edge when she responded, "Lovely."

I'd forgotten this kind of elegance was her daily experience.

When she spoke, her voice washed over me like cold water. "There's an opening in my office. Your education and research skills will be used to the maximum. It includes a generous wage and the opportunity for making important connections for the future. If you insist on staying with the man you married, you can commute. With this job on your résumé you will be able to make your way in most political circles."

As she spoke, I watched her scan the room, one shapely brow raised. That was part of her job - to seek out opportunities to recognize a constituent, shake a hand, compliment a potential donor, or catch a competitor on what she considered her turf. Something she saw didn't pass her inspection and a frown crossed her lips. I pitied the manager.

In my lap, my hands grew damp, and I bunched the linen napkin into a tight ball. My pulse throbbed and a line of sweat broke out across my upper lip. *Why do I always feel this way? She's my mother and will understand.*

I took a drink of ice water. My shaking hand caused the ice cubes to tinkle a bit louder than normal. They sounded like church bells in my head. Setting the goblet down, I shook out my napkin and touched it to my lip, wiping away the perspiration.

"Eve, I need to tell you something."

"Of course. What?"

"Mike and I are separated."

"I'm not surprised. What's his problem?" A slight smile moved across her lips.

The waiter arrived with our food before I could reply.

She irked me. *How can my mother gloat when my life is breaking apart?*

Tiny pink shrimp nestled into a bed of greens with vinaigrette dressing on the side. Our politically correct lunch-no woman could be too thin or too powerful. Eve sipped white wine while I gulped ice water. My empty stomach gurgled. We ate in silence. I finished first-I mean really finished. Only the olive oil I couldn't get to attach to my lettuce shimmered on the plate.

"You shouldn't devour your food, Stacie. You are an adult- you don't need to clean your plate. Manners are an important part of success in the political world. I trained you better than this."

"It was a very small salad, and I was hungry."

"A little self-control goes a long way. You do, however, look thinner. New diet?"

"No. I haven't felt well lately."

"Have you seen a doctor?"

Her little bit of concern undid me. Hope rose in my chest. *Maybe she really wants to know.*

"I'm struggling to recover from an abortion," I said.

She stabbed a shrimp with her fork and I jumped.

"What do you mean *recovering*?"

"I hemorrhaged and it takes time to recover from the loss of blood, and I'm a little depressed."

"When did you have it done?"

"A couple of weeks ago. I can't sleep or focus at work. Mike is upset because I didn't tell him before I went ahead with it."

We talked about "it." A nameless entity. A legal right shrouded in shame.

"Stacie, it's a simple procedure. I didn't raise you to be weak and out of control. You need to get over it."

"Did you ever have an abortion?"

"Of course not."

Her sarcasm and disdain chafed me but I couldn't seem to stop confiding in her.

"There's more. I feel sad. Empty."

"You need a change. A new job-new place to live. A city with a pulse."

"I need Mike."

As soon as the words left my mouth I trembled at the power they held over me. Then I glanced at Eve. My trembling turned to shakes.

I watched, fascinated, as she set her fork down beside her plate, wiped the corners of her mouth, and folded her napkin, placing it with exaggerated care beside her plate. I was secretly glad I'd breached her public facade. I knew her proper movements were an attempt to gain control of her surging anger.

"I knew it. You're dependent on him." She snarled still smiling just in case anyone who counted was watching.

"He's my husband."

"So? Women enjoy more opportunities to expand and grow than ever before. Why waste your life in a nowhere job with a nowhere and now absent man?"

"Eve, I love him."

"It will pass. There is no future for you here. It is time. Divorce is easy and quick. It will also put you in a unique position to understand the many women in the nation who, like you, who are expanding their horizons beyond men."

"Did your love for Dad pass? Are all men a hindrance to women?"

"No. Your father and I are fortunate to enjoy a different kind of relationship based on personal freedom."

A waiter interrupted our discussion as he refilled my water glass.

"I won't stop loving Mike."

I recognized the look on her face. I'd seen it in press conferences when a reporter asked her a question she wanted to bypass. "You can fly back to sign the divorce papers."

Standing up, I somehow pulled on the ivory linen tablecloth. My goblet jumped while ice and water tumbled over the edge. Eve looked at me, her fingers gracefully interlaced as she anchored the tablecloth with her elbows.

"I didn't agree to a divorce or the job. I don't want either."

"Quiet, Stacie," she hissed, her professional smile still in place.

My voice had risen above the acceptable level of country club etiquette and the standard of public performance set by my mother. The room fell silent and heads turned and watch us. Of course Eve didn't want her famous face connected with an emotional outburst or a clumsy daughter. She preferred good press.

Our waiter returned and asked, "Can I help you?"

"Please clean this up. Stacie, you are disrupting other people's meals and embarrassing me. Sit down."

My obedience was expected. Instead, I ignored her command, swung my purse onto my shoulder, and ran from the elegant room. In my car, I took a few deep breaths, almost hoping she would follow me and make sure I was okay. I studied the stucco building I had once considered my second home. After tennis lessons or playing golf with Dad, he always bought me lunch. Anything on the menu was mine for the asking. Until today this place was a safe haven. Now it represented the court my mother's judgment and betrayal.

As I drove toward home where no one waited for me, an internal battle raged. *Can't she be liberated, a senator, and my mother? She never asked why I bled. Why isn't it enough for her that I love Mike? Who does she think she is? I don't fit into her perfect daughter mold. I'm more like Dad. But, I'm like her too-I have a vision and passion. It's never good enough for her. What does she know about abortion anyway? It's just an issue to her-it's my reality. Why can't I please her and be loved by her? How can she judge me so harshly?*

I heard my own voice above the traffic and wind blowing in my open window. Great. I hoped no one saw me talking to myself. My stomach growled as I approached Juan's drive-thru. I ordered a bean burrito and a large cola.

I wanted to talk to someone. Jonica? Maybe she'd understand but, then again, maybe not. If the women who were supposed to be on my side didn't comprehend me how could one from the other side? Perhaps no one could.

I pulled into a spot at the park and watched a solitary old man feed a demanding bunch of geese.

Thunder rolled in the distance. Emptiness and loneliness battled for first place in my heart.

CHAPTER 7

Jonica

The dreams exhausted me.

Sometimes the memory lingered in my mind all day.

I resisted going to bed. Instead, I'd pick up a new book to read, start watching a long movie, or get back to work on my current writing project.

Every day I begged, please, not tonight!

Each one started the same way. My tummy protruded and so did my belly button. My skin was tight and I couldn't bend. Ben was somehow just out of sight but his voice teased me about bursting at the seams.

Then a low backache, the gush of warm water down my legs, and an all encompassing pain took over the nightmare.

Next, without knowing how I got there, I was in a delivery room with my bare feet in stirrups, my body in a hospital gown, and a sheet draped around my knees. An urgency to push demanded my attention.

From behind the sheet Dr. Steele's voice commanded, "Not yet, Jonica. Don't push. Breathe."

There were people all around me, I listened to them but they never came into view.

Ben's gentle voice encouraged me through breathing exercises as another tidal wave of pain hit.

Finally Dr. Steele said, "Push now."

I pushed with all my might - so hard my teeth and jaw hurt.

"The head is out. Take a deep breath. Now, Jonica. We've got to get the shoulders through. Push. Push. Push."

I obeyed, reaching my chin to my bent knees. Things happened fast then. The child left my body and so did the pain. Someone wrapped the infant and handed it to Ben, who finally came into view as he carried the baby to me.

This was the only place the dreams varied. Some nights I "delivered" a girl, others a boy. I saw their faces, counted their fingers and toes. The healthy cry ended as he or she began to seek nourishment. I felt the tug and sting on my breast and woke up.

The moment my eyes opened, grief washed over me. These pains and the wonder of bringing a new life into the world would always be a mystery to me.

My womb remained hollow.

Stacie

The nightmares always left me quaking.

They were always the same. Each evening I sought a new diversion-anything to avoid sleep.

I heard myself say to an empty room, "Please, not tonight."

Inside the dream, a baby's scream woke me. I wiggled my feet into my slippers. A strange hazy light flooded the hallway making all the edges blurry. As I walked toward the crying it began to get softer and farther away. Someone was taking the baby.

My feet stumbled as my terror grew. The pounding of my heart echoed off the walls, making it even harder to hear the baby. In the center of the room where I was sure the cries came from stood a crib. It felt as though I walked in slow motion as I struggled to get there in time. I saw a blanket inside the crib. It looked like it was wrapped around a small body. I saw my hand pull back the soft covering. It was empty-except for the stains. Blood - lots of blood. In the dream, I heard myself cry out, "No!"

My own voice woke me. My cheeks were wet with tears. I clutched the sheet so tight my hands ached. I'd never been aware of my womb-suddenly that vacant place was in my thoughts day and night.

CHAPTER 8

Jonica

For weeks after the Bible study incident, anger kept us home from church. We lounged around, watched TV preachers, and went out for dinner late so we missed the church crowd. And we were crabby.

"Ben, maybe we should look for a new church."

"Do you think there is a place where all the people understand what it's like not to be able to have children?" he asked from behind the Sunday paper.

"No."

"Has sulking helped us?"

"No."

Ben continued to read as I pouted. *Why is he so ornery with me? Since when did all this become my fault?*

He got up and tossed me the comics and said, "Maybe these will perk you up."

"Me? It's you who's in such a bad mood." I snapped the paper up in front of my face as he climbed the stairs. Where should we go for lunch?" I asked his disappearing back.

"Nowhere, if you don't cheer up. It's bad enough staying home with a grump-I don't want to go out with one."

I fumed. *Me a grump? Right. He's the champion grouch!* Then, as if to cancel out my silent complaint, he started the hot water for a shave, singing, "I've got a tiger by the tail it's plain to see..."

When I heard the shower spray begin, I stomped upstairs. Making the bed, I took my frustrations out on the sheets and comforter. I yanked and smoothed everything into place. Then I got out a clean pair of jeans and a white T-shirt, and looked in my jewelry box. The light shone on my mother-of-pearl earrings. Ben had given them to me as our first "just because I love you" present. Picking them up, I admired the silver setting. The hard spot in my heart melted just as Ben turned off the water. Rats! I could stay not mad at my man.

I waited outside the bathroom door. When Ben opened it, I grabbed him in a bear hug around his waist.

"Is this because you love me so much or want to go out to eat?"

I looked into his eyes feeling a surge of defiance I hoped he'd translate as bold flirting. "Both."

As I turned away, he swatted me and said, "Hurry-I'm starved."

We drove to a little café on the river. After ordering hamburgers and shakes, Ben reached across the table for my hand.

"Joni, it's time to go back to church. We can go to the first service, and you can choose a different Bible study."

"I know."

"What? No argument?"

"No, I don't want to be a victim anymore."

"I also want to stop by Natalie and Dave's house. I miss the boys. I miss my sister and brother-in-law."

"I know. But . . ."

"What?"

"How do we do this? How can Natalie and I understand each other?"

"You can't. But you can both choose to be kind. You don't even have to like each other. But I need you to be nice and treat her with respect. So do the boys."

"I know."

"This is too easy, Jonica. What's really on your mind?

Tears welling up in my eyes, I told him the truth.

"The boys are so special to me. I long to love them and be loved by them. I want Natalie to let us be part of their lives. I need her to understand I don't want her boys in my life as substitute sons, I want them to be my nephews. I'm still scared of her judgment, but I'm more afraid of not having Jeremy and Kevin in my life. I want to be the best Aunt Joni I can be!"

Ben called his sister on his cell phone. She agreed it was time to see each other.

When Dave opened the door, Natalie peeked out from around him and said, "Hi guys." She was scared too. Her unkind words echoed in my mind. *Lord, help me choose not to be angry anymore.* Before I could say anything, Jeremy and Kevin ran to us for hugs.

"Please can we go to your house and play computer and stay overnight?" Jeremy asked, standing on one leg then the other.

"Please?" Kevin echoed.

Dave pulled his wife from behind him and held her at his side. "Give them a break, guys," he said to his sons. "Let them get in the house before you take them away again."

Natalie hung onto Dave's shirt the same way Kevin held onto her purse strap in the stores-for dear life.

"I miss your hugs, Natalie. I think I'm way overdue."

She released her grip on Dave and flew into my arms. "I'm sorry," she whispered in my ear.

I'd let hurt simmer into anger and was treacherously close to bitterness. Its huge talons released the death grip they had on my heart.

"Forgiven," I whispered back. "And I'm sorry for my anger." This simple apology set me partially free. There was still Della.

We talked and ate cherry cobbler hot from the oven. We were on the mend.

Later, at our house, Jeremy played games with Ben on the computer while Kevin and I rocked.

Kevin took my face in both his hands and asked, "Why don't you got kids?"

Ben missed a turn at the game and Jeremy won. The little boy's question hung in the air as he continued his search of my eyes.

"Well, we asked God for them and He said no."

"Why don't you buy one?" he asked.

"Uncle and I will talk about it later. How would you boys like to play a game of cards?"

Little feet scrambled to the kitchen table with Ben right behind them. After we let each boy beat us at Go Fish, I read them a bedtime story, tucked the covers around them, knelt at their beds to pray for them, and kissed warm cheeks.

In his arms later, I asked Ben, "Why don't we adopt?"

"Jonica, I've thought about it. I don't have a strong desire to adopt."

Silence surrounded me as I waited for him to say more. Then, I heard his soft snuffling snores. How could he fall asleep in the middle of an important discussion? The truth settled into my heart before I could rouse him. *As far as he is concerned, there is nothing to talk about - he's decided.*

This submission thing is so not for me Lord!

In the morning I watched cartoons with the boys while Ben walked. I fixed them all breakfast and let the kid noise fill up the quiet spaces between my husband and me. As soon as the car backed out, I got the boys started on a coloring project and called my mom.

She listened, then said, "Honey, give it time. The Lord will either give Ben a desire to adopt or lessen yours."

We hung up and Natalie came to get her sons. After hugs all around, they left. I went to my office and pounded my computer keyboard, journaling my guts out on to the page. While they printed, I paced. Sitting down with a cup of coffee, I grabbed my orange highlighter. If Ben could "see" my anguish, it might make a difference. I underlined key portions to speed up his word intake. As I read my words the wind went out of my sails. Sure, I detailed my desire to experience hearing my child call me "Mom." However, something else stood out. Over and over again my orange lines highlighted the same phrase, "And what will people think?"

The evidence of my pride hit hard. Tears marred the typed page, and I dialed Mom's number again.

"Jonica, worrying over what other people think is the wrong motive for adoption. What does God want? What does Ben want?"

Ben wants us to love the kids we already have in our lives. I'm not sure what God wants."

"God gave you a good and wise man. Neither of them would intentionally lead you the wrong direction."

"I know, but what about what I want?"

"What do you want?"

"I want to be a wife, mom, and writer. I want to give you grandbabies. And I want people to approve of us-I want to be a normal family."

"Do you feel confident God wants you to adopt?"

"No. But isn't it the right thing to do?"

"Joni, I'm not convinced it's right for everyone."

I'm so confused."

"Does the chaos you're experiencing come from God?"

Her question sliced right to the truth. "No."

"Honey, we love you and Ben just the way you are. Whatever is right for the two of you as a family is right for us."

After we hung up, I slid to my knees. *I love You and Ben so much. Please remove this confusion and replace it with Your peace. Give us both clarity and unity about adoption. And please don't let others misunderstand. Help them to see this as God's will and accept us as we are-a family of two.*

The distress, anger, and rebellion lessened as I opened myself more fully to God.

As I started to let go of what I assumed were other people's expectations, relief took a couple steps into my soul.

Stacie

I avoided everyone from my past. Jonica and I took our morning coffee breaks together via the telephone.

We kept our discussions on surface stuff and rarely talked about the news. We held opposing political views and chose not to talk about them. But when a local woman drowned her infant son, I wondered what my new friend thought. So I asked her. Here was her opportunity to label me and this woman as baby killers.

She said, "I would love to have a little boy. And it makes me angry she got one and then took his life. I will confess to you sometimes my faith isn't all I hope it will be. I looked at the photo of her little boy and raged at her out loud for a while. Then I asked God why. But none of that matters now-her little one is gone. I cannot understand her, but I will pray for her."

"What do you pray?"

"For her to find peace with God and for justice."

Her answer shocked me. Not the justice part-even I felt the law demanded a stiff penalty. To pray at all boggled my mind, but to pray for a murderer was beyond my comprehension.

"You tell me, Counselor. If you were the prosecutor, how would you handle this case?"

The other line clicking in rescued me from having to give her an honest answer. I was relieved. My legal opinion on this one strayed from my liberal training. I was thinking death penalty.

"It's Mike. I gotta go."

"Talk to you tomorrow."

I switched over to Mike.

"Hi." Did he hear the shiver that ran up my spine and spilled out into my voice?

"Hi, are you busy for lunch?"

Excitement bubbled up inside me. Mike had contacted me a month earlier, and asked me to join him for counseling. Though we didn't agree on everything, we were making steady progress. We went out on dates and talked about when he might move home. He didn't commit, although we held hands and savored sweet kisses good night.

"No, I'm free."

"Can we meet at the condo? I'll bring a pizza."

"Sure. What time?"

"Will twelve fifteen work?"

"Sure." Why couldn't I think of anything else to say?

"I have to go, Stacie. I'll see you then."

Panic surged through my body and my heart raced. *Does he want to move more stuff out?*

My intercom rang and I was asked to report to my boss's office. Walking down the hall felt like the one time in grade school when I was sent to the principal's office for kicking a boy on the playground. My steps were slow and deliberate. His assistant told me to go right in.

Chandler Daniels is not one for small talk and he got to business as I settled into the chair he motioned to.

"Stacie, how are you? You've missed a lot of work the last month."

"I haven't been feeling well, and Mike and I are separated."

"Do you need a good lawyer?" Looking into his eyes I saw he wasn't joking. He was ready to step in if invited.

"No, we're getting counseling and hope to reunite." *Please let it be so.*

"Is your counselor a good one?"

"We're seeing Donna Jacobson."

"I know Donna and recommend her to many struggling couples. Will your health continue to disrupt your work?"

"Maybe. I don't know." From somewhere deep inside me, courage rose and I told him about the abortion and my depression- even the dreams.

"I know you hired me as a favor to my mother, Mr. Daniels. I appreciate it and I know I've let you down."

He smiled and rose, coming around the desk to the chair beside me.

"Stacie, I know your mother and like her, although our politics are different. I looked into hiring you because I read about your graduating with honors in the paper. We're always looking for the best and brightest. I think you should also know I respect your dad. He told me you were full of potential and I believed him.

After I reviewed your resume and references, I hired you because of your own accomplishments. Always remember, your merits earned you this job-not the family connection.

I have some very firm beliefs about work. One of them is you need to do the work you were made to do. Are you doing what you love?"

"No."

"What do you want to do more than anything Stacie?"

"To help kids and battered women. I want to be the voice of the voiceless."

"Then what are you waiting for?"

"Cases. A partnership."

"A partnership here will not bring you any closer to this dream, Stacie. As much as I hate to admit it, we don't handle family law cases unless one of our current clients needs us. Then we will handle their wills, pre-nuptial agreements, and divorces as a convenience for them and charge them astronomical prices for it. Corporate cases bring in the big bucks and that's what we've always been about. We don't handle the kind of litigation you dream of."

"What do you advise?"

"Open your own practice. You're educated, possess leadership skills, are gifted at communicating, and possess the desire to make a difference."

"I don't know where to begin."

"Your dad and I will help if you're serious. I'm at the end of my career and so many dreams have expired - the time for making them come true is gone. I wanted to help people too...but I took the path to wealth instead. Don't let the lack of it stop you."

I heard myself say, "I'll do it."

"We've already farmed out your work to others. So what are you waiting for?"

"Are you firing me?"

"No, that wasn't the plan. I had a sense you needed some time off and was going to offer you a medical leave."

"I don't know if I can afford to do this."

"You get one life to live your dreams. Can you afford not to?"

"You mean I'm not fired but I can leave today?" I asked.

Smiling, he replied, "Yes. You write me a letter of resignation, I'll have bookkeeping cut you a severance check. You did a lot of extra work around here before your current struggle. It's money you've earned.

"By the way, I own some downtown real estate and have a two-room office space available next month. It needs someone to pick out paint and carpet. Are you interested?"

"How much for rent?"

"I'll make you a deal you can't refuse. Now, go make your dreams come true!"

I looked at him and saw it. He had the same light in his eyes Jonica did. "You're one of them aren't you?"

"One of who?" he asked.

"A Christian."

"How did you know?"

"I have another friend like you. It shows."

"Here's my personal card, Stacie. He wrote the address of the building and a cell phone number on the back. I'll call you in a few weeks to sign a rental agreement. You can go by the office anytime and check it out. The dentist's office has an extra key. I'll let them know you'll be stopping by in the next few days. E-mail or call anytime. Just keep in touch."

"Thanks. I will."

Back in my cubbyhole I packed my personal stuff into two boxes I found in the supply room. Another researcher helped me get them to my car. Driving home, I couldn't believe how good almost getting fired felt.

I shoved the second box into the living room just as the door bell rang.

"Hi," I said, staring at Mike's hands. In one he held a pizza box and in the other his suitcase. I wondered if it was empty-if he needed more of his stuff.

"Can I come in?"

"Please!" I said, stepping back, my eyes still on the bag, and reaching for our lunch.

"Moving out?" He asked pointing at the boxes.

Looking into Mike's eyes I saw a shadow of what clung to me-fear.

"No. Moving in." I almost choked. "Mike, I'm so sorry!"

During counseling we had promised not to make any major decisions without consulting each other. I told him about my conversation with Chandler Daniels and my new plans. My tongue went tingly from the sheer speed I used to get the words out and not taking any breaths. I reminded myself of the commercials where the voice reads the "fine print" at warp speed.

"I'm sorry too, Stacie. At my personal session with Donna, she asked what I wanted to do - what next step I wanted to take. I told her, 'I just want to go home.' She said she'd asked you the same question and you said you hoped I'd just show up on the doorstep one day."

We stared at each other for a moment. Then he said the magic words, "Here I am, Stacie, if you'll have me."

He reached for the pizza just as it started to slip from my hand. I watched as he set it on the credenza and then reached for me.

As I released the anger and confusion, gladness flooded the place they vacated. I set my love for him free - no more holding back - I was going to give him one hundred percent of me. For the first time since the abortion, no one else's expectations mattered.

Relief tried to sneak into my heart.

I let it.

CHAPTER 9

Jonica

"What did you do for Mother's Day?" Stacie asked.

I don't remember all I said but I let things fly I never intended. A lot of it was anger and the leftover residue of pain held on to for far too long. I even told her about Della and Bernice.

After she left, I got scared. "What if she doesn't believe in God because of my outburst?" I asked Ben. "What if in my anger I sinned?"

His response surprised me. "She needs to see the real you-the whole woman. True friendship demands honesty and the freedom to share your life experience - even the hard stuff. It's part of who you are. You don't need to protect Stacie from you."

I chose not to listen to Ben's words of wisdom and instead continued to anguish over my behavior. I hated letting her see my unhealed wound. It was one thing to listen to her struggles, but I was the Christian, the victorious one. How could I put the garbage in my life on display like that?

Ben saw the determined look on my face, and knew I wasn't done fretting. "Jonica, no one comes to Christ because of you. God is working these things out in Stacie's heart. You are His instrument but you cannot save her. It's also possible she won't believe if you aren't transparent with her on a deeper level. By not letting her see all of you, your relationship will always be surface level. If you keep this space in your life away from her, she may always see God as distant too."

After hours of worry I called her.

"No. You didn't sound wimpy or whiny," she assured me.

Then in typical lawyer fashion she asked one last question. "So what did Ben do for you today?"

"How did you know?" I sniffed.

"It's his way with you."

Her confidence in us gave me courage-maybe I hadn't ruined everything. Tears burned my eyes as I remembered his gift to me, his declaration earlier in the day.

"Good morning, my love-Happy Wife's Day!" On the card he gave me, he'd whited out the word "Mother's" and had artistically drawn in "Wife's." Then he stepped back into the hall to get something. He brought in a tray with cinnamon sugar bagels, walnut honey cream cheese, and coffee.

On the tray rested a rectangular box. It held a new silver Sensa pen, my favorite brand. It wasn't the pen-although thinking back I know he meant it to re-affirm his faith that my writing was a vital part of me. This went beyond a material gift. His sweet act of marriage carried our relationship around a new corner. I took owner-ship of the fact that I was Ben's first choice for all time. No more doubts about us, just a simple peace as I held on to the man God had given me.

And yet later, the same day, I gave a great big blues bash in my honor in front of Stacie. *Good going, Johnson*, I chastised myself.

Then I heard Stacie say, "Jonica, I have to tell you something I couldn't say to your face and I need to tell you right away."

My hopes sank. I was right. I'd disappointed her and jeopardized our friendship. Then her words tilted my world slightly off center again.

"Please try to understand. This is hard for me to say. I don't want to make life any harder on you."

My spirits continued to sink even lower. "You can tell me anything," I said, trying to sound strong.

"I want a baby."

"Oh," was all I could muster for a second. The pause left her free to talk about her desire and her fear of judgment from her mother-and from me.

She started to cry and said, "I woke up feeling so empty today and for the first time Mother's Day meant more to me than a day to make sure I did my duty and called Eve. Is it wrong for me to want this after what I did?"

Only one word came to mind. "No."

"Jonica, I need this to be okay with you."

"I'm fine. Just because I can't get pregnant doesn't mean you shouldn't."

When we said goodbye, I was exhausted. This emptying myself out to her left me feeling vulnerable to the point of naked. I'd have preferred keeping my mask on a little longer-like until after she'd become a believer. I knew it had taken a lot of courage to admit her desire for another baby.

While I respected her for that, when I hung up I still had one question for God. *Why today?*

Stacie

I didn't intend to trip Jonica up with a trick question.

When she slammed her glass down on the table it was like seeing a volcano erupt from a long sleep without warning.

"I despise the day," she blurted out as she squeezed more lemon into her iced tea then stirred it, the spoon clanking on the glass and the ice cubes swirling as if trying to get out of the way. My silent shock allowed her to continue. The words came out sharp and staccato.

"Don't get me wrong, I love honoring my mom and Ben's, and we do. In our own way-at home. Not in church. We don't go to church on the 'parent holidays.' I don't want to stand up to be honored as a 'spiritual parent' although I might well be. It shines a spotlight on those of us struggling without children-or parents. There are a lot of grieving people in the pews on these two days of the year.

"Parents fit the normal profile. When invited to stand with them or stop in at the welcome center in the foyer and get a flower, I feel like a 'glitch' in the system. Standing with the parents is not my place. I am Jonica, childless woman. Aunt to many, mother to none. The day is all about women who have kids - not women who can't. If I join the moms, I stand as an imposter. I can't-I won't do that anymore. I will not pretend it isn't uncomfortable or that I am honored."

Sheesh. Who knew?

Then she told me about the ladies at church. They didn't surprise me-this was the kind of behavior I expected from Christians.

"Finally," I whispered with pride. Thankfully, she missed it. *The old bats!* A new emotion caught me off guard as she let the truth rip. I wanted to protect her from any more harm. Of course, not having any other close friends, I had no idea how to go about doing such a thing. No one can protect her friends from mean people, but, I was suddenly capable of wanting to punch out the two old biddies who seemed to think they could say anything they wanted to Jonica in the Name of Jesus.

She tapped the tea off her spoon and slammed it on the table. "Anymore questions?" she demanded.

There was no way I wanted to probe any further. Her anger made me realize I'd never asked her how she was feeling. Other than Ben and her mom, I knew it was possible no one else had either.

For the first time, Jonica was uncomfortable and unsure of herself with me. In every other conversation we had, she said all the right things at the right times, always soothing and encouraging me. Now, I watched her fidget, and she didn't look me in the eye.

I left shortly after she presented her case against the parent holidays. On the way home, I started to worry. Had she noticed I'd never asked about her pain before? Was she sick of listening to me dump my problems on her without giving a second thought let alone a first to hers? Did she ever resent my neglect? I'd treated our friendship like it was all about me. And up to that day, it was.

I knew our relationship had changed. She got real with me and that took courage. She shed some of the "victorious Christian" veneer I'd started to resent. I saw something beyond the anger that shocked me to the core: her wound.

I acknowledged something else; until that day, Jonica had still been on trial with me. When she let loose with the truth, I liked her more. As she poured out her frustrations, I began to respect her on a new level. She'd said all the right things this time too - she just didn't know it.

After berating myself for not being a better friend for a while longer, I decided to call her, but she beat me to it. Hearing her voice and her worry over how I'd taken her "outburst" as she called it, reassured me. I could count on, my friend to do everything she could to make it right. She tried harder than anyone I knew.

Comforted by her call, I decided to take a risk and be totally open with her too. I told her about my deep sadness and my secret yearning to have a baby.

So, in typical Stacie fashion, when my friend was most vulnerable, I put my burden on her. I tested her again, and she passed. I knew I was safe with her-at the very least, her religion demanded it- but it was more than that. Nice was as much a part of her as her DNA.

I was confident in one person I knew she'd been with that awful Mother's Day. Ben. Those two kept teaching me lessons in real love.

Later, as I considered the high cost of friendship, I realized that even in her hurt and anger, she didn't blame God. Her religion wasn't a surface thing. It seemed ocean-deep.

I wished I could put her God on the witness stand. I had one question for Him. *"Why Jonica?"*

CHAPTER 10

Jonica

Going back to church was easier than I expected. Sort of. We headed for the pew we often occupied-middle section, middle row. Several people stopped to say hello and said we'd been missed the past few weeks. We smiled and let them know it was good to be back and that we had missed them too. I was comfortable with surface comments, but had no desire for anyone to go deeper.

I'd known several of them since Bible camp and youth group. But our lives had changed direction after they started having kids and we didn't.

The organ music started, and I opened my bulletin. As the swelling music surrounded me, I read the prayer request insert. Descriptions of job losses, cancer, deaths of loved ones, and sick babies filled a page. . *Lord, the needs of our people are so many and so great. Help me to remember to think more of them than about myself.*

The pastor stood, greeting the congregation, and made an announcement. "Today our service will be different. We have folks who want to share what the Lord is doing in their lives. Mixed in with the testimonies, we will sing praise songs, and experience a drama."

The praise band opened with "Majesty." We stood to sing, and I listened to the teenage girl who sat beside me-a perfect alto. Behind us Della's and Bernice's soft sopranos filled with vibratos floated on the air. A writing idea came to mind and I grabbed an index card and a pen out of my purse and wrote myself a note: *yesterday and tomorrow blending in perfect harmony-just like the Old and New Testaments.*

People shared how obedience to God had changed their lives. Some spoke about mission trips, others about their marriages, and still others about issues of purity. Then one woman stood up and shared how God had used one person's act of forgiveness to bring an entire family to Christ. My shoulders tightened and my jaw flexed as I resisted the Holy Spirit.

The drama portrayed the need to forgive others if we expect to receive forgiveness from God. Behind me two old ladies sniffed and I knew they held lace-edged hankies to their noses. The cotton drip catchers were legendary in our church. Della and Bernice made them and sent them in get well cards or handed them out whenever they saw a need. Lace always peeked out from the pockets of their handbags and the sleeves of their sweaters. The ladies always came prepared.

Oh crud, I feel something for these two and I don't want to. I also wondered if maybe conviction about the way they treated me was the reason for their tears.

My attention returned to the stage as the main character asked the congregation, "What about the plank in your own eye?"

Mine? Lord, they don't even think they did anything to me. Can't they see how wrong they are? Can't they at least try to understand?

A still small voice asked me, *Do you understand them?*

My stomach churned and I reached in my purse for a tissue. A new lace trimmed hankie fluttered over my shoulder. As I dabbed away my stray tears with the fresh cotton, I smelled the gingersnap-scent of Della.

Shoot! I do like some things about her - she has wonderful soft white hair. She is part of a vanishing breed. Grandmas nowadays don't look like her. They play golf and run marathons; she makes hankies and puts up preserves. They wear shorts; she wears print dresses and aprons. They tan; she wears corn-silk powder. They have long acrylic nails; she buffs her short ones to a natural shine. They drink lattes; she drinks Earl Grey-properly prepared. There just aren't many like her left.

'I love her. She is my child. My Son died for you both.'

Father, when two of Your children don't get along is it called sibling rivalry?

Movement interrupted my discussion with the Lord. I'd missed the closing prayer and hymn.

As I exited the pew, I reached for Ben's hand. He wasn't there. No he stood where we'd sat-holding Della's hand in his. Bernice's was in his other. He bent toward them as if not wanting to miss a word. I watched him woo them with kindness. Their eyes sparkled at him from wrinkled faces. Rhinestone earrings glistened as their heads bobbed in agreement with everything he said. I found myself moving back into the pew to avoid the crowd.

He is conspiring with the enemy. He is way too charming for my own good.

Letting go of their hands, Ben stepped toward me and both women greeted me in unison, "Jonica." Neither of them made any attempt at an apology. Seemed like a waste of a good sermon to me.

"Ladies."

Before I could utter another syllable, Ben put his hand on my elbow and guided me out of the pew. When I shook hands with the pastor he held both mine in his and said, "Welcome back, you two. Jonica, my wife told me what happened at Bible study. I know this is a rough time. Is there anything I can do?"

Looking into his caring eyes, I said. "Please thank Janice for calling. I didn't return the calls, but I knew she was praying. And no, I just want to let it go for now. If I need to speak to them, I will when the time comes."

"I think you need to. The damage will always linger and the distance between you expand if it isn't settled."

"I know, but to be honest, Pastor, I have some things to work out in myself first. It's going to take time." *Like how I was going to get past their bad behavior if they were never sorry.*

He smiled and said, "God bless you, Jonica." I was glad he couldn't read my mind.

At home, I set the table with our china, lit candles, and put a pot roast and vegetables on the table. Ben and I chatted about our week and the one yet to come. Life settled back into our normal routine. The food was good, the company great. Some of the edge eased off until I brought up the ladies.

"It seemed easy for you to be gracious to them."

"Joni, they are my elders. Dad drilled respect for older people, especially women, into us kids. And besides, what they have to offer us will be gone with them. They are unique creations of God, deeply loved by Him too. No one can give me what they can as individuals. I don't like what they did to you-to us. But for my life to move ahead with Christ, I am required to forgive them."

"I know." I couldn't keep the resignation out of my voice. "But, why is it so hard?"

"I'm not sure. Maybe because it is so important."

Ben cleared the table while I cut generous slices of peach pie, heated them up, and dropped a big scoop of vanilla ice cream on each. I promised Ben, "Tomorrow I will walk four miles instead of three."

"Whatever, Hon. The game is about to start." Ben looked like an imp wearing a Red Skelton smile.

"Go on."

I watched him walk away in his stocking feet, taking his first big forkful of dessert. *Would our little boy look just like him, Lord?* I wondered as the desire to have a son from our bodies again overwhelmed me and the invisible hand of despair gripped my stomach.

I poured a fresh cup of coffee and carried it in one hand, my pie in the other, to the living room. With my feet tucked under me, I dug into the treat. A huge bite in my mouth, I started another silent conversation with the Lord.

I'm uncomfortable so what are You trying to tell me. What plank is blinding me? I've always treated Della and Bernice with respect and kindness. They talk to me like I'm still a little girl. I'm a married woman. Their words prove they don't get it. I don't understand why they are so mean.

"Lean not on your own understanding."

It feels like they think they're superior because they are mothers. It makes me so stinking mad. They know it all. Wasn't there sin in their lives? They still conceived. None of us are blameless and if sin is the cause of infertility, every woman in the world would be barren. They are Christians, so where is their love? Your Word says we will be known by our love for each other.

"A new commandment I give to you, that you love one another; as I have loved you, that you also love one another."

I'd also memorized this verse-it precedes the one I reminded the Lord of. He seemed to stress the "as I have loved you" part. That's the thing about memorizing verses - when you least expect them - there they are.

Am I capable of this love, Father? Are they? Is anyone? You are God. How can I possibly love the way You do?

"With me all things are possible."

Before I could continue our argument, the phone rang. I carried my empty plate to the kitchen, annoyed because I didn't remember eating beyond the first bite. Shoot. Rich, creamy, fruity, and crusty was my favorite taste combo.

"Hello."

"Jonica, this is Bev. I have an urgent request for all our prayer chain members."

Grabbing a pen and notepad, I said, "I'm ready."

"Della's son, Don, was killed in a car accident today on the way to his mom's for dinner."

I couldn't think of a single word to say and was glad Bev continued with information.

"Pastor is with Della now. So is Bernice. Please pray for her and Don's family. I'll call back when I know when the funeral is. Please pass it on."

"I will," I promised and hung up. I dialed Natalie's number.

"Hi, Natalie. It's me."

"Jonica. You sound so far away."

"Just very sad. We have a prayer chain request."

As I gave her the news, Natalie started to cry. "I can't imagine anything worse than your child dying." She sobbed. I spied my purse sitting on the counter with a tiny edge of lace peeking out.

"Me neither. Please pass it on."

I reached for the hankie and held it to my nose and inhaled. The words of the Lord came back to me, *Lean not on your own understanding.*

"Lord, I cannot know what Della is going through right now. I can know she's hurting, but I cannot understand her pain. You can and do. Your Son died. Please, Father, hold her in Your tender loving care. Thank You for being near her right now. As only You can, please give Don's death eternal value. Please forgive me for not forgiving her as You forgive me."

"Joni?" Ben's voice interrupted my prayer. "Who are you talking to?"

"God."

"Who called?"

I told him and tears filled his green-gold eyes. "I guess there are some things worse than infertility."

The white light of truth burned into my heart.

Oh God! This is worse. She carried Don in her womb and delivered him in pain.

I know she loves him deeply - his death doesn't change that...except now she can't tell him. She's going to be so lonely for him. Please shelter her in the shadow of Your wings.

Anger is stressful. As I released my resentment, the burning in my stomach eased, my jaw unclenched, and my shoulders relaxed.

Lord, thank You for setting me free-again.

Stacie

Mike woke me up on Sunday morning with breakfast in bed; coffee and an Egg McMuffin-fresh from the golden arches. "Breakfast is served."

I sat up and pushed the hair from my face. When he bent over for a kiss, I tried to dodge him and muttered, "Morning breath."

"Kiss me, Stacie."

I did. .

"Dig in. I'm starved. Want to do something today?" he asked as he moved a big bite of muffin to his cheek.

"Don't talk with your mouth full."

"Okay, Mom."

"Mike!" I put down my half eaten muffin and burst into tears. Surprise and concern washed over his face.

"Stacie, I'm sorry. It was a joke."

I sniffed. I was as sensitive on this mother-thing as Jonica.

"I don't know what to say. I feel like I'm walking in a mine field without a detector."

"It's fine."

"No, it's not. Tell me how to fix the hurt I caused just now."

"Take this," I said and handed him the food.

He punched it into the bag, set it on the dresser, and looked at me. I opened my arms and said, "Hold me." He did.

"I'm serious. How can I make this better?"

"I don't know. Strange things bother me now. Will I ever be normal again? I wonder if I will ever make you happy. Your mom and I are so different and she's special to you. I wonder if I'll ever 'qualify.'"

"I don't want you to be anyone else. I have a mom- you are my wife. But I wouldn't mind if you knew her better. I think you'd enjoy who she is."

"I guess I've kept my distance on purpose. You know how good I am with my mother."

"Our mothers are very different - and that's a good thing. Besides, you and Jonica are nothing a like but it still seems to work. Override those arguments, Counselor."

"Your mom is one of them, isn't she?"

"A Christian? Yeah. But she won't push her beliefs on you."

"How can you be so sure?"

"Has she pushed yet?"

"No. I don't give her any chances."

Silence reigned for a moment. Then I asked the question that seemed to bother me the most. I wasn't sure which answer I wanted to hear.

"Do you believe in God?" I asked him.

"I don't know. Sometimes I want to. At one time I did. Then I found so many other things to consider at college. I guess I don't know what to believe. What is truth? Are there absolutes? If there is a God and He is love, what's up with this world?"

"I don't have any answers. But it sure seems like *someone* is circling the wagons-there are Christians everywhere right now."

Later we took a long ride, and Mike called his parents. We fell back into our normal Sunday routine with no effort. Late in the afternoon, the phone rang. It was Eve.

"Stacie, I'm calling to ask how you are."

"Fine."

"Have you thought any more about what we discussed?"

Anger flared. "My answer is no."

"Go ahead and take some more time to consider it. I can hold the position open a few more days."

"No. I've made other arrangements."

"And they are?"

"I'm opening my own office."

"Whose idea was this?"

"It's always been my dream. I never hid this from you. Chandler

Daniels helped me remember my passion. Mike agrees and so will Dad."

"Mike?"

"We've reconciled our differences."

"Well. Your father is waiting to talk to you."

"Thank you for calling, Eve, for asking how I was." I don't know if she heard me. I could only hope so.

"Hi, Stacie. How are you?" Dad's deep voice surrounded me in comfort. It was like an umpire yelling, "Safe!" over the runner at home plate.

"I'm fine, Dad. Mike is back home and I have so much to tell you."

"Are you two free for dinner tonight after I take your mother to the airport?"

I asked Mike and he agreed.

"Dad?"

"Yes, honey?"

"Give the Senator a hug for me."

"Sure. Where to you want to eat?"

"Bob's Truck Stop on highway fourteen?"

Mike gave me the thumbs up.

Dad laughed. "My country club girl has gone country."

At the truck stop we sat in vinyl booths and ate BLTs and onion rings and drank chocolate malts. At the end of the meal, Dad said, "I love you both. You belong together. Do what it takes to make it work."

"Dad, you love Eve, don't you?"

"I've never loved anyone more."

Back home, Mike and I snuggled on the couch and talked about our plans to make my private practice a reality. I rested my head on Mike's chest and let the beating of his heart comfort me.

"I know it's going to mean less money than we planned for the rest of our lives," I said. "I had no idea what it costs to advertise."

"Can you live with that?"

"I think so. Cutting back on most things won't bother me."

"What do you mean?" he asked.

"You know. There are always things we want."

His arms tightened around me. "Like what?" I heard a knowing smile creep into his voice.

"Like to love you forever and ever. Like to be the best legal advocate this county has ever seen. Like to get my mother to love me and keep my dad smiling. And you know...just more."

"Look at me, Stacie."

I sat up, faced him with my legs crossed yoga style.

"There is more," he urged. "Tell me."

The longing I was afraid to voice was almost constant, and I didn't know where to start. Fear welled up inside me and tears slid down my face. Mike handed me a tissue and waited.

"Honey, do you want a new car? A new house? Those things will come but it's going to take some time."

"No. They don't seem as important as they did before."

"Since when?" The two most beautiful eyes in the world to me squinted as he pulled his brows together.

"Since recently." I sniffed and was rewarded with the box of tissues.

"So, what's on your mind?"

"I'm afraid to tell you."

"Do you want to wait until our counseling session on Thursday?"

"No. We need to learn to share without a third party. I just don't know how."

My hands shook and a trickle of sweat ran down my side. I knew my face was flushed, my eyes and nose red. *So much for bewitching him with my beauty.*

I felt him waiting. It was hard to begin. Jonica accepted my desire as natural and didn't resent me, but the abortion had left Mike feeling betrayed. How could I tell him *this*?

"Mike, I have this intense yearning . . ."

"Is it something I can give you?"

"Yes. But I don't know if you will understand."

"I won't if you don't tell me."

"I want to have a baby," I whispered.

"What?"

He released me and lifted himself off the couch careful to avoid touching me. I looked up. He stared down at me. "I don't know what to say."

"What are you feeling?"

"Angry- way too angry."

"Please hear me out."

"Right, Stacie. You aborted our first baby just a little over two months ago. And now you want another one?"

"I know," I sobbed. "I have these dreams . . ."

"What dreams?"

"Please, I can't talk to you when you're physically looking down on me."

He walked over to his recliner and sat down. "The dreams?" he asked.

I told him about the cries, the crib, and the bloody blanket.

"I know the cry-it is as familiar to me as your voice-it is our baby's. My arms ache for him. I can't hold him, kiss his cheeks, nurse him, or change his diapers. I can't make him stop crying because he's gone."

"You think it was a boy?"

"For some reason I do."

I looked at my hands amazed at the way they were clenched to the point of white knuckles and yet I didn't seem to have any feeling them. Everything in me was focused on the stabbing fear in my heart.

"Stacie, I can't explain how much I miss him; the opportunity to see if he would have your eyes or my nose."

"What are we going to do?" I sobbed.

"I don't know. We can't replace him or her with another pregnancy. We were given one chance to have that particular child and it's gone."

The loss in his voice frightened me but his next words crushed me.

"I don't know if I can trust you."

"Trust me?"

"Yeah-to get pregnant again."

"What do you mean?"

"I have to know-will you change your mind and get another abortion?"

His question stole the breath from my body. My lips went numb and my head spun. My stomach rolled and I felt hot all over. As the room started rotating I put my head between my knees.

"Take some deep breaths, Stacie."

"I'm trying."

"Do it. I'll get you something to drink."

It was difficult to breathe with my head on my knees and my heart in my throat. I did my best.

"Drink this."

I took a few sips of fizzing Diet Coke.

"Better?"

I nodded my head.

"Stacie, I have to know."

As I looked into his dark blue eyes, the truth almost blinded me.

"You really think I'd do that to you or to me again?"

"I can't be sure. You made a life-changing decision without me. I'm angry - I'm trying not to be but everyday I still fight feeling betrayed. The trust I once had is gone."

"How can you love me and not trust me?"

"Do you love your mother?"

Puzzled, I answered, "Yes."

"Do you trust her?"

"To hurt me."

"That's where I'm at."

"You think I'm like my mother?" Anger started to bubble inside my gut.

"I think you bought the lie. I did too for a long time."

"*The lie?*" I asked as I narrowed my eyes along with my heart. *Great. Here comes a pro-life lecture.* I braced myself and prepared to do battle.

"The one about us-about married people. Where you have your life-your body-and make your own decisions and I do the same."

"If we aren't individuals, who are we?" This new direction threw me but I was pretty sure I could hold my own in this argument as well.

"I hope we are two people who are slowly growing into one. If we are always going our own way we will become strangers. We will be the next statistics and signing divorce papers stating irreconcilable differences. Our friends will ask, 'What went wrong?' and we'll say, 'Nothing, we just grew apart.'"

"So you agree with our counselor-there is more than equality to a marriage?"

"All success demands common goals and dreams. This is true in the marriage partnership as well. For example, I understand you making the decision to open your own office without me. I left you. The opportunity came and although we were in counseling, you didn't know for sure where I stood about us.

But, the baby-we were together and you chose not to talk to me. Not to find out how I felt or what I thought. You didn't even know how concerned I'd be for your health. Or if I wanted a child."

"So, whose dreams do we give up?"

"Neither. We adjust them to fit together. You want to protect children. I want you to. I want you to defend them and make the bad guys pay, and . . ."

As his voice drifted off, I watched him drop his head into his hands.

"And what, Mike?"

"And we both want a baby."

I was out of words but Mike wasn't.

"I have dreams too . . . about little kids. Sometimes I see a little girl who looks like you except she has my eyes. Sometimes I see a little boy who looks like me, but with your shining black hair. They reach for me and I go to pick them up . . . and they disappear. I can never reach them, never hold them." Tears escaped from the corners of his eyes.

"Mike, no!" I got up and went to his chair. I knelt in front of him and took his hands. "Can you ever forgive me?"

"Yes, Stacie I can-I choose to. Can you forgive me?"

"For what?"

"For not telling you how I felt months ago-about abortion, marriage, and staring a family."

"When did you know you didn't want to wait any longer to have kids?"

"I watched you finish getting ready for work one morning. I relished the way you moved, your eyes and smile. Your grace and beauty have always fascinated me but in that moment you were never lovelier to me. I found myself wanting children-little replicas of us. More than wanting-I desired for them. But your goals were crystal clear. I couldn't let what I wanted come before your dreams. Now I know you were pregnant at the time."

Tears rushed down both our faces and I was forced to sniff. It was either that or rub my nose on his knee. There wasn't time for anything else so I sniffed again - harder. We were on a relationship roll and I couldn't let anything, not even a snotty nose, get in our way.

"Mike, please forgive me. I've lived as if abortion were the right choice for a long time. I had no idea I'd regret it. Until this last month I didn't know how much I wanted a child - our child. I need your forgiveness like never before."

"I forgive you, Stacie. I love you. I need to ask again, can you forgive me?"

"Yes!" I murmured as I climbed into his lap. As we held each other, I felt freedom knocking.

CHAPTER 11

Jonica

My birthday and Father's Day fell on the same day.

Ben told me to go all out on a new dress, and gave me a gift certificate for "the works" at my favorite salon. Then, he invited Stacie and Mike to supper at Gabrielle's, our favorite fancy restaurant.

On Saturday I found the perfect dress. The navy velvet bodice and flowing mid-calf skirt fit like it had been designed for me. After lunch, I went to City Looks. I picked out a rose-colored polish for my nails. While the manicurist massaged and polished my fingers and toes, I relaxed. Then I met with the hair stylist.

"What should we do today?"

"Short and stylish." I said.

"Are you sure? We'd be taking off more than twelve inches of hair."

"I'm sure. Can't we donate it to some wig organization?"

"We can."

"Go for it."

I hoped to find a new me. Even though I knew a haircut wouldn't change my childless condition or bring healing to Della or Stacie- and it surely wouldn't bring about world peace-I wanted to look and feel different. I was tired of braids and clips to hold back my long hair.

Walking around the mall again, I found the right shade of navy shoes and a matching clutch bag. As I walked, my hair danced to the beat of my movements instead of hanging. I headed for Mitchell's department store. I purchased a set of dangly sapphire earrings, and had a makeover at the Este' Lauder counter. I purchased an eye shadow, blush, lipstick, and a bottle of *Beautiful* perfume.

Smiling as I headed for the car, I wondered where I could talk Ben into taking me so all this would pay off.

At home, my man gave me the once-over and teased, "You look great. You want to go out? It'd be a shame to keep all this beauty to myself."

"Sure." A shy feeling stole over and instead of the flirty promises I wanted to make, I blushed. The changes were big. I wasn't sure what other people might think. Ben's comments and kisses gave me a partial peace. There were still those church ladies to consider.

We ate at our favorite pizza place then went to the bookstore and drank fancy coffees. Later we held hands and walked around the lake, sneaking in kisses when we thought no one was looking.

I dreaded the next day. Even though I had a gift for "Husband's Day" hidden in my drawer, I didn't want my husband to hurt anymore. *Father's Day is so hard on Ben. He tries so hard to keep it to himself to protect me, but I see it. Please Lord, give us a break.*

A cool breeze moved across the lake and we listened to the quiet honking of geese as they settled in for the night. The popcorn man shut off his light, and street lights flickered on.

In the morning, I woke Ben with breakfast in bed. I had to get up before the sun peeked over the horizon to surprise my early bird husband. His singing is the only alarm clock I needed. But on that morning, I beat him.

He enjoyed his scrambled eggs and toast. For awhile, he played with the music computer program I bought him. We skipped the Father's Day service at church and later met our parents to celebrate our dads and my birthday. My folks gave me a new burgundy study Bible. Ben's gave me a china teapot decorated with wild roses. We gave our dads gift certificates to the local tool shop.

Back home, Ben told me to go to my favorite spot in our yard. Sitting on the bench, surrounded by rose bushes, I waited. Ben brought me coffee on a silver tray. In the center sat a square blue box topped with a silver bow. It was almost too pretty to unwrap except it was obviously a jeweler's box. Nestled in the navy velvet a band of diamonds and sapphires sparkled.

"Happy Birthday, Jonica!" Ben reached for my right hand and slid the ring onto my finger.

"I love it!" I said holding my hand so the stones could shine in the light.

Ben lifted my hand to his lips and kissed it.

The little boy next door saw us and yelled out, "Happy Father's Day, Ben!"

"Get in here, Brady. He's nobody's father," his dad grouched.

In the second before Ben moved away, I wondered, *Is that man just plain mean or incredibly stupid?*

Ben went inside. For a moment, I sat in the garden numbed by shock. Then I followed my husband into the house. I found him sitting on the stairs his head in his hands, shoulders shaking.

"Please look at me."

He did. Nothing in our journey so far had prepared me for the savage pain in his jade eyes. Tears flowed down cheeks usually upturned in a big smile. Never in my life had anything hurt me as much as his anguish. Not even when my beloved grandparents died. I could handle the arrows flung at me-but not the ones they hurled at Ben. He stood and held his arms open. I slid inside them, and we hung on tight to each other as we grieved. My cry changed from *Why me?* to *Why Ben?*

"We will never hold babies born of our love. Would our little boy have your smile and my eyes? A little blond-haired girl will never look up and call me Daddy."

I wanted to say something-anything to comfort the suffering man in my arms. No words came. So, we continued to cling to each other, praying we'd survive this shipwreck we called our lives.

A few minutes later, he held me away from him and said, "Thank you for saying nothing. Your quiet love is all I needed right now."

Dressing for our night out, I tried to put the pain aside. The new dress, hairstyle, and makeup helped me feel feminine. In recent months I'd come to see myself as less of a woman. I patted my empty womb, expecting an echo. There was only absolute stillness.

"Ready?" Ben asked as his arms slid around me from behind.

"Almost." I left his sweet embrace to fill my little clutch with powder, lipstick, and a lace trimmed hankie. *Please be with Della, Lord.* Since Don's death, I found myself uttering little prayers for her often. When I saw her at church she looked thinner, and her voice wobbled when she spoke. I was afraid she was fading away.

At the restaurant, the Cutters waited in the foyer. We met Mike for the first time. His dark eyes danced as he took my hand and said, "Hello."

Stacie hugged me. "I love your new 'do.' It's so different and yet so you." Her reassurance mattered.

She wore a black, fitted sheath dress that stopped just above her knees. She'd pulled her hair back into a silver clip. Her red nails and lips glistened in the soft light. When she took Mike's arm, they looked like movie stars-all elegance and glamour.

Our husbands pulled out our chairs for us and we all settled in to study the menus. After ordering, the guys talked about work while Stacie and I sipped lemon water and listened.

I ate succulent shrimp and filet mignon well-done. For dessert the waitress brought pieces of turtle cheesecake-mine decorated with a single candle. As I blew out the burning light, I breathed a silent prayer. *Please let me shine for You into the lives of Mike and Stacie.*

As my first bite of rich caramel, pecans, chocolate, and cheesecake melted in my mouth, I watched my friend. She seemed to glow more than ever before. Mike is so good for her, *Lord-thank You for bringing them back together.*

I couldn't keep from complimenting my beautiful friend. "Stacie, you look more stunning than ever-it might be the light in here, but you literally shimmer."

She looked at me and smiled. "Thanks." In her eyes I saw an intense joy and an equal amount of sadness.

Mike signaled to the waitress and she brought a small gift on a tray to the table.

Mike and Stacie smiled and said, "Happy birthday."

Inside another jewelry box was a necklace.

"The jeweler said it represented friendship. Something about two guys in the Bible named Jonathan and David. It seemed a perfect gift for you." Stacie said.

"Thank you both." I said as Ben got up and attached the clasp.

"You're welcome. And thank you for supporting me these last months. I didn't know friends like you existed." Stacie said.

Looking at her, I saw it again. Radiance. Gladness and a deeper love for my friend flooded my heart.

Joy from the Lord who is my strength.

Stacie

Father's Day dawned bright and beautiful.

While Mike showered, I made the bed and prepared my surprise for him. I released a bunch of pink and blue balloons I'd been hiding in the guest room closet. I paced the room, batting at the helium-filled plastic bubbles. When the door opened I stood still holding my poster. It read, "I'm positive."

Mike stepped out of the bathroom, rubbing his hair with a towel.

"What do you want to do after brunch?"

"Celebrate."

"The brunch is the celebration."

Then he lowered the towel and saw the balloons.

"Stacie?"

I held the poster higher and peeked out around the side. His whoop echoed in the tile bathroom behind him.

"Happy Father's Day, Mike!"

We hugged, and his kiss held a tenderness that seemed to me reverent. Then, our stomachs growled.

"Are you sick yet?"

"No. Not all women get sick. Maybe I'll be lucky. Right now I'm starved. Let's hurry. I don't want to miss a morsel, just in case my luck changes."

In the car Mike instructed me on my new health regimen. "No coffee or wine from here on out. I won't drink them either. That should make it easier on you.. And I think you should walk instead of jogging. And no lifting."

"Yes Sir." I giggled at the look on his face. He hadn't expected me to give in so easy. Surrender was not one of the main goals in my life but I wanted to give this baby the best chance possible to be healthy, and I intended to be an excellent mom from conception on. I didn't tell him, but I'd started drinking decaf the moment he said he wanted children too.

My dad joined Mike's parents and us for breakfast. I handed our dads foil-wrapped boxes. A silver one for my dad, gold for Mike's. They pulled out engraved money clips.

A second of silence followed, then the two men asked in unison, "For real?"

"Uh-huh."

Mike's mom whooped when she read the engraving and grabbed her son in a big hug. I had a moment of staggering fear. What if she found out about the grandchild she'd never know? Would she be so happy for us then? I forced the anxiety away.

"Now I know where you learned to whoop," I muttered to Mike with a wink.

"What do they say?" asked a confused Mike.

"Grandpa."

My dad took my hand, his eyes guarded. "How are you, sweetheart?"

"Fine, Daddy."

"I'm so happy for you. For us." He said as he kissed my cheek.

At home we rode the elevator with a woman and her young son. "Happy Father's Day, mister," he said as they exited on their floor.

"Thanks, pal," Mike said as the door closed.

Getting ready for Jonica's birthday dinner, I patted my tummy. It already felt fuller.

I longed for Jonica to be all right with my news, but intended to keep it quiet at least for today. I didn't want to ruin her party. I knew she and Ben would have made great parents. A shiver of sadness ran through my body as guilt gripped my stomach. If there was a God why would He let me get pregnant after what I did and not her-the innocent one? I let it go. First of all, I didn't believe in God, so I was uncomfortable with even thinking about Him. And second of all, no one could figure out all the mysteries of life-so why should I try? It was too complicated, messy, and painful. Jonica would make the best of it like she did all things.

We arrived at the restaurant early. Mike wanted the waitress to bring Jonica's present to the table later. I was excited. I knew I'd found a special gift. In the mall was a wonderful jewelry store full of original pieces. I asked the jeweler for something out of the ordinary for a close confidante. He delighted in showing me a necklace he said represented a story of great friendship. When he told me there was a biblical connection, I was convinced Jonica would love it for more than one reason.

I clung to Mike's arm after he spoke with the waitress. "You are such a nice man."

"I'm glad you think so."

I met Ben for the first time. I knew he knew about me, so I was nervous. He shook Mike's hand and gave me a quick hug. "I'm so glad you are in Jonica's life. You mean so much to her."

The moment was easy - as if we'd been friends a long time. I watched Jonica and her husband. He had it too-the look I now called "the Christian glow."

Her beauty lit up the room. Her new hair, dress, and makeup were only part of it. She knew exactly how to dress, and carried herself like a queen totally in love with her kingdom.

This shining thing that radiated from deep within her mystified me. I couldn't point it out and say, "See?" Yet it was as real as the floor beneath my feet. I knew they were sad. These were hard days for them. Yet here they sat, loving everyone who crossed their paths. Even waiters, waitresses, and busboys received a word of thanks and praise. Weird, a little whacky, and wonderful at the same time.

We ate, talked, and laughed. Our husbands hit it off and made plans to play golf. Mike wanted to know more about guitars. I was glad he passed on asking about motorcycles and helicopters. One adventurous man in our lives was enough. Besides, mine was about to be a daddy and if I had to be careful, so did he.

When she blew out her candle, I wondered what Jonica wished for. I hoped with all my being she would get it-my friend deserved to have her dreams come true. By the time we tasted our cheesecake, my nerves nearly caused my tummy to revolt.

When Jonica complimented me, bubbles of uncertainty gurgled in my stomach. I knew something showed. *Please let everything be good with her*, I begged whatever power of the universe that might hear me.

The waitress interrupted our stare. Jonica loved the necklace and knew the meaning behind the design. When she looked at me again, I knew somehow she knew.

"I'm pregnant," I said as she whispered, "You're pregnant."

Her eyes shone with sincere love for me.

Where does she get such joy? Such strength?

CHAPTER 12

Jonica

Infertility was a continual process.

Just when I hoped things were better, the grief came back with surprising force.

As I was getting ready for bed a few nights later, I decided if honesty was such a stinking good policy, it was Ben's turn. Once again, raw anger at the situation started a slow burn deep in my belly. Words pelted out of me like a sudden summer hailstorm. I gave him no warning as emotion spewed out of me with a vengeance.

"You know I'm happy for Stacie. She longed for this pregnancy."

"I know."

Slamming my pillow instead of plumping it, I threw back the covers and continued. "It's not fair. I love her and I want all her dreams to come true."

Hot tears ran down my cheeks. I pressed them away with the heels of my hands. I paced the room and continued ranting while Ben watched, propped up in bed. His quiet spirit did not calm my storm.

I raised my face to heaven. "God, my life is still in pieces here. I don't know how to live with this gut-wrenching pain or this constant emptiness. Will it always be like this? Do You even hear me?"

"Come here, Jonica." Ben spoke in a gentle tone of voice that usually drew me straight into his arms.

"No. I don't want to be comforted. And if you're looking for romance, think about another night, Buster. I want answers. How can God say, 'No' to us? What is He thinking?"

"About you."

"Pardon me?"

"Remember when we found that verse in Jeremiah twenty nine? For I know the thoughts that I think toward you, says the LORD, thoughts of peace and not of evil, to give you a future and a hope. Then you will call upon Me and go and pray to Me, and I will listen to you. And you will seek Me and find Me, when you search for Me with all your heart."

"He gave those words to the Jewish nation."

"He is the same yesterday, today, and tomorrow, Joni. God gave the message first to His chosen ones, but He has a plan for all His people. And remember the study we did on being grafted in as Abraham's children?"

I could only nod. The study made the Bible promises more real for me.

Come to bed, honey. It's late." Ben invited once more.

His faith and the Word of God quieted most of my anger.

So, instead of stomping my feet and shaking my fist at heaven, I slid under the covers feeling better but knowing I was still holding on to a little corner of resentment.

In the warmth of Ben's arms, I asked, "What do you do with all the hurt?"

"I think not having kids is always going to impact our lives. With time and space we will deal with it better, but it will always be here." He pointed to his heart.

"I know and I hate it. Are you ever angry?"

He shrugged and my head bobbled. "Sometimes. Mostly, I'm sad. I'm learning it's hard to fight facts."

"I don't want this to be our truth."

"Me either, but it is. Accepting that is essential to us living in freedom."

"Do you think that's what the Bible verse about the truth setting us free means?"

"The Truth there is Jesus. I believe that trusting the One who is Truth is freeing even when we don't know why something happens in life, because we know He does, and that is enough."

"Like we have any chance against God."

"Joni we're not against God and He's not against us. He is not the enemy."

"No infertility is."

"Honey, sometimes the enemy we battle so hard lives within us."

"Don't you think if God gave us a miracle child, Stacie would see and believe?"

"Do you want a miracle for Stacie or for you?"

"Both."

"Maybe the greatest miracle is when we don't get what we ask for every time, and keep believing anyway."

"I want you to be wrong. I'd love to show Stacie something only God could do so she'll have to believe. I long for her to see His power and to feel it displayed in my life so she can't resist accepting Him."

"Faith in things unseen is the greatest of all. When you live your beliefs out in front of Stacie, she may resist and even disagree. Just remember, her dispute is not with you - it's with God."

"Are you counting on her to reject Him?"

"She's a skeptic, it will take time for her allow the facts to trans-form into faith."

"I'm not sure I'm up to being a steady witness to her. I mean, look at the way I handled her Mother's Day question. Why did God choose me? I'm really not the best woman for this job."

"I think you're the perfect woman for the job. God wouldn't have it any other way."

Sudden hot emotions rose in me.

"Hey, Mrs. Johnson, I thought romance was off the menu for tonight."

"It's back on."

When the alarm went off, I swung my feet to the floor and my heart filled with urgency. Stacie needed Jesus.

After my morning routine, and seeing Ben off to work, I grabbed a cup of coffee and headed for my office. I pulled opened my Bible and went over the familiar salvation verses. While I knew their truth and power personally, I sensed I was in the wrong place. For some reason, I flipped over to where Paul was speaking to the leaders about his imprisonment. *What a good lawyer. Lord, I wish I could communicate Your truths to Stacie like Paul.*

The sunshine warmed my head as I bowed in prayer. Seconds

turned to minutes without my awareness as I lifted my friend to the lover of her soul. *In Your time, not mine, Lord.* I sighed as sweet surrender brought peace.

The phone rang.

"Jonica, they finished painting and carpeting the new office space. Dad had the furniture delivered too. Can you come and see it?" Stacie's voice bubbled.

"I'd love to. When?"

"Now? We could meet at the office and walk to Wong's for lunch then take a tour?"

"Sure."

"I'm starved and need an egg roll. Does this really work for you?"

Laughing, I agreed. "I wouldn't want to come between a pregnant woman and her egg rolls."

She chattered as we walked to the restaurant. My tirade at Ben the night before had left me with little to say. I wanted to be quiet. I hoped she wouldn't take it the wrong way or ask any questions.

She told me about her new business cards, her visit to social services, and her contact at the women's shelter.

In mid-sentence she pulled her top tight and we looked to see if her tummy had changed since the last time we'd checked. The bulge was so small she could still wear her jeans in comfort. I prayed for the tiny one nestled safely in his or her mother's womb. In the quiet of the moment, God filled me with genuine gladness as only He can.

She mentioned the women's shelter again and had my full attention. "It was one of Eve's first political missions. Years ago she raised money to get a newer facility."

"I'm deeply committed to the shelter too. In fact, I'm writing an article for the newspaper about it and how we can all help."

"Imagine that-you and Eve on the same side of anything."

I liked the idea that the most liberal senator in Washington and I held a common passion. Maybe I'd try and set up an interview with Eve Dunbar focused on our common bond instead of our political differences. My editor was always looking for the fresh angle. This qualified.

We ate and talked, and inside me I sensed the Lord restraining my tongue. I yielded to Him.

Inside her new office, I understood Stacie's excitement. Chandler Daniels had kept his promise. After consulting with Stacie on her favorite colors, his painter and carpet layer had finished the project. The front office featured one small window facing the courtyard, comfy chairs for clients, and a reception desk.

"Won't my 'someday assistant' enjoy this view?"

Before I could comment, she moved right along. "Now for my office." She swung open etched-glass double doors and we stepped through.

Her space included built-in floor-to-ceiling bookcases already lined with her intimidating law library. Bright colored rugs rested under her impressive desk and in front of other furniture. A bay window also faced the courtyard and I noticed bird feeders and blossoms just outside.

"This room is huge." I saw trim around what looked like a large doorway but from my angle couldn't see inside. "What's behind door number three?" I asked.

"The best of the best-tadaaaa!"

She opened the double clear-glass doors to reveal a large closet turned nursery. A new, full-sized window faced the back of another building but gave the tiny room a sunny glow.

"I wondered what you were going to do with Baby," I said. "This is great."

"Most of my work will involve research and phone interviews. When I do home studies and visits or have court dates, or meetings, I will need someone who does part-time childcare, but whenever possible, I want him or her with me."

"Very cool. I can baby sit sometimes. I know Natalie is looking for a little one to take care of now and then to help make ends meet. She's flexible and wonderful with kids."

"Thanks. Write down her number and I'll call her."

After jotting down the information, I returned to exploring Stacie's brave new world. Her desk was a piece of art, a large glass oval rested on black metal legs formed into intricate swirls.

"This desk is great."

"I think so too. Eve sent it. That makes the whole thing even more amazing."

"Is the lamp designed by the same person?"

"Yes. She ordered them made for my Washington office. When she realized she couldn't change my mind, she shipped them here."

"I'm glad."

"Me too. I love them. I just don't get it."

I pondered my response to her Eve comment carefully. "I know you and Eve aren't close, but it's pretty cool she knows your style and got it for you. I mean, she wasn't planning your office to be a carbon copy of hers right?"

"Your point is interesting and this is nothing like she'd choose for herself. She's into old. Antiques trip her trigger. But that doesn't prove anything. With Eve, everything comes with strings."

A laptop computer, the silver desk lamp, a crystal vase filled with daffodils, some photos in silver frames, and a clock with a timer rested on the desk. Near the window sat a round, glass-topped table with four matching black leather chairs. In the center of the room was a black leather couch with yellow, red, green, and blue throw pillows. In front of the couch sat another table. Rather than magazines or knickknacks, a stack of puzzles and a pail of markers waited for small clients' hands to use them.

Time to change the subject. "This office is so you, Stacie."

"Thanks."

"What are you going to put on the walls?"

"Pictures of things children enjoy and that are emotionally safe. Beach balls, sand castles, that kind of thing."

"Cool."

"I'm excited. Dad bought me the rest of the furniture-even the things for the baby and the kids' corner. Sit on this couch-it is so soft."

She looked at her watch and then stroked her smooth leather couch. "Do you need to be anywhere right now?"

"No. Want to talk?"

"I guess." Grabbing a pillow and hugging it close, she took a deep breath. "So I wonder-what does Eve want in return?"

"You're so sure this isn't a gift from a mother to her daughter?"

"You don't know Eve."

"You're right. But maybe you being pregnant touches her, and this is the only way for her to let you know."

"She can communicate with everyone but me."

"Relationships are strange sometimes. She seems like a woman who has a reason for everything she does."

"That's what I mean-what does she want in return for this gift?"

"No, I meant something else. I don't think Eve wastes time or opportunity. I wonder if she is trying to say something to you she can't find a way to put into words."

"Like what?"

"Maybe that she is proud of you even if you aren't following in her footsteps. Or she might be saying, 'I love you'?"

"You think?"

"Could be."

"I don't know what to believe."

"What do you trust?"

She shrugged. "Usually, I don't."

"Speaking of trust, we've shared almost everything else in our lives except my faith. I'm not sure it's safe to talk about what I believe."

"Why? I knew we would eventually."

"I don't want to offend you. I'm also afraid my evidence or closing arguments won't convince you."

She hugged the pillow tighter and waited. I tried to swallow what felt like a rock in my throat.

"It's all right, Jonica, go ahead." Truthfully, I think she just wanted me to be done. I sat in full agreement with her. I'd rather be at home telling Ben how it went than living this moment where I could fail in a big way.

" Here is the evidence I hope you will consider." I pulled a small Bible out of my purse. "I'd like you to read and deliberate the first four books of the New Testament, especially the trial and execution of Jesus. If you decide not to believe what's recorded here is the truth, you aren't rejecting me. You're disbelieving the Word of God"

"And if I agree to do this, what do you expect from me?"

"Your honesty. I marked a special place in John; the third chapter. I think it'd be interesting to hear your take on what Jesus told Nicodemus-a ruler of the Jews-a man of the law. I'd like to know how you would have represented Jesus if He'd asked you to be His lawyer. Your opinion of Pilate also interests me. And I'd like to know, after you read these books as a lawyer, who you think Jesus was and is. If you want to read further into the New Testament, you'll meet a man named Paul. He was well acquainted with Jewish and Roman law."

"They had lawyers in the Bible?"

"Sure. This one wrote several of the books in the New Testament."

Her eyebrows rose as I handed her the Book. I don't know if she noticed my trembling hand, or heard the shake in my voice.

Good grief. I sounded like a law professor giving an assignment- not a friend asking her to consider my faith.

"I also marked a couple of spots where Jesus interacted with women. I think you'll be interested in how He treated them. He has never been the chauvinist some want to make Him into."

"I'll think about it." She said as she took the Bible from my hand.

With a simple sentence and not the detailed excuse I'd braced myself for, we were done. Whatever she did with the challenge was up to her.

Watching Stacie run her hand over the cover, I was reminded again of her beautiful mother. Eve's public service didn't reveal the mystery woman behind the persona. Who influenced her life the most? What experience had forged her heart of steel? Where would she be without her drive? When alone, did she miss her daughter? How could I find out so my friend could know she was loved? I could hear Ben in the quiet place of my mind urging me to stay out of their relationship. Shoot. All I wanted to do was make my friend happy.

We sat in comfortable silence. Stacie had accepted my challenge and in her hand rested the Word of God, which He promised would not return void. Did she realize the power she was unleashing in her life?

Stacie

Pregnancy changed me body and soul.

Sometimes a soft fluttering caught my attention. I'd wait to feel it again, barely breathing, afraid I'd miss it. I vacillated between slight nausea and extreme hunger. I cried without warning, and at the most unexpected times loneliness for the fetus I'd aborted washed over me. The sudden bursts of grief stunned me. Mike and I no longer talked about it-the other child. I kept the sorrow to myself, tightly bottled

in a secret chamber of my heart. We focused on the current pregnancy. Our baby...alive and well. Nothing else could matter. To face
the past meant to shatter and I needed to be whole.

Chandler Daniels called to let me know the office awaited my
inspection. Dad called to ask where I wanted my desk. The delivery
guys were on their way with it, and I met them there. Four weeks
earlier Dad had taken me shopping. I kept the colors basic black and
white with primary colors as accents. Dad had the kid's table
custom-built. It sat low to the ground and big, colored print pillows
served as chairs. The tabletop performed a dual function. A whiteboard framed in painted wood, it was strong enough to color on, put
puzzles together, play games, and would also serve as a drawing
board. It provided a safe place to express emotions and then wipe
them away. With the legs painted black, it matched the decor. The
white walls were bare.

"It looks like you're specializing in children," dad commented.

"I think I am. The anger that drove the woman-defender thing I
had going seems to have evaporated."

"That could be a very good thing."

"Mike agrees."

Then I had to ask. "How is Eve taking my pregnancy?"

"She'll get used to it. Don't worry." He drew me into a hug. "Your
mother will fall in love with this baby."

"I hope so."

"I must go. I'm meeting Chandler Daniels for lunch."

"Do you know him well?"

"Yes."

"Does he ever share his religion with you?"

"Every chance he gets."

"Are you ever offended by his preaching?"

"He doesn't preach, and when he does mention his faith, I don't
find it offensive. It's just part of who he is and, he has good inten-
tions."

"Do you agree with him?"

"No."

"Is he getting to you?"

"No again. Is Jonica's getting to you?"

"She doesn't talk about it much either although I know it's important to her."

It almost made me sad but what I knew of her religion made no sense to me.

When dad left, I grabbed my phone and called Jonica. I could hardly wait for her to see the office. Of course, the tour had to wait. I was hungry. The little morning sickness I experienced came for me in the evening, so by lunchtime I was famished. She came right over and we walked to Wong's. The waitress, Linda, remembered us. When she asked if we both wanted coffee, I said, "No. I'm pregnant so no caffeine for a few months."

"Congratulations. Two egg rolls?"

"Yes." Our voices blended in a sweet harmony.

"Jonica, I want everyone to know. It's too early but I'm dreaming about my belly showing the world I'm pregnant."

"Then you'll be uncomfortable and dreaming about your size four jeans!"

"I know. Nuts, huh?"

"No. It's just part of the whole process."

We ate and caught up, then returned to my office.

"Stacie, I'm impressed. You make black and white look inviting instead of stark. You did it in your home and again here. I love it. The way you made the kids' table the center of the room, will show your young clients right away this is a special place for them."

She liked the nursery too. I couldn't tell her how the crib brought me both joy and horror. I longed to see my baby curled up in sleep there, eyelashes resting on chubby cheeks. But the lost one in the nightmares haunted my daydreams.

We talked about the desk from Eve and she brought up a lovely scenario about my mother. It was easy for Jonica. Her mother showered her with love and acceptance. She had no idea who mine was.

I wanted to stay in my little corner of the world a while longer and we settled in on the couch. After all my chatter, I quieted down to enjoy just being with my friend.

When I mentioned trust, our conversation headed in a new direction. Jonica took a deep breath and reached into her purse. Out came a small Bible. I braced myself for condemnation and a stiff sentence if my response was outside of her religious law.

I was relieved by her approach. No sin or hell talk. She asked me to read four books and report back my findings. She talked sort of like a teacher handing out extra credit. She seemed more interested in a conversation than a conversion. When her voice shook, it revealed her nerves but I sensed she was hopeful I'd accept her challenge. To be honest, the idea of studying ancient law, lawyers, and a trial intrigued me.

She handed me the small purple book. It wasn't as intimidating as I remembered Bibles looking.

"It's a gift to you. If you ever want to know more, you can look."

"It comes with strings."

"It does. But you might find these strings set you free instead of binding and gagging you."

I noticed my first name embossed in gold on the front as I rubbed my hand across the leather cover.

We sat quietly together, at ease even in our diversity.

I wished her God had the power to change my mind. I hoped she wasn't counting on that.

CHAPTER 13

Jonica

Our friendship grew and we were both more comfortable since I'd shared my faith. She'd wondered when it might happen, and I'd felt tense waiting for the right time. What Stacie did with anything she learned wasn't up to me so I left it all in her court. It was between her and God.

I had moments when self-doubts stabbed and jabbed their way to the front of my mind and brought on times of regret. Maybe if I'd shared the traditional plan of salvation I'd have 'closed the sale' and she'd already be saved. I doubted my adequacy. Then I'd release Stacie to Him again. The God who created her could surely speak to her with or without my help.

Stacie shared each phase of her pregnancy with the joy of a child on Christmas Day. Hearing the heartbeat, feeling the movement, and seeing her rounded tummy brought giggles and amazement. One day, shopping for nursery furniture, she grabbed my hand and pressed it to her belly.

"Feel that?" she asked.

"I do," I whispered. The movement fascinated me. A life being formed by God rested inside my friend and under my hand.

"Mike gets the same look on his face you do."

She ooohed and aaahed over the multitude of baby things - each one cuter than the last.

Watching her, I understood Mike a little better. Both of us stood on the side lines mesmerized by the mystery of life as Stacie experienced it as only an insider can. With Mike in my corner, I wasn't alone in the by-stander business.

I knew the little room at home had a purpose. It would always be a safe place for other people's babies. A new kind of hope rose up in my chest. I looked forward to rocking them, singing to them, and loving them. I was inching toward healing and acceptance.

"This is it, Jonica. Look!"

I turned to look and found her sitting in an oversized white wicker rocker. She looked at home.

"My Aunt Jenny is making a quilt in bright yellow, green, and white. She also offered to cover the cushion of any rocking chair I found. This is so perfect. What do you think?"

"I think it's the one."

Stacie purchased two child-sized easels, extra pads of paper, and markers.

I bought the rocking chair. It seemed the perfect gift-a place for my friends to rest while they cared for their little one. A gift for all three of them.

Stacie made delivery plans for the purchases and we hurried on our way. The next stop was my parent's house.

Mom welcomed us both as daughters. The house smelled of baking, fresh coffee, apple cinnamon potpourri, Odyssey perfume, and Old Spice aftershave.

"I love your hugs, Rose," Stacie said.

"I love yours too. Now you two get in here and eat some of these homemade cookies."

"Hi, Girls," Dad hollered from his computer room downstairs.

"Jonica, will you run these cookies down to your dad for me?"

"Sure."

"Special delivery, Daddy."

"Your mom makes the best cookies."

"She sure does. What are you doing?"

"Playing Monopoly with the computer."

"Who's winning?"

"Not me."

"I'd better get upstairs-I don't want to miss anything."

"You enjoy your visit."

"We will, Daddy. I love you."

"I love you too," he said, the words muffled by his first bite of cookie.

Mom arranged chocolate chip, peanut butter, and oatmeal raisin cookies on a plate and asked, "How did your shopping trip go?"

I watched Stacie blossom when we visited my parents. As Mom touched, chattered with, and served her, the tension often evident in Stacie's shoulders and jaw melted away as she absorbed the sweet mothering.

Stacie picked up an old photo of me. I stood beside my new doll highchair with my favorite doll Betsy in place. My smile was huge. I was big on playing Mama.

"Please tell me about Jonica as a little girl."

"Our daughter bubbled and waltzed her way into the hearts of most people who knew her. She charmed her grandparents the moment they held her. Blond hair and blue eyes got her out of some of the trouble her bright mind often got her into. Her favorite things were talking, playing house, singing, hearing stories read out loud—and did I mention talking?"

"Some things never change," Stacie teased. "I wonder if this one will have a strong will. I'm reading the book you gave me on raising children and I can't help but wonder." She brushed cookie crumbs off her tummy.

"Joni was strong-willed. She knew right from wrong and sometimes chose wrong even though she knew it meant discipline."

"Jonica-strong-willed? No way! How did you handle her?"

"We stayed consistent even when blue eyes danced, blond curls bounced, and pink cheeks rose in sweet smiles. At first, her determination surprised me. When I asked my mother about it, she just smiled and said something about history repeating itself."

Dunking my cookies into my coffee, I remembered feeling naughty and deciding a moment of disobedience was worth the punishment. Later a new emotion had entered my mind then reached into my heart. I watched Mom's face when she disciplined me and saw disappointment. It bothered me to make her sad. One day I challenged Dad and saw the same look in his eyes. From then on, I wanted to make my parents proud of me. I didn't always succeed, but their love and praise rewarded me even when it was hard to be good.

"I wish my mom loved me the way you love Jonica. I'm not out-and-out jealous, but I do envy your relationship."

"I pray for your mom everyday. I believe she loves you and I hope one day you will know how much."

"You pray for me too, huh?"

"Yes, and for the little one in your womb. In fact, we bought a gift for you."

Mom walked to the bedroom and came out with a large package wrapped in bright green paper.

"Jonica, call your dad. He's part of this gift too."

We watched Stacie as she held the unwrapped print up and read the words of Psalm 139 in a whisper.

For You formed my inward parts;
You covered me in my mother's womb.
I will praise You, for I am fearfully and wonderfully made;
Marvelous are Your works,
And that my soul knows very well.
My frame was not hidden from You,
When I was made in secret,
And skillfully wrought in the lowest parts of the earth.
Your eyes saw my substance, being yet unformed.
And in Your book they all were written,
The days fashioned for me,
When as yet there were none of them.
How precious also are Your thoughts to me, O God!
How great is the sum of them!

"The same God creating this baby in you, created you. With love, detail, and knowledge of who you would be. He loves you, Stacie, and so do we," Mom said.

"The book of Psalms is a book of poetry, right?"

"Yes, or song prayers inspired by God and offered back to Him by David and other writers. And now it is our turn."

"Thank you, Rose and Carl. This will hang near the rocking chair Jonica bought today, and I will read it to him or her often."

On the way home after dropping Stacie off, I thanked God again for my parents. They always knew how to touch people with genuine love.

Stacie

After Jonica shared her religion with me, I relaxed. We were past it. We could agree to disagree and still enjoy our friendship. She accepted me even though I didn't embrace her beliefs.

I decided to keep my end of our bargain and bought the works of a historian named Josephus and several books on Jewish and Roman law. Everything I'd read so far was interesting but I hadn't touched the Bible she'd given me. I was doing my homework before I read the fable. For me it was a case of facts versus faith. I hoped she wouldn't be disappointed when we finally talked about it all again.

In the past, I'd built relationships based on total agreement. Anyone who disagreed wasn't worth the effort. I lived the "them and us" mentality. I'd always envisioned Christians as closed and unsociable- living apart from the real world in some religious la-la land. Jonica and her family welcomed me with hearts and arms wide open. I was never an outsider with them.

Their social involvement surprised me. They went to movies, concerts, restaurants, and were politically, albeit misled, involved. Jonica spent hours in art galleries. Ben invited Muslims, Jews, believers from all denominations, and many non-believers into their lives. From one photo I'd seen, a cook-out at their house resembled a mini United Nations meeting. They helped out at the soup kitchen, cleaned ditches once a month with their church, and Jonica had a curious habit of stopping to offer the homeless food gift cards. I'd never seen any of the politicians Eve wined and dined in elegance and extreme wealth, do any of these things. Did they know that for some people of faith this was a way of life? It was news to me.

Eve had kept me sheltered from friends as a much as she could. Only people whose influence furthered political and social status gained entrance to our exclusive lives. Private schools, tutors every summer and heavy class loads assured excellent grades and early graduation. It also meant no time for shopping at the mall or sleepovers. Birthday parties included kids from the same financial and social background. We dressed for the occasion and stayed on our best public behavior. Competition, sarcasm, and conceit took the place of giggles and shared secrets. The rules remained rigid into adulthood. I broke only one- I dated and then married a man who laughed, loved, and taught me to do the same. A man not handpicked by Eve. She wasn't sure how he voted and that burned her.

As a young mother, Eve spent her time raising me. We did normal things for a while. We went to the park, the zoo, and on picnics. The memories lingered at the edges of my mind. Sometimes I thought I remembered her laughter-as clear and sweet as the tinkle of a small wind chime. When Mother left for Washington, Dad and I developed new habits. We ate in front of the TV, rented silly movies, ate popcorn, and told jokes.

After I told him about the baby, Dad had dropped off a boxful of my old baby things. I wondered if Eve remembered them. After shaking out and refolding tiny dresses, bonnets, and buntings, I found an old shoebox of photographs. In the first few Mother and Dad gazed into each other's eyes-their look so intimate I felt like an gawker. A young Eve held a small girl child-a copy of herself. My smile beamed at the camera. There was also a picture of Eve holding an infant. She didn't smile into the baby's face. Her arms held it loosely. Curiosity drew me to the unknown child.

I flipped through more memorabilia. Another photo showed Eve on a lounge chair, with me in a small wading pool next to her. I knew that was about the time things changed.

After Grandma and Grandpa died in a car accident, we moved to their mansion. Dad worked longer hours, and Eve read more books. We no longer went to the park. A nanny, housekeeper, and cook took care of me and the house. My mother went to meetings and marches. If anyone ever experienced a conversion, Eve did. She preached feminism to anyone in listening range. Her clothes went from cotton pedal pushers to linen slacks and silk blouses. She took speech lessons and practiced for hours in front of me, delivering her message of equality and women's rights. The only time she smiled was for campaign photos. When I turned seven, I started at a private school and Eve ran for office the first time. When she won the state representative's position, I went to the State House with her. She let me sit in on the proceedings. The big words and long speeches bored me. I fell asleep.

"Stacie, you embarrassed me today. I will not bring you back until you can pay attention. You behaved in an immature, rude manner."

I'm just a kid. The silent rebuttal never reached my lips. I didn't understand why I should care but I knew from then on I'd better. Disappointing Mother was bad. I decided I try hard not to let her down again. Most of the time, I failed.

One picture remained in the bottom of the shoebox. I stood in front of Eve while Dad held the infant. The snapshot resembled a family picture. Somewhere along the way I'd forgotten these moments in our lives. I tried to figure out how old I was in the photo. It was shortly before we moved so I had to have been around four.

At the very bottom of the big box rested the blanket from the photo. Perhaps the baby came to visit and needed to borrow my blanket. I tucked everything back in the box.

Determined to make our home a wonderful place for our child, I reviewed the list of things I needed to buy for the baby's room. Since I was only five months pregnant, some people might consider it premature. I just wanted to be prepared. We opened up the small bedroom we'd never used. Mike painted the walls white and put up a baby border-wild animal babies including my favorite-an elephant. Not quite Noah's Ark but almost. He also put up a green shelf and Jonica filled it with stuffed animals and birds. Mike's mom brought over his old Tonka trucks and Hot Wheels. Some of us were counting on a boy and if it was a girl, I hoped she liked earth movers and cars.

At the Baby Warehouse, Jonica and I wandered from one room group to another. Nothing hit me as different enough. Then I saw the old-fashioned white wicker rocker. The soft round lines and texture drew me in. So did the wall hanging and mobile that matched our wallpaper. My dad and Mike's folks had given us some money, and I added the numbers in my head. Everything, including the easels I found on the way in, the art supplies, and small accessories fit the bill. I'd wait for the chair.

"Stacie, I'm buying the rocker."

"No way!"

"Yes way. We want to. Ben told me when you found something special to get it. Please don't deny us this pleasure."

"Are you sure?"

"I am. We want to give you something you can all enjoy. When you or Mike get up in the night, you can settle into this rocker and know you are loved."

She left me with no defense.

On the way home, we stopped to see Jonica's folks. In the short months of our friendship, Jonica shared her parents with me. A visit to their house included a meal, treats, or both. Cookies just out of the oven, homemade soup, pies, cakes, or sweet breads. Rose served generous helpings and gave great hugs. When our plates were empty she'd ask in what sounded like one word, "Gonnabeabletoeatsomemore?"

She almost filled the empty spot in my heart. I'd found a real mom. It didn't lessen my desire for a relationship with my own, and in fact the longing for Eve's love grew as the baby did. I wanted to call her with every new report. I didn't take the chance she'd reject my joy.

When I'd asked Eve to feel the baby move and put her hand on my belly, she pulled back saying, "I'm not comfortable touching your stomach."

Dad put his hand on the spot she'd vacated and smiled. "Eve, remember the first time you held my hand like this and we felt Stacie move?"

Her half smile didn't reach beyond her lips as she walked away.

Jonica's giggle brought me back to Rose's kitchen. We sat at the oval wooden table and munched on cookies, talking about raising children and my concerns about a strong-willed child.

It was hard to picture Jonica stomping her feet, a defiant pout planted across her face. Rose said it was true so it had to be. I learned her nickname was "Chatterbox" and that her grandparents had to hang up on her when the long-distance telephone conversations got too long. I liked that story best.

Rose delighted in sharing stories about her little girl - one of her precious golden children. Jonica's brother received equal time in his mother's stories and love.

Rose assured me my mother loved me. Then she and Carl gave me a print of a Psalm framed in bright yellow, matted in green. She had gone to so much trouble to match the nursery. The words moved me in a strange way when I read them. But I was most touched by the pencil drawing at the end of the verse. A newborn rested in a hand. I knew it represented God's hand. I wanted to ask, "Does He hold my other baby in His hand too?" The words stayed hidden.

Always these two women used gentle persuasion to direct my thoughts to God. At times I resented their faith - their confidence that God cared on a personal level. I held my grievance at bay and with a starving heart I accepted their love, but not their religion.

Looking at my friend and her mom, I realized I trusted these two women to love me and all the children I brought into their lives. I knew they would share their love and faith with them equally.

My heart filled with thanksgiving for the way Jonica and her family touched my life.

CHAPTER 14

Jonica

As more of my friends became moms, I saw them less. I knew they didn't know what to do with me. Baby showers came more often, and my attendance halted. I was different and that made people uncomfortable. No one wanted to make it worse for me, but for awhile, everything did. It was no one's fault. I grieved these losses too.

Kelly, who was in charge of scheduling nursery duty, asked if she could add my name to the roster.

A mom overheard and said, "She isn't a mother. I'm sure she doesn't know how to do these things."

I faked a gracious attitude, said a no thank you to Kelly, and went to powder my nose.

Mom met me there and I fumed, "What about the teen girls who help? They aren't mothers yet but are most welcome. What's the deal? Does she have any idea how many babies I've cared for? How many diapers I've changed? How many wobbly heads I've supported? How many snotty noses I've wiped?"

"No. Are you going to tell her?"

"Oh, sure. Like that will make any difference."

"Do you want to work in the nursery?"

"No. But I don't like my non-motherhood disqualifying me either!"

"Honey, I think you're in a lifetime battle."

Organ music interrupted us, ending my opportunity to keep dumping my pain on my mom.

Monday, I let it rip with God again.

So, Lord, what's up with this? Will they always misunderstand? And will it always be me and them? Thank goodness for Stacie- without her I'd be friendless.

The loneliness was staggering. Tears flowed, and I did nothing to stop them.

The heartache was exhausting, and dehydrating. I got up, blew my nose, and watched water tumble over ice cubes in my glass. I paced the house taking big gulps, hoping to eliminate the huge lump in my throat. It didn't work. Tears flowed again as I admitted to the things I longed to do for my children.

Lord, I will never nurse my babies or fix them grilled cheese sandwiches with lime Kool-aid for lunch, or peanut butter cookies for an after school snack. There won't be any school supplies shopping, first days of kindergarten, graduations, or weddings. No children who look like Ben will call me Mommy or need me to kiss away their hurts. Never will I experience the mysterious moves of a baby in my womb. I won't wipe their runny noses or bandage their skinned knees. And You know what else God? I know not all days with kids are fun- they are filled with work and sometimes tears. So see-I'm not just thinking about happily ever after here! I need an answer Lord-what is the purpose of all this?

"If you abide in My word, you are My disciples indeed. And you shall know the truth, and the truth shall make you free."

Setting my empty glass in the sink, I went upstairs. In our bedroom, I curled up in my chair. Lord-here I am. Do You have anything special-just for me-in Your Word today? Opening the burgundy leather cover to the day's reading, I begged, *Please Father, give me something real from You. Something I can't get anywhere else. I'm tired of clichés meant to help but that really hinder. I don't want to be a whiner and I know I'm getting really good at it, but I want more - something that means I'm not useless and this isn't all for nothing. Show where You are in this.*

God's timing is always perfect.

My Scripture for the day was John 9:1-4. The disciples asked Jesus about a man born blind. They wanted to know if his sin or his parents' sin had caused the man's sightless condition. Jesus' answer to them changed my life forever.

He said, "Neither this man nor his parents sinned, but that the works of God should be revealed in him. I must work the works of Him who sent Me while it is day; the night is coming when no one can work. As long as I am in the world, I am the light of the world."

I held my breath as I reread the passage. I read it yet again.

I declared, "Father, sin didn't cause me to be infertile! Thank You. Like this blind man I am part of the work You are doing in this world. You're trusting me with infertility, so through it I can bring You the honor and glory."

I looked to the man's history again. They cast him out because Jesus healed him.

This is how I feel-like an outcast. Even knowing this is Your will for me doesn't change the fact that I'm different and will always be outside 'normal.'

When I read how the man believed and worshipped I slid to my knees.

Lord, like this man, I believe You are the Son of God. If You can use me for Your kingdom in a greater way childless, I'm willing. You tell us we all have a cross to bear. If this is mine, help me carry it well to the end. You didn't deny or cast off Your own-You hung on it, bearing my sins, and You didn't get off until Your death. From the day You were born until the day You died, You knew this was Your destiny. You chose to take my place. Your Word that convinces me that if You are trusting me to be childless, I can do this. I want to do it for You for the rest of my life if this there is glory in it for You. Please, Father, don't let me waste it-may it have eternal value.

After this prayer, I again picked up the Word, looking forward to finishing out this quiet time with the Psalm for the day. Nothing could prepare me for His next blessing. I rejoiced with the psalmist as he declared, "He raises the poor out of the dust, and lifts the needy out of the ash heap . . ."

"Oh Lord! You do!" I kept reading.

". . . that He may seat him with princes-with the princes of His people."

The next verse sent a jolt through me. "He grants the barren woman a home, like a joyful mother of children." I read it again-out loud emphasizing the word like.

Father, sometimes this verse is quoted at me as the answer to all my prayers-if I only believed more or stopped sinning, or whatever... I would receive a house full of my offspring. It doesn't say that! You say, like a joyful mother of children. My home will be comparable to or approximately like theirs but not identical. You will fill our home with joy when the children we love come to visit. Father, I want to be this woman!

Stacie

My pregnancy and desire to be a mom separated me from my old acquaintances. They found my intentional pregnancy uncomfortable and my abortion regret unbearable.

Baby clothes and nursery plans were not their idea of fun. I blamed no one, and accepted the parting as differences of opinion. I was isolated except for Jonica.

After spending time with Jonica and her mom, I returned to the box of old pictures. I found more wedding pictures of my parents tucked under one of the box bottoms, the word "extras" printed on the envelope in Eve's handwriting.

"Extras for who, Eve? Me? At one time, did you hope for more than just me? I was certainly never enough for you."

A picture of my parents coming back down the aisle grabbed my attention. Until now, I'd never seen their wedding pictures. Photo albums weren't displayed at our house. The only pictures displayed in frames were the "official family sittings" we had taken each year for Eve's Christmas mailing to her generous campaign contributors.

With smiles radiant and hands clasped, the couple in the photo appeared to run toward the camera.

"You seem in such a hurry to begin your life together. Eve, you were deeply in love-what happened?"

I looked into my mother's shining eyes, her smile so full of joy that I smiled back. Black curls danced under her veil as they rushed down the aisle. Dad gave the photographer a full smile, happiness alive in his dark eyes. He reminded me of an Olympic winner accepting the gold medal-my mother. Unbelievable.

"Dad, where did this joy go? Why didn't it last?" I asked the young man in the picture.

I put this photo beside the box and looked at Eve feeding Dad cake, them signing the marriage certificate, and running to Dad's convertible as onlookers tossed rice. A last wedding photo showed the back of the car with a sign reading, "Happily ever after!"

"Yeah, right!" I muttered. "Whoever wrote this didn't know Eve at all." The back of the photo read in Eve's precise printing, "Sign made by Steven." My dad wrote that? He didn't seem like a fairy tale kind of guy. Confused, I put it back in the box.

Next came one of a small stucco house, "Our first home" printed on the back in blue ink by Eve. On the corners were black tips used to glue photos into old albums.

"These aren't extra copies," I muttered. "Why did you remove them Eve? It's as if you don't want to remember these times at all."

I sifted through pictures of my parents smiling at each other, holding hands, hugging, and Eve with her hands on her rounded tummy. Rubbing my own tummy bulge, I studied the photos of my mother pregnant with me. She seemed to like the condition then. Next came images of a blanket wrapped newborn in the arms of various friends and relatives.

I held up one of Eve cradling me while I slept. "You loved me!"

The beautiful face of my young mother blossomed with love for the child in her arms. A smile lifted the corners of Eve's mouth as she looked at me. Tears rolled down my face, and I put it with the wedding photo.

"What did I do to make you stop loving me, Eve?"

For a few minutes I sobbed-grieving for a love lost so long ago.

"I promise, I will always love you, touch you, and accept you," I told my unborn babe.

I wiped my eyes and picked up another pile of pictures. One showed me laughing with my mouth wide open, splashing in a wading pool while Eve grinned at the photographer. In another Eve held me wrapped in a big white towel.

Prickles shot to every nerve ending in my body. I nearly dropped the picture.

"You're hugging me!"

I started to cry harder as it dawned on me - I missed something I once knew - her loving touch. I put this one with the wedding picture.

Next, I pulled out the mystery shot to study again. The blue blanket was tucked tightly around the tiny body even though Eve wore a white sundress and sandals. My chubby legs stretched as I stood on tiptoe trying to gaze into the face of whoever slept in her lap.

Eve looked off into the distance. Her jaws were clenched and she looked completely detached from both of us. Why don't I remember this baby?

Another picture in the pile was of Eve and Dad. She was wearing the same dress and shoes. His arm reached around her slender waist. Her arms were crossed in front of her as if she needed to hold herself up. Dad still looked like a man in love, although sadness now shadowed the once dancing eyes. She looked like a woman ready to do battle. Hardness replaced the tenderness once captured by the camera. And she was thin-so very thin.

"Bad day, Eve?" I wondered out loud.

I put them back in the box, slid on the cover and put it in the closet. The pictures continued to play across my mind like an old 35mm movie. I wished for a turn-off button. Instead, my mind seemed to have only one called "replay."

I decided to frame the ones of Eve and me and put them somewhere I could look at them often.

I didn't understand it all but I comforted myself. She had loved me for awhile. It was better than nothing and would have to be enough.

Later, showing them to Mike, he looked into the face of my bride mother and said, "This is what your dad holds on to, Stacie- this beautiful woman in love with him, his daughter, and life. Whatever happened to take her happiness away, he hopes it will come back every day of his life."

"She loved him too-you can see it-feel it."

"Yeah."

I told him about the strange baby in the other picture. "It bothers me. I don't have a younger cousin, so who is this?"

"Maybe it belonged to a neighbor or she might have been taking care of a friend's kid."

"Possibly, but why keep the blanket?"

"Maybe it was a gift when you were born and she let this baby use it on a visit."

Looking again at Eve with me as a newborn, I wished I knew this woman so full of love and life.

CHAPTER 15

Jonica

The day God blessed me with the truth in His Word, the burden of infertility lightened.

I didn't say anything to Ben, Mom, or Stacie. I wanted them to see my changed heart-not hear about it. I was sure it showed on my face. I hoped everyone would notice.

"Joni?" Ben asked the next day. "Can we talk?"

"Don't you have to go to work or did I forget a day-off?"

"I have to go in but I called and let my assistant know I'd be a little bit late."

"You want a cup of coffee?"

"No. Do you have time to sit here on the couch with me?"

"Sure."

He reached for my hand and said, "I see a change in you. Your eyes shine again, your smile comes easier, and your laugh isn't forced anymore. What happened?"

"The Bible. God touched me with His Word. The other day I was so down I wanted to quit. I let Him have it- again. I asked Him to give me something special - an answer. I threw all my doubts and questions at Him.

I didn't hear anything in the stillness so I decided to read the Word from my One-Year Bible. I didn't open and point to a verse as my message. Instead, I asked Him to show me something special in my scheduled reading."

I took a deep breath as tears of joy sprang into my eyes and splashed down my cheeks.

"Did He?"

"Yes. He spoke to me."

"What do you mean He spoke to you?"

I heard the skeptical tone creeping into his voice.

"I promise, I'm not losing it. It wasn't an audible voice. He used His Word and gave me a peace passing all understanding. I am comforted and confident He has a reason for us not being able to have kids. He is not punishing us-He is trusting us to live through this experience and bring Him honor and glory."

"What Scripture did He use?"

"I think it will have more impact if you let Him show you the same thing. I'll get my Bible so You can see what I mean."

Running up the stairs I prayed for God to use these verses to comfort Ben too. I hurried back down and handed him my open Bible and said, "I'm going to get us some coffee."

In the kitchen, I got out our extra big mugs. I messed around mixing Ben's coffee, cream, and sugar just the way he likes it. I arranged muffins on a plate, waiting for Ben to call me back.

When he did, I grabbed the coffee and plate. He reached for his cup and said, "I see it."

"You do?"

"You're right, Jonica. He's trusting us with this. I've often wondered why God lets good people get horrible diseases, live through accidents only to find themselves paralyzed, or why He held back the blessing of children from us. I watched your grandparents suffer through cancer and it only made them stronger in the Lord. They brought Him honor and glory as they faced the disease, treatment, and lost the battle. God found them standing true to their faith. This hurts, but I want Him to find me trustworthy too."

I took a sip of coffee before responding. "I still feel bruised inside. Infertility tests my faith. Do I really believe God is who He says He is? If I do, my faith says His will is always His best for me. I know He wants me trust Him with everything-especially when I'm worn out in my heart and don't understand."

"We're experiencing the death of a dream and grieving is hard work."

"That's it exactly. It seems like one great big loss. I didn't know if I could be victorious in this battle."

"We can't on our own. But we know God is the victory."

We sat holding on to each other, my hand resting on Ben's chest. "I love the feeling of your heartbeat."

Ben held my hand in his and took a deep, ragged breath. "Honey, it's not always going to be easy, but I want us to honor God through this. I think we need to find the courage to talk about it to other people - to be honest even when they can't understand. Not to strike out in anger or defense but to explain to those who really care, so they won't hurt another couple in ignorance. We can pray and trust the Lord for opportunities to share not only the hurt, but the Healer."

Ben left for his office, and I climbed the stairs to mine. After answering some e-mail, I got to work. Part of writing is reading and studying what kids like. I picked up one of my favorite children's books, *A Duck Named Quacker*, by Ricky Van Shelton. *Lord, help me to express Your love this way through the characters in my books.* I wrote for a few hours, stopping only when the phone rang.

It was Stacie.

Stacie

Stepping into the ultrasound room, my head started to spin, my stomach did a somersault, and my legs shook.

I was going to lose it.

"I don't know if I can do this."

"Sure you can. It's painless." The technician assured me.

""We need a moment here," Mike told her.

"I'll take a quick break."

Mike's eyes never left my face. Stacie, I'm right here. What's wrong?" he asked, guiding me to a chair.

"They used a machine similar to this on me right before they did the abortion," I whispered.

"We don't have to do this."

When it was time for the first ultra-sound, I made excuses for the test not being necessary. As time went on, I knew Mike was looking forward to seeing our baby for the first time and we both wanted to know if we were having a boy or a girl.

"Stacie, don't do this for me. We can get through the pregnancy without it."

"Somehow I need to get past this."

The technician returned. "Mrs. Cutter, do you want to reschedule the test for a day you're feeling better?"

"No, I'll be fine."

I rested on the table hoping I'd be able to hear the baby's heart beat over my own. A pumping heart was just the beginning of what our little one had to show us.

The technician explained the procedure then lightly pressed the senor on my abdomen, stopping immediately to let us gain some perspective to the world inside me.

"Whoa, Stacie-do you see it?" Mike asked.

"Yes."

In front of me on the screen, I saw a tiny body.

"Hi, Baby."

Hot tears ran down my cheeks, cold by the time they ran behind my ears and in my hair.

The technician zoomed around and we saw tiny fingers, toes, ears, and a profile that reflected his dad's already.

"Look Stacie, he's sucking his thumb."

Just then the baby made a stretching move and turned over.

"You're right Mr. Cutter. You are looking at your son."

Mike reached over with a tissue and wiped my face while tears of joy ran down his own.

"I love you, Mike. I love our son."

"I love you and him too."

"Can we take some of the pictures home?"

"You sure can-I'll make some copies for you right away."

I carried the envelope clutched to my chest with one hand- the other gripped Mike's with all my might. It kept me grounded - I thought without his touch I might float away on a cloud of giddy joy.

We went home and spent the afternoon looking at the ultrasound copies, talking about our dreams for him, and picking out names. We settled on one we both liked, and promised to keep it a secret until he arrived.

"I feel so bad that Jonica will never know this joy or experience childbirth."

"There's one way she can experience part of it."

"How?"

"We could invite her to join us in the delivery room." Mike suggested.

"I'd love that but are you sure? This is our first time not only to have a baby but to share his first moments of life outside me. Will you be okay sharing such a private family moment with someone else?"

"Isn't she just about as close to us as family?"

"To me, she is."

"Do you want her there?"

"I do. She's my only real friend besides you and after all the hurts she's had, I'd like to prove how much I trust her with our son from his first breath. I just don't know how hard it might be for her."

"You won't know until you ask."

"Do you mind if I call her now?"

"Go ahead. Knowing Jonica, she won't want to intrude, so let her know we both want her there."

My excitement soared and I sounded a lot like her when I began a bubbling conversation.

"Hi Jonica! Guess what? We know he's a boy."

"I'm so glad for you-for us."

"Jonica, Mike and I want you in the delivery room."

I heard a sharp inhale and a slow exhale. "Jonica?"

"I'm here. This is such a private time-are you sure you want another person there when you see and hold your son in his first few minutes after birth?"

"We're sure. You're like a sister to me. You are going to be a big part of his life, Jonica, and we want you to know him from the very beginning."

I heard her crying and my stomach fell. "Jonica, what's wrong?"

"I feel so honored. All of this is such a mystery to me. On my own, I'll never enter a delivery room, see a moments-old baby take his first breath, or hear his first cries. You cannot imagine what an honor this is."

"You accept?"

"I wouldn't miss it."

CHAPTER 16

Jonica

As I wandered along my garden path, the little "gardening angel" from Stacie caught my eye. The resin character stood about three feet tall. She held a rosebud, and her mesh wings reminded me of my grandma's screen door. I couldn't stop a smile from creeping over my face. I remembered the night we heard people sneaking around in the garden.

"Stay quiet, Jonica," Ben whispered.

I sat on the edge of the bench in the dark ready to run if he gave me any encouragement.

"Where to you want to put it?" a male voice asked.

"Shush. They'll hear us."

Footsteps crunched on the pea rock pathway.

"Here! This is the perfect spot."

I recognized the female voice at the same moment the motion-sensor yard light went on.

"Stacie?"

Her squeal covered Mike's mumble.

"Jonica! You scared the daylights out of me! What are you doing out here?"

"It's my garden," I managed between hysterical giggles.

The bright beam shone on them like an interrogation light in a bad movie. They squinted and squirmed. Mike held a goofy looking statue.

"That looks heavy. Want to put it down?"

"Yeah. Is this a good spot?"

"Sure. What is it?"

"Your new 'gardening angel.' I wanted to surprise you."

"You succeeded."

"The light gave us away."

"That'll teach you to do your deeds in the darkness. Besides, you make really noisy thieves."

"We aren't stealing something; we're leaving a gift and it's not like we make a practice of this kind of thing," Mike said as he set the angel down more gently than I expected.

"I guess we'll let you off on a technicality."

"Thanks," he muttered.

Ben sat on the bench laughing. He'd catch his breath and then start again.

Stacie stood as if frozen in the light.

"Are you okay?" I asked.

"Sure. Just a little spooked I guess."

"Honey, we need to go," Mike urged.

"Where's your car? We didn't hear anyone pull up." Ben said.

"A block away," Mike answered, hands now stuffed in his pockets, he looked at his shoes.

Little giggles continued to escape as I told my friend I needed a hug before she left.

"I can't see you," she said blinded by the bright beam.

"Come toward my voice." I snickered.

She did.

Grateful for that sweet memory, I opened my Bible and journal.

Today is the day I go see Eve, I'm nervous. We're poles apart politically, except for the women's shelter. I'm glad for this open door into her world.

I went into the house and dressed with care. Simple and I hoped elegant. Ivory linen slacks and a pale blue silk blouse. I transferred my tape recorder and notebook from my beat-up leather backpack to my soft leather briefcase.

"The Senator is expecting you." Eve's assistant knocked twice on the door and held it open.

Eve stood and joined me in front of her desk. We shook hands.

"Jonica. Welcome."

"Hello, Senator. Thank you for seeing me."

She appeared cool, dignified, and distant. Her assistant brought a tray with a carafe, china cups on saucers, sugar, and cream.

"I believe you enjoy hazelnut coffee?" she asked.

"I do. Stacie told you?"

"I asked her, yes."

"That's nice."

"You didn't expect me to be nice?"

"I don't know what to expect - you have a reputation for being tough on your opponents."

"Are you the enemy Jonica?"

"I sure hope not."

Being in her presence I felt like a little girl getting grilled by a stern teacher. My professional abilities disintegrated and my insides turned to gel.

"Please sit down."

We sat across from each other in tapestry-covered wingback chairs-not soft like Stacie's couch. They were stiff and not broken in - comfortable for short visits only.

The small round table between us fascinated me. "I like this piece."

"Thank you. It was my mother's tea table."

I never knew there was a special table for serving tea. My confidence continued to dwindle. I was all middle-class in the presence of high-class.

"I read some of your articles and interviews. Many are posted on the Web. I'm impressed with your work. I appreciate the research you did even if I don't agree with your conclusions."

"Thank you."

"You brought a recorder I assume."

"Yes." I reached for it obediently and set it on the table ready for the slight push of the on button. I took a deep breath.

"You're nervous."

"You're famous."

"If it helps at all, interviews always make me apprehensive."

Her frank comment eased some of my shakes.

"I've watched you several times. You cover it well." I took a sip of the delicious brew she'd poured for me.

"Keeping up with the opposition party?"

"I suppose in a way. However, I enjoy hearing honest debate. It's the only way to get a fair take on any issue."

"You're into 'fair and balanced' news?"

"I am."

"Much of what we say is taken out of context. The media twists things to fit either their conservative or liberal bias. Neither pleases me. I'd like them to let the discussion play itself out for the voters to decide. But, I'm also a politician. We're great pretenders who know how to spin the moment to our party's advantage."

"I'm not the media. I hope to do all I can to help raise awareness for the needs of the women's shelter. If I can show the readers how two women so divided on most issues can come together and make a difference when they are united in a cause, the reward will be doubled."

"An idealist. How refreshing. I forget how contagious genuine enthusiasm is."

I knew she was busy, and I needed to move on or lose the interview, but my writing hand seemed attached to the handle on my dainty china cup. The tiny cracks in the finish revealed that it too was an antique. I wondered these were family heirlooms as well or something she picked up along the way-part of her senatorial persona.

It bothered me that I was curious about things not important to my article. I had the feeling I was supposed to ask her something not on my list but, I had no idea what. My lack of focus and concentration frustrated me.

Soft track lighting on the ceiling revealed something startling. Eve's cool demeanor, careful coiffure, and expensively dressed body didn't distract me from noticing the way her hand shook as she lifted the cup to her mouth. Her makeup could not conceal her pale skin. I knew that something was terribly wrong. In her eyes I caught a reflection her campaign posters and TV interviews missed. Sadness.

"Stacie mentioned you are a Christian."

"Yes."

"Tell me. Are you trying to convert my daughter?"

Her hard veneer barely concealed her protective instincts.

"I'll leave that up to God."

"No hell-fire and brimstone scare tactics while she is in her present hormonal state?"

"It is never my intent to manipulate someone into a decision. I love your daughter. And though we do not believe the same way, I intend to be a good friend to her."

"Interesting. So you agree to disagree?"

"We don't talk about it much."

"So your religion isn't your passion?"

"I don't have religion, but my faith is very much a part of who I am. I love the Lord."

"So, you do intend to convert Stacie."

"No. But I hope she finds Christ. Conversion is His work, not mine. Only He can change a heart."

I squirmed in my chair. The overhead lights seemed to spotlight me and the chair warmed up under my thighs.

"Are you hoping to share your testimony with me?"

"Do you want me to?"

"No."

"Then I won't. But if you ever do open up that door to me, I will walk right in, sit down, and tell you about Jesus."

"You remind me of my mother."

"Your mother was a Christian?"

"So was my father. They raised me in a faith-filled home. Believers surrounded me. If the church doors were open, we were there."

"So what happened?"

"Nothing. I just didn't buy Jesus."

"Of course not."

"What?"

"He isn't for sale."

"No, as I remember He's a gift from God."

"He is."

"If that's true, He's the one gift I've left in the package. Although my parents went to their graves praying for my soul, I never had any desire to know Him."

"Can I ask you another question?"

She smiled and raised a pencil-groomed eyebrow. "Isn't that why we're here?"

I leaned toward her and swallowed hard. "Eve, are you okay?"

"You Christians think you know it all don't you?" She stood and put her hands on her hips.

"No. But my intuition radar is sensitive."

She let her hands fall to her sides and looked at me wide-eyed with tears suddenly spilling over.

I knew I'd just found the question I was here to ask. Today would result in a byline for me, but it was mostly about a woman in need of prayer.

"I have breast cancer."

"Does Stacie know?" I asked.

"Her father is telling her as we speak. For right now, this part of the conversation is off the record. Is that understood? I'll be giving a press conference in a day or so to inform the public. My family and I need a few days to let it sink in and figure out a treatment plan I can live with. Literally."

"Of course. My editor wants the piece in three weeks."

"By then it will be public knowledge so you can use it in the article if you wish. Maybe it will bring in more awareness and support for the women's shelter. I'd feel better if I knew this could bring about some good."

Eve's assistant interrupted our conversation. Someone else was waiting for the Senator and it was time for me to go.

I watched her carefully pat away the tears. "I'm sorry you didn't get your interview. I'll have my assistant fax or e-mail you the information. I trust you to quote me correctly. Please let her know how you'd like to receive the release."

We were back to business as usual and I'd just been dismissed. As I moved toward the door, I stopped and turned around. "Senator, I'm going to pray for you."

"Of course you are."

"Do you mind?"

"No."

Stacie

I found another angel for Jonica's garden. This one sat cross-legged and held a butterfly on her finger. The same wire wings decorated her back. This one had short tightly curled hair. I knew she would bring a smile to my friend.

None of us will ever forget the night Mike and I sneaked into my friend's garden. I hated getting caught.

A knock at the door interrupted my walk down memory lane.

"Hi, Dad. Come on in. I know Jonica isn't home today. So, you won't get caught carrying this statue into her garden."

He smiled. "And where do you want me to leave this cherub?"

"Right by her swing is her rose garden. In the front and center is a spot where she lost a bush. Put her there."

"And if Ben is home?"

"He won't be. He's on a business trip. The timing is perfect."

I fixed coffee and Dad pulled a bag out from behind his back. "Morning glory muffins sound good to you?"

"Sure do."

"Stacie, you look great."

"Thanks." I swiped his cheek with a kiss and set the muffins on a crystal plate.

"You should visit Eve's office sometime. You might like the changes."

"She redecorated?"

"Sort of. She bought some chairs and some had some artwork commissioned. I guess your new office inspired her."

"I thought I only inspired disapproval in her."

His face grew sad at my comment and the phone rang.

A sweet female voice told me a social worker had referred her to me. She and her husband were caring for a brain-injured child and wanted to adopt her. There were extenuating and complicated circumstances and she needed a lawyer who specialized in advocacy because of the girl's mental, emotional, and physical condition. I agreed to meet them at my office the next day.

I turned to my dad. "My first case."

"Good."

Something in his voice wasn't right.

"Dad, are you upset?"

"Stacie, did you ask Jonica to visit your mother?"

"No. Jonica told me about her hope to write an article about the women's shelter. I let her know she and Eve shared this passion. She called Eve herself and asked for an appointment. I later told Eve about our friendship."

"That's good."

"Why?"

"I know Jonica is a Christian and if her motives are other than the shelter, your mother will see right through her."

"You mean did she go there to testify to Eve?"

"She's very aware of people approaching her with a hidden agenda. It happens to her all the time. They don't usually come to her for help because they like her. Her name gives their issue power, and influence via her voice. So, she is accustomed to smooth attempts to manipulate her."

"You make it sound like politics is lonely. Eve is surrounded by people who believe like she does."

"Sure. She selected her staff. She sees some dear old friends. And she has us. But honey, politics is lonely. For most of the causes she believes in she is the mouth piece-the classy woman who can deliver the message and bring in the bucks."

"Isn't that the goal?"

"Sure. But it gets old after a while. Those groups she works so hard for don't know your mother. They don't understand what she sacrifices to carry their message to the masses. They don't know she wishes she were here instead of there. or how sick she is. They just don't get it."

"Sick? Eve is sick?"

I watched a horrible sadness creep into Dad's eyes followed by tears. A crying daddy is scary. He reached for me and held me close.

He whispered, "Honey, your mother has breast cancer."

The babe in my womb moved as I started to weep.

Dad held me close.

I asked him, "Do you know how to pray?"

"No."

CHAPTER 17

Jonica

Hope blossomed in my spirit as I sat in our garden and looked at my new angel. In reality I pictured angels as strong warriors fighting the spiritual battles I knew raged just beyond my vision. But these silly statues never ceased to bring a smile and thanksgiving. Stacie had found a Christian symbol she was comfortable with and didn't resent.

I thought about the mother and baby elephant statue I had taken to Stacie's dad to sneak into her home for me. He got a kick out of being my secret agent. I pictured the porcelain figurine in her office nook at home, right under the print of an elephant charging. In the animal's dust you could see other adults and two babies. I knew the art represented Stacie's desire to protect women and children.

All the furniture in my friend's home was metal, glass, or leather. She added color, warmth, and zip with teal, purple, gold, and red rugs, pillows, and pottery. Elephants of all shapes, sizes, and colors stood in corners, held plants, or stood holding glass on their backs as end tables. It was all beautiful, passionate, and elegant.

For a few minutes I let myself get caught up in the flutter of activity at the bird feeders. Goldfinches, chickadees, and a sparrow feasted. A robin worked the freshly weeded flower bed while a wren sang from the top of a birdhouse. A hummingbird hovered by the sugar-water feeder before settling in for a drink, and an oriole savored bits from an orange slice. So much beauty in feathers.

I wondered how Stacie was doing with her new client. Unable to share any of the details, Stacie had told me the case would put her skills to work and get her started in the direction of her dream. She was thrilled to be in the arena doing battle for someone unable to fight for themselves.

I turned to the essays sitting in my lap. After finishing the editing on my new book, I had volunteered to lead a creative writing class for the teens at church. The kids asked hard questions and sought honest answers from God's Word. Some wrote about mission trips and lives changed forever by the poverty and disease they saw and the simple faith they encountered. Others fought temptation while some failed the fight then regained lost ground with God's help. Most wrote poetry. They filled their folders with the reality of their faith, dreams of love, secret hurts, and the hope only they could offer their world. As their edifier, I wrote only comments of encouragement to each one and let them know I kept them in my prayers. Sometimes I noted places they could submit their work, leaving the decision up to them.

After reading the last essay I headed for the house. I set the folders on the counter where I would remember to take them to church and deliver them to the teens on the way to Bible study.

The phone rang.

"Hi Jonica. I had to call someone. I'm confident my first case is going to succeed."

"I'm so glad."

"Until now, it's been a dream focused on me. This afternoon, it was all about a client who needed a voice."

I heard her ruffling papers. "Doing paperwork?"

"Just going through my mail."

"Well, it's time to head home. Dad said he might drop off a package today. He's always picking something up for me or the baby."

Wishing I could see her face when she saw her dad's delivery, I said, "Thanks for calling."

"Figured you'd want to know and celebrate this victory with me."

Up in my office later, I started a new Bible study about the life of Jesus. One thing I found clear. He often withdrew and prayed. After these quiet times with His Father, the Son returned to His ministry refreshed.

I was experiencing a normal down feeling after the elation in

finishing a book and sensed a deep inner need for renewal. A new
outline rested on my desk, but I knew it wasn't the right time to work
on it.

At supper I asked Ben, "Honey, do you mind if I take tomorrow
off?"

"Sure. It's always fine with me if you take time away from writing."

"This time I want to do something different, like go to the cabin
and spend most of a day in prayer."

"Alone?"

"Yes. Mom and Dad spent last weekend there so it's open and
clean. Betty and Dave are going up so they'd be right next door."

"Do you want to stay overnight by yourself?"

"No. I thought I could go up with them and you could drive up on
your cycle after work and join me."

"You know, this is beginning to sound like a win-win situation." I
heard the smile in his voice before I saw it on his face.

After the ride up with my aunt and uncle, I withdrew to the cabin.
While the coffee brewed, I put my supplies-Bible, journal, and my
favorite pen-out on my favorite Adirondack chair. The wide arm
provided a perfect table. Grabbing a pillow and a cup of hot coffee, I
headed for the porch. My time started with writing a love letter to
God. When the page was full and the mug empty, I put the pillow on
the floor in front of my chair and put my knees on the pillow.

*Father, spending this much time in prayer is new to me. I don't know where to
begin except with my needs and burdens . . .*

In the midst of some hard praying an unexpected joy came and
things took a turn. Songs of praise and thanksgiving flowed from my
mouth in a worship service of one for One.

When my stomach growled, I fished a peanut butter sandwich out
of my bag and poured another cup of coffee. After a short walk in the
woods to work out the kinks in my legs, I started back toward the
porch. On the path in front of me, sunlight filtered through the trees.

"Lord, I need Your wisdom in all things."

"My Word is lamp to your feet and light to your path . . ."

"Oh God, I want to be full of Your wisdom."

I hurried back to my Bible and opened to the book of Proverbs -

the book of wisdom. When I got to the last chapter, a verse stood out as if it had been printed in bold letters: "There are three things that are never satisfied, four never say, 'Enough!' The grave, the barren womb, the earth that is not satisfied with water-and the fire never says, 'Enough!'"

Jumping out of my chair, I exclaimed, "God! You understand!" For a moment, I stood still, hugging my open Bible to my chest, and then knelt again. *Thank You for meeting me where I am-for drawing me out here. Thank You for this verse. Lord, thank You for opening my eyes to Your Word.*

It took awhile for my enthusiastic joy to quiet and my spirit to settle into an unearthly peace. But my legs felt as though I'd plugged them into an energizer, so I turned toward the lake. As I walked along the shore, my thoughts turned back to Him. The God who is love.

I stood on the sand and waited. The sunshine soaked into my body like warm oil. A warm breeze hugged my skin. *Lord, I feel Your presence. What's next?*

Stacie

Hope seemed to wilt before my eyes.

To her, I was just another stranger with lots of questions. She swayed back and forth in her chair to a secret rhythm. The doctor's report stated she'd reached her learning capacity. At fourteen she was fast becoming a woman physically, but no matter how long she lived, she'd remain ten mentally. Now, after a devastating fire and severe burns on her legs, she was silent. Her injuries didn't include damage to her vocal cords, and although mentally alert, Hope no longer spoke. Something inside her shut down and we needed to find a way to open the door of communication.

Peggy said that before the fire, Hope liked to draw pictures and write simple stories. She looked at the whiteboard table and back at me. I smiled. Her mouth turned up on one side. I found her beautiful. Long, shiny black braids, olive skin, and coal black eyes told the story of her ancestry. I envisioned her grandmother long ago following a hard but simple life in the Badlands. *Thank You, for sparing her face in the fire.* A prayer? I guess. To an unknown God I didn't believe in. Again.

"Any improvements, Peggy?"

Her foster mom replied, "Yes. It's a tiny thing, but Hope now grunts when one of the other kids bothers her. And the other day she laughed at something silly Stevie did."

"Great."

"We think so. For whatever reason, Hope and Stevie are more bonded. He's her protector and instinctively interprets her needs. He's more emotionally mature and seems to grasp some of the horror Hope feels. There was a fire on TV the other night and he quickly shut it off. He often tells her he is her big brother and will always take care of her."

"How developmentally challenged is he?"

"He has Down syndrome."

"And he comprehends this much?"

"He has learned many practical skills, but his greatest strength is his tender heart for the hurting."

I turned my attention to the girl across from me.

"Hope, this is a drawing table. It is for you to use when you visit me. Here is a box of brand new markers. You can draw anything you want to on this table. Then, if you don't like it, you can erase it.

"Sometimes we need to speak and we can't find the words or our voices. But we can draw those words and it's a different way of telling people what is happening in our hearts. Do you want to try?"

She shrugged her shoulders.

"Sweetheart, your doctor told me you used to be able to talk, and he believes you can understand me now. We want to find a way for you to tell the judge where you want to live. It's really important. If you can't say the words, I get to be your voice. The only way for me to do that is for you to find a way to tell me so I can tell him."

She answered by swaying a little harder.

"I'm going to get Peggy and me a cup of coffee. Do you want something to drink too?"

Eyes still glued to the floor, she nodded her head yes.

"Does a Sprite sound good to you Hope?"

Again, she gave a positive nod. Every response equaled a success.

I set the drinks down and settled into the couch. I started getting to know Peggy and her family a little better while Hope continued to listen in. Peggy listed the first names of the kids she and her husband had adopted. Each one lived with a different handicap. Most people saw only their disabilities while Peggy and John saw their possibilities. The birth of their daughter Faith, also a Down syndrome child, had motivated them to adopt other challenged children into their family.

"Tell me a little bit about the house you live in."

"Can I also tell you how we got it?"

"Sure."

"We prayed for it."

Oh boy. I felt a fake smile stretch across my face, making my cheeks feel tight. *Here we go again.* Prayer meant faith. Faith meant God. The One I didn't believe in had no intention of leaving me alone.

"I see."

"We knew we'd need a house with several bedrooms, easy access, a dining room to seat us all, and a fenced yard. If it had two floors, we'd need an elevator for the kids who have wheelchairs. It needed to be up to code in every way."

I smiled, a bit more genuine, to encourage her to keep going.

"Our pastor called on the congregation to pray together for us and this dream. A woman called me later and told me she'd heard about us from her attorney, who attended our church. The women's shelter had a new building and their old one was going up for sale in a week."

Out of the corner of my eye I saw Hope open the box of markers. I looked back to Peggy so I wouldn't get caught watching her.

Peggy blinked back tears. She'd noticed too.

"The realtor called and we took a tour. It was everything we needed and wanted. Even to the Victorian design and a modern elevator. The doorways, bathrooms, and entryway were already handicap accessible. There are eight bedrooms and four and a half bathrooms. I had a Goldilocks-moment - everything was 'just right.' Except for the astronomical price."

"So, how did you swing it?" I asked as I saw Hope slide down to the floor and put her hand on the whiteboard table.

"More prayer, some fundraising, and a huge donation from an anonymous source."

"Any idea who?"

"No. The lawyer told us the donor was a very wealthy individual who simply wanted to help. This person wanted to purchase the house in our name and would cover maintenance costs for the next twenty years. A trust fund was set up for us."

"So, you were up and running."

"We were."

I watched Peggy observe Hope. Love shimmered through her tears.

Turning my attention to the picture taking shape in front of me, I moved behind the young artist.

"Hope, may I watch you draw?

She nodded.

A little white house scribbled over in red squiggles stood by a bigger green house. An arrow connected them. I knew the little one represented the fire where her parents had perished and she received her injuries. The big one must be Peggy's house. Silent tears splashed onto the whiteboard.

"Is this where you want to live, Hope?"

Instead of a nod, she wrote the letters h-o-m-e under the big house.

She drew a cloud over the little burning house and from it fell big drops.

"Did it rain that day?"

She shook her head and whispered, "Tears. From when God cried."

She spoke. It was all I could do not to grab her in a big hug. I resisted scaring her and losing all sense of my professional distance.

"Hope, may I take a picture of your picture to show the judge?"

She nodded and I snapped the photo. Then Hope wiped the board clean with the eraser and snuggled up to Peggy.

After passing out tissues, I asked, "When can I come to your house? I want to see it so I can make a full recommendation to the court. I want to be able to tell the judge I've been there and fully understand Hope's desire to live there."

Hope went back to swaying.

Peggy said, "As soon as you can. Hope is the last child we're adopting. We will be all full then. She will be our third daughter."

"Did you complete the questionnaire I sent you?"

"Yes. And I brought you copies of the home study in case you hadn't heard from the county yet." She pulled a large file from her bag and handed it to me.

"Here are the kids' histories, medical records, and all the information you asked for."

"Lots of reading."

"We keep excellent records. It's important for their guardians to know everything just in case anything would happen to John and me."

"I probably won't get to these until after I see the house."

"It's time to go home, Sweetheart," Peggy said, standing and holding her hand out to Hope.

Hope hugged me goodbye. I guess the little bulge under my shirt was bigger than I realized because she pointed to my stomach and said, "You got a baby in there."

"Yes. I do."

"I'll never be a mommy because I'll always be a little girl."

I didn't know what to say to the once silent girl who now stood before me speaking with such profound understanding.

Peggy gazed at the child. "Your voice is so pretty, Hope. Please try not to hide it from us again, okay?"

"Okay, Mommy."

Her simple reply undid us both. Peggy hugged Hope to her side and said, "This day is truly a miracle." We wiped more tears away.

As they walked to the elevators, Peggy turned back. "Stacie, there is one person who lives in our home we will never be adopting. We are taking care of him on a permanent basis for his dad. He's just as much ours as the others. But his dad is deeply in love with him-he just can't care for him on his own."

"It's in the file?"

"Yes."

"Thanks. Will tomorrow afternoon around two be good?"

"The bus brings the kids home at two-thirty. I can give you a tour first. You will get to meet us all."

"Great. See you then."

To get myself back in control, I flipped through my mail. An official looking letter from the United States military was addressed to Stephen Dunbar, Jr. There is no such person.

My dad called to see when I'd be home.

"Later. I have a lot of reading to do. Hey, Dad, guess what? The U.S. military is looking for Stephen Dunbar, Jr. Talk about a glitch in the system."

A strange silence filled the air.

"Just toss it." His voice sounded stretched. Huh. Maybe my dad wanted a boy and ended up with me. For the first time, I worried about my place in my dad's heart.

We hung up and I wondered, *So, what's up with this?*

CHAPTER 18

Jonica

"Mom, I need to talk-is this a good time?"

"It is. I just poured a fresh cup of coffee."

"God is at work in me."

"How?"

"He's renewing my spirit."

"An answer to our prayers."

"I know. I figured when this happened I'd feel ecstatic and I am but I'm worn out."

"Tell me about it."

"It started in church yesterday. Ben and I went to the early service. After we sat down, for some reason I looked toward the door instead of reading my bulletin. Della and Bernice entered the sanctuary holding on to each other. Grief lines pulled down on Della's pale skin. Her usual determined step now slowed to a clumsy shuffle. Bernice watched her friend closely. Mom, I felt something besides anger toward her. As they settled in front me, Della slumped into the pew, keeping her head down. The soft curls in the back of her head were uncombed. You know that is so not like Della. Compassion moved me into action.

"Leaning forward I said, 'Good morning ladies. Della, your hair is so lovely and soft.' Even though it seemed sort of familiar, as I chattered, my hand fluffed out the tiny sausages of hair left by her rollers."

"Thank you," she answered, "not seeming to notice my touch."

"Thank you, Jonica," Bernice mouthed pointing at Della's curls.

"I'm praying for you, Della," I said and sat back.

She nodded and the ladies leaned into each other.

"Mom, I cannot tell you how the relief surged through my whole being. The anger is gone."

"Good! You aren't accountable for her actions, and holding a grudge only impacts you."

"God wasn't done. After church, we met Natalie, Dave, and the kids for brunch. While we visited, the kids colored and placed their stickers strategically on their placemats.

"Here, Jonica, I did this for you," Jeremy said.

"Me too," Kevin chimed in.

"Won't they look nice on Joni's fridge?" Natalie asked, smiling at me.

"Yes, they will," I agreed. "Thank you very much."

Two little faces beamed at me and I looked back at her. "Are you sure?" I asked not wanting to overstep my bounds.

"Very sure," she answered. "And I need to ask you something. I have so many 'treasures' from the kids I don't know what to do with them. You're so organized; any ideas?"

So I told her how I had bought several plastic drawers on sale and put them in the extra closets. And how I used recipe cards to label the contents in each drawer, some for memory boxes, crafts, journals, et cetera. She liked the idea.

"Natalie is welcoming me back into the kids' lives. She doesn't seem threatened or afraid of me loving them. She asked me for advice."

"She cares for you Jonica. Your situation is so far outside her comfort zone she doesn't know what to do or say. I think she's afraid she'll hurt you again, and she might but it won't be on purpose."

"I think you're right. They shared some news with us. She's pregnant."

"How did you take the announcement, honey?"

"I was able to feel true joy for her. I'm happy for them. For me, it's another baby to love!"

"What did you say to Natalie?"

"Well, when she told us, she looked straight into my eyes. She saw the prick of sadness before I could hide it, and waited. I told her I was truly happy for them and I am.

For a second I felt the sting we will always carry in our hearts. But, the joy of a new niece or nephew is a sweet balm to my heart. Isn't it strange? Sometimes the very thing hurting us can be the same thing God uses to bless us if we let Him?"

"Maybe that's why we often lean so heavily on Romans 8:28. How's she dealing with the pregnancy?"

"I think she's feeling overwhelmed by the responsibility and work load another little one will bring. She really didn't want to be pregnant again. Two was enough. I know she's being careful around me but, I also saw a sweet joy in her eyes when she touched her tummy tenderly. I think she's going to do just fine."

"I'm so glad for you, and proud of you. You are allowing God to work His miracle in your heart."

When Mom said these kind words, the floodgates opened up, and I started crying. "I'm still disappointed for me."

"Of course you are. You will always feel a pull on your heart at this kind of news. Don't feel bad about it - your pain is nothing to be ashamed of. Just like you did this time, acknowledge it and celebrate the Lord's goodness to those He sends children to."

"I will. I decided I'm going to pray for the parents of the kids I love."

"Good for you and them."

"Their responsibilities are huge."

"I know." She answered with a smile in her voice.

"Was I a lot of work?"

"All kids are but most of the time you were a joy."

"There's one thing that's a little hard to think about. Ben and I are pretty sure we need to be open with others about how infertility feels. I haven't put that part of this together in my mind yet."

Mom sniffed and answered, "God is growing you, Jonica, and as you share with me what He is doing, He grows me too. I hurt for you and can't imagine your pain. I only know He has a plan for you. I believe it with all my heart."

"Me too. I know He's not going to give us children. I am learning to accept His answer. In the hollow place, I feel Him filling me up with something wonderful."

"What?"

"Hope."

Stacie

Sitting on our couch, my toes curled and my shoulders tightened as I read the caller ID. Taking a deep breath, I answered. "Hello, Eve."

"How are you?"

"Growing bigger everyday and feeling great."

"Are you watching your weight? You'll want to be back in your regular clothes soon after the delivery."

"I've gained a few pounds less than the doctor thinks I should. I have so much energy and feel absolutely wonderful. Did you feel this way with me?"

"I'm sure I must have. How many clients are you working with right now?"

"One. A young person seriously damaged and silenced by life's circumstances who needs an advocate."

I took the quiet on the other end of the line as interest and began telling Eve about my hopes for success.

"I feel like this is what I was born to do. Right now my client needs a voice. I'm it. This is a win-win for the court and for the client."

As I talked about my work, my body relaxed and my excitement about the case grew. Stretching my legs out in front of me, I propped my feet up on the glass-topped coffee table. I savored a moment of intentional disobedience-Eve couldn't see me breaking one of her rules, "No feet on the furniture."

"Are you sure it's healthy for you to focus so much attention on one person?"

I pulled my legs under me again as the tension crawled back into my neck and across my shoulders.

"And what about income? Can you make ends meet? Being an advocate doesn't pay much. Many times it's little better than social-working."

"I had enough in a small savings account to pay the office rent and insurance for a year. Chandler Daniels took care of the redecorating. You and Dad bought the furniture. Besides, there is more to this than financial consideration."

"For example?"

"Personal satisfaction. My client is coming out of a shell of sorrow and starting to live again."

"Live? How much living can a severely damaged person do?"

The ice in Eve's voice shocked me. This was cold even for her. Sitting no longer comfortable, I wandered around dusting the edges of picture frames and the leaves on the plants with my fingers.

"My client is a person with feelings including the ability to love and be loved."

"So how long will you have only one client?"

"Until after the baby is born and I go back to work. Even then, my load will be light. I want to focus on giving him my time and care. By handling a few clients I can serve them better."

"I suppose you resent me working instead of caring for you."

"No. Your work and time away from home was our way of life. I don't resent it or blame you. You had a calling and answered it. You left me in the care of the best. No one molested or abused me. While I missed you, I'm proud of you and grateful for a good life."

"I suppose a nanny is out of the picture financially. Have you found qualified daycare?" Had she missed my compliment or was she avoiding it?

"Yes. Jonica's sister-in-law is a licensed day care provider and willing to take our little guy part time."

"I hope you won't waste the benefits the woman's movement worked so hard to get for you."

"It doesn't have to be one or the other. This is an opportunity to answer a call to help society, use my education, and give my best to my family. I'm thinking of specializing in advocating for special-needs kids. I'm so drawn to them."

"Why?" her voice rasped with surprise.

"What's wrong with wanting to help, Eve?"

"It's fine. I just don't understand. Can't you leave the flawed to their trained caretakers?"

"You make it sound like my client is not worth the effort - as if we should 'shelve' the crippled and hurt. We're all broken in one way or another. Injured people have so much to offer anyone interested in working with them. This client is free of any agendas, and is incapable of manipulating people. The vulnerability I see in this life is a strength. I'm legal counsel to the voiceless. It's what I've always wanted to do."

"How will you afford it?"

"Mike's advancing in his job, and his pay increases are generous."

"Well, good."

"Eve, being an advocate gives me something I haven't had in a long time. Something I need and want to pass along to everyone."

"What?"

"Hope."

CHAPTER 19

Jonica

I parked my car in the grocery store lot and hurried toward the door. I met Norma, our church secretary, coming out.

"Jonica! Did Della get a hold of you?"

"No. Why?"

"She called the office this morning needing a few things from the store, and you're next on our list of folks to call when a shut-in needs help. I gave her your number. She listed only a few items. Folger's coffee, sugar cubes, white bread, strawberry jam, a half gallon of whole milk, and a few cans of tuna in water. She was specific about the water."

"I'll pick them up and take them to her today. If she called someone else, I can use them anyway."

"Thanks. Don used to run her errands. It's incredibly difficult for her right now. Depending on her son was one thing. Needing others is harder for some than others. Della's always been independent."

We parted and I pushed the cart around the store picking up the things Norma mentioned. My list would keep for later.

The guy at the checkout was in a chatty mood. "I overheard you talking to Norma. I'm not much on organized religion myself but I've always admired the way you do things for each other. Almost makes me wish I was one of you."

I smiled and kept my words to myself. *Yeah, yeah I know. You're always watching for us to mess up. Thank goodness you can't read minds. If you knew how I used to feel about Della it would justify your opinions about religion. Today I could prove to you that Pharisees are alive and well.*

Second thoughts hit as I pulled up in front of Della's. *What am I doing here Lord? We went to the funeral - wasn't that enough? And why would You send me?*

"In honor prefer one another . . ."

I get it.

The soft tan stucco and dark brown trim made the house unique on a street of white-sided homes. The grass needed mowing and the red geraniums in the window boxes needed a drink. I stepped into the screened porch and knocked on the wooden door with an oval, beveled window.

"Jonica. What are you doing here?"

I tried not to notice Della's curls mashed from sleep and her wrinkled dress. I also chose to ignore her rude greeting.

"Norma told me you needed a few things from the store." I said, holding out the plastic bags.

"Come in."

She shuffled through the living room to a tiny kitchen in oversized plaid men's slippers, threadbare in places.

"Put them here. What do I owe you?"

Setting the sack on the counter beside some dirty dishes, I handed her the receipt.

"I'll be right back."

She went into another room. I heard a soft mewing from the hallway. A small calico cat approached with caution.

"Hey, pretty kitty, what's your name?"

"Her name is Patches. Somebody with no sense of responsibility dropped her off. She yowled half the night. When I opened the door to tell her to 'hush' she snuck in. Don took her to the vet and picked up a large bag of litter. Tuna is her favorite," Della answered, as the cat rubbed around her legs, purring.

"Is there anything else I can do for you?"

"No. This is fine. Thank you."

"You're welcome."

She handed me a check and walked toward the front door. As I followed, we passed a beautiful antique buffet. In the center rested a recent picture of Don and her. I stopped. "This is a wonderful photo."

"Don insisted we get a family photo taken the week before . . ." Her unspoken words dangled between us. "They came back yesterday."

"What a precious keepsake."

I watched her sink into her rocker.

"I miss him."

She pulled a hankie out from her sweater sleeve and dabbed her eyes. The flow could not be stemmed. Instead of heading for the door and leaving the woman to grieve as I intended, I heard my voice ask, "Can I do something for you?"

"What?"

"Do you mind if I stay for a few minutes?"

"Why?"

"I'll leave if you prefer, but it seems grieving alone all the time must be a big burden to carry. Perhaps for just a little while I can share the load? And maybe you'd like me to water your geraniums. They are wilting."

"Fine."

She directed me to the watering can and the spigot. I went back in after giving her flowers a good long drink, and asked if I could do anything else.

"Like what?"

"I'm not sure. Would you like to talk about him?"

"What have you heard?" Her voice was so sharp, I jumped.

"Only good. How he worked hard and many believe he was the best mechanic who ever worked on their cars. I heard he spent a lot of time with his kids. And how much he enjoyed visiting his mom."

"He was a good son. The gossip hasn't reached you."

"Where would I hear it?"

"Church."

"I'm not very involved so it's not likely I'm going to hear anything there."

I reached for another photo of Don from the bookcase. Four smiling teens surrounded him. Two girls and two boys. "His kids?"

"They came with us to the photographer the same day." On the piano sat a single, framed picture of Della, Don, and the same teens.

"I'm sure you noticed there is no wife in these pictures. She left them broken-hearted a few months ago. She didn't even bother to show up for the funeral. I knew she was a hussy from the beginning.

He was crazy in love and wouldn't listen to a word we said. How can a woman walk away from her children? We kept it as quiet as we could. No one needs extra judgment heaped on them."

How well I know.

My gaze fell to her slippered feet. The scruffy flip flops were faded gray and red. The ends extended way beyond the heel of her foot.

She noticed my stare.

"These belonged to my husband. He died almost ten years ago. I gave his tools to Don and his clothes to the homeless shelter. I couldn't part with these old slippers, his bathrobe, or his books. I've always been angry he missed out on so much of life. Now, I'm grateful he's not here to grieve for his son. Parents aren't supposed to outlive their children. What you see in these photos is my whole world."

I didn't know what to say.

She looked at the slippers again and said, "These old things will fall apart one day. My feet will miss them. His robe doesn't smell like him anymore."

I started to cry.

"Why are you bawling?"

"I can't imagine not having Ben. I can't grasp your sorrow or your loneliness. I'm glad you have your grandchildren. They must be a comfort to you."

"His oldest daughter just turned twenty-two. She wants to be the other kids' legal guardian and raise them. With Don's life insurance and her job as an RN, they should make it. The house is paid for. I'll help too."

It struck me her oldest granddaughter was only two years younger than me. With three siblings in her care, she didn't define a "normal" family either. I hoped I'd get to meet her.

"Their mom doesn't want to be an active part of their lives at all?"

"She told Alisha she doesn't want the life insurance, the house, or them.

There is a new man with lots of money. She flashed a huge diamond at the kids the morning she left and drove off never looking back. I know because they watched until she was out of sight hoping it was some kind of bad joke. It wasn't."

Della reached for the photo in my hands.

"I just don't know where he is now."

"What do you mean?"

"He wasn't interested in what he called 'my religion.' I don't know if he ever made it right with God. And now I have to deal with this." She pointed to a large manila envelope.

"Someone needed to identify the body. To spare his children that horror, I went. They gave me this. I can't seem to open it."

"You will when the time is right."

The doorbell rang.

"Would you get that? I know I look a mess."

The mail carrier greeted me, eyebrows raised. "Hi. How's Della?"

I shrugged. "I brought her a few groceries from the store, watered her blossoms, and am visiting for a while."

"Good. I've been worried about her. Every day she seems to sink a little lower. Don was a good friend. I try to keep an eye on his mother."

"You two quit talking about me," Della scolded from inside.

He raised his eyebrows and his voice. "Della, you settle down in there. You know we do these things because we care. I've got one letter for you today. It's from the garage.

"What do they want?"

"I don't read your mail, so you'll have to open it to find out."

"Jonica, bring it in here and, Bill, you get on with your work."

"Yes, Ma'am. Please take care of yourself."

"Get along now!"

"I'll be back after supper to mow your yard. I'll bring Katie along. She'll be glad to help you in the house for awhile if you'd like."

"That will be fine," Della said.

Bill stepped off the porch then turned and said to me, "Good luck." He left with a brief salute.

I went back in and offered her the letter. "You open it and read it to me," she demanded.

"Are you sure?"

"You asked if you could do anything. Is opening a letter too much for you to handle?"

I choked back an angry retort. She was old and grieving and I didn't have the heart to say what I was thinking.

She handed me the brass letter opener from the table by her chair.

After slicing it open, I offered the opened envelope, but she waved it off.

"I asked you to read it to me, Girl."

"This might be business. I'm uncomfortable delving into your personal stuff."

"Please, Jonica."

As I pulled the single sheet out, the smell of oil, grease, and exhaust entered the room. I heard her take in a deep breath.

Dear Della,

I know this is a difficult time for you. I put Don's toolbox in the back room. Someone will need to come and get it. Maybe his boys will want to look through it. One of the guys can deliver it to you if that's more convenient.

Sincerely,

Cliff

"Give me that."

She snatched it out of my hand and held it to her nose. "It smells just like Don."

As she held the letter and frame to her chest, I remembered when Don had worked on my car. He had greeted me politely, all the while looking at my car as if he couldn't wait to get under the hood. After handing me a coupon for a free coffee at Millie's down the street, he pulled the car into the garage. When I came back, his head was buried deep inside the guts of another car. I shared the memory with Della.

"And you know what is so neat about it all?" I asked.

"What?"

"He did what he loved."

She smiled. "He excelled in school and we offered to send him to college anywhere he wanted. We promised we'd support him no matter what he wanted to be. It stretched the limit of our under-standing when he wanted to work at Cliff's and drag race in the summer. For a long time I thought it was a phase and would pass. It didn't.

"Was that hard?"

"Not after I watched him work on my car. He loved the old thing and kept her running for years."

"Did you ever watch him race?"

"Every chance I got. Open the closet door and pull out the leather jacket on the right side."

I did and held it up. On the worn black leather, embroidered in red letters, it read, "Della, Pit Crew Chief-in charge of prayer."

"You wore this?"

"I sure did."

"I love it. Do other people know?"

"No, and don't you go telling them."

"I won't. Except Ben. I tell him everything."

"Marty and I were like that too." Again her eyes drifted to the slippers.

"Where are your pictures of you and Marty?"

She waved toward a door. "Our wedding and anniversary photos are on the wall in there. Go ahead and look."

I couldn't believe my eyes. A straight silk gown pooled at the bride's feet. A veil circled her upswept hair, and white lilies and ivy cascaded down the front of her dress. A tall handsome man stood by her side. Don was a replica of his dad. I found myself mesmerized by her smile. Where did this joyful woman go?

Family pictures taken every five years or so lined one wall and anniversary pictures taken every ten years lined the other. Decades of devotion.

On her bedside table sat a trio-frame that held a series of photos of Della and Don in their racing jackets, including one of her in his race car. I wondered what she'd think if she knew we both liked black leather.

When I went back to the living room, she held the large envelope with Don's belongings inside. "Please open this. I can't put it off and I can't do it alone."

I took it and pinched the metal fastener together.

"Here you go."

She shook her head. "Would you mind handing them to me one at a time?"

First my hand found his billfold. She gripped the leather in her right hand and waited for me to continue. Next I found a full ring of keys. She held it in her other hand. The only other belongings were a comb, a wedding band, and a separate brass key. She pointed toward the table, and I set them down.

"Wonder what the key is to," she said.

"I don't know. Ben's friend is a locksmith. I could take it to him and he might know at least what kind of lock it goes to."

"I'd appreciate it."

Tears welled up again and she asked, "Did a sin I committed cost Don his life?"

Her question seemed to suck the air out of my lungs. I inhaled and choked before I could spit out, "No, Della! You didn't cause the accident."

"How can you be sure?" Watery pale blue eyes begged for an answer.

"May I show you from your Bible?"

She nodded and I picked up the worn black book. Turning to John chapter nine, I read aloud the story of the man blind from birth.

"See Della? God allows some bad things into our lives and trusts us to bring Him honor and glory through them. Infertility is not God's way of punishing me. He is using it to draw others to Himself. I don't know how He can use Don's death, but I believe He can and will."

"Jonica, I'm so tired, I don't know what to think anymore."

"I'll go and let you rest. I'll leave your Bible open to this passage so you can take another look later. As soon as I find out what this key goes to, I'll stop by again."

"Can you hand me the blanket behind you?"

I picked it up and held it toward her. She reached for it, her hands still full of Don's things. She wasn't ready to let go of the little bit of her son she had left.

"Here. Let me tuck you in."

I drove toward home in a daze.

I'm not sure where all this is leading Lord. Thy will be done.

My cell phone chimed. I heard Stacie's sobbing voice. "Please, Jonica, can you come over?"

"Sure. I'll be right there."

Please God, keep the baby safe.

Stacie

I parked the car and looked at the sage green house with rose red trim. Bay windows, a wrap-around porch, and gingerbread added dimension to the large square building. Jonica would love this place, I said to myself. Walking up to the front door, I took in the hanging pots with bright red blossoms, the yellow rose bushes along the walk, and the wooden porch swing, chairs, and tables. Red, green, yellow, blue, purple, and orange paint splashed, swished, and zigged without a pattern across each piece of furniture. Braided rugs decorated the dark sage floor.

"Hello, Stacie!" Peggy greeted me opening the screen door. Its squeak welcomed me.

"Hi. Who painted your furniture?"

"Flashy, huh? One day I mentioned these pieces needed paint and the kids volunteered to do the job. I primed the wood to match the house then gave each one a can of their favorite color and a brush or sponge. They did the rest."

"I love them. May I hire them to do mine?"

"You're kidding."

"I mean it. We enjoy our balcony and bought plain white metal furniture I need to do something with. I think this is wonderful. Joyful. Where did you get all the different styles of chairs?"

"We were driving by a yard sale and saw them all lined up. They reminded me of our kids and us-all different but together. We let each kid pick out the one they liked best. The lady laughed when we piled out of the van and tried them all until we each found one that that fit. Come on in."

The oak staircase, floors, and wide trim invited me into another era, when building a house was a work of art.

"Let's start with something to drink then I'll give you a tour."

"Sounds good. Where did you get all these wonderful antiques?" I asked, running my fingers across a lovely old dining room table. "My grandmother owned one just like this."

"It came from a secret donor. A delivery guy dropped it off one day just when we needed it for our first meal."

"What a strange coincidence."

"We believe it was God working anonymously."

In the soft, butter-yellow kitchen, we enjoyed fresh lemonade over crushed ice and talked.

Pulling out my legal pad, I asked Peggy to refresh my memory on

Hope's injuries.

"She suffered from a severe lack of oxygen shortly after her birth and sustained permanent brain damage. Her parents taught her to speak, color, and write simple words. Eventually, she learned to read simple books and write basic sentences. She stopped progressing at the third grade level, although she never mastered math beyond easy addition and some subtraction. We still reinforce those with flash cards a couple of times a week as her homework."

"The record states a fireman rescued her from the burning house, and that she suffered third degree burns on her legs."

"Her favorite blanket was on fire. She tried to put out the flames by kicking at them. She screamed at the fire fighter briefly when he took it away from her. She couldn't understand it was no longer her security but a deadly enemy. As far as we know it's the last sound she made until recently."

"Who told her about her parents?"

"Her case worker, Rebecca, who also had the job of making all the funeral arrangements and finding a foster home for an orphaned, injured, and very frightened child. Rebecca called us and asked if we'd like to meet her. I visited the hospital where she sat in a pool to soak the skin before they sloughed off the burned skin. I watched a child suffering torture in absolute silence. At times I wondered if I'd survive and couldn't believe she had. I went back day after day. She wouldn't look at me. I kept talking to her, praying for her out loud, and singing to her about God's love.

Two weeks later we enjoyed our first breakthrough. She looked at me before staring into the water. Her therapist and I danced a little jig out in the hall later. Then came her first smile. We were on hold there for a long time."

"And yesterday was the first time she spoke?"

"Yes."

Tears welled up in my eyes.

"What you are doing for us-being Hope's advocate-means so much to us as a family. We all love her. Last night she said only two words but we went out for pizza and ice cream to celebrate."

"What did she say?"

"Hi, Stevie."

"You should have seen him do his happy dance for Jesus. He jitterbugged around saying, 'I knew it.'" Peggy said with a smile.

"He knew what?"

"He believed that Hope would talk again. Stevie's faith in God runs deep. He prays until something happens, never doubting."

Changing the subject, I asked, "How many bedrooms does this house have again?" All the God talk made me uncomfortable. Like Jonica, Peggy talked about Him as easily as she breathed.

"Eight. We all enjoy our own rooms with one left over for guests. We are thankful for four and a half bathrooms."

"Who handled the sale for you?"

"A lawyer our pastor referred us to. He offered to work with us pro bono which fit our budget at the time. Shortly after we approached the realtor with an offer to purchase it for a reduced price, someone else made a higher offer.

The second party wanted to turn it into a bed and breakfast. We figured we were finished and that we'd have to keep looking for a property we could fit into and somehow afford. Then our secret donor made an even bigger offer and before we knew it, we closed. Right away, we started going to auctions and garage sales looking for sturdy old furniture. Again gifts poured in.

Two people who reupholster furniture took old chairs and couches and made them new again. Five women volunteered to refinish the old, worn pieces of oak furniture we were given or found here and there. They turned our basement into their workshop, and recruited teens from church. Together they also redid the kitchen cupboards and all the wood trim.

Later, a childless couple in their sixties from church volunteered to be grandparents. They remember each birthday with a card and special cake, and they share holidays with us. She makes pajamas for the kids- cotton in the summer and flannel in the winter."

"This story is amazing. People are usually so disconnected from each other nowadays. What motivated them?"

"Faith."

"As in your daughter?"

"No. As in God."

"Can I see Hope's room?" I had to find a way to turn off all this God-talk.

In the long hallway upstairs, several doors stood open. Peggy paused in front of one with a piece of paper taped to it that said, "Welcome Stacie" several color crayon smiley faces circled the words.

"Here we are. Hope made this and taped it up here last night. I helped her with the spelling."

Inside, a purple crazy quilt rested on an iron-rail bed painted lavender. Soft purple lace curtains edged the long window, a deep purple crocheted afghan rested over a wooden rocker. On the wall by the chair hung a large photo-a family portrait. Hope stood in the middle, between Peggy and John. The rest of the kids surrounded them. On the nightstand was an older photo of a younger Hope with another couple. Her birth parents.

"Hope knows her mommy and daddy loved her very much. We haven't told her this, but the firemen found their bodies in the hallway outside her room. Their attempt to save her life cost them everything. Before they went after Hope her dad called 911-if he hadn't, she would be gone too. They should have waited outside but they couldn't. The fireman grabbed this keepsake as he carried Hope to safety. He is now her beloved adopted uncle." She held out a picture to me of a brawny young man holding Hope's hand.

I gripped the banister on the way downstairs, tears threatening to blind me. In the entryway, I noticed a wooden cabinet on the wall by the door.

"What's this?"

"My husband made this for the kids. Sometimes people send them cards and letters. They enjoy getting mail themselves, so, these are their mailboxes."

I read the names and one jumped out at me. Stephen Dunbar, Jr. My stomach lurched and my throat tightened.

"Who is this?"

"Stevie. The boy we talked about before."

"How old is he?"

"He just turned twenty-one."

"Why is he here again?"

"Stevie has Down syndrome."

"Do you know his parents?"

"Only his father. He comes to visit every week. In fact, I hope they get home soon. Mr. Dunbar should be here in about fifteen minutes. Stacie, are you okay? You look so pale."

"I'm not doing pregnant very well. I just need to go home and rest. Please explain to Hope and John for me." I grabbed the old doorknob and stepped out. "Thank you so much for the tour. You are a special woman."

"So are you, Stacie. The silent kids of this world need you to be their voice."

I tried not to run down the sidewalk. I hurried to my car and threw my briefcase onto the passenger seat. My rush woke up the baby, who let me know with a swift kick. I rubbed my stomach, hoping to calm the child in my womb and my racing thoughts. *He will come from behind me.*

I turned my car around in a driveway a few doors down and parked on the other side of the road. A vanload of kids pulled into the driveway and right behind them followed a black Catera. My dad got out of the car and a blond man-boy raced into his arms.

I don't remember driving home, letting myself in, or dialing Jonica's number. I do remember hearing her say, "I'll be right there."

CHAPTER 20

Jonica

Blooming roses, book sales, and Della filled my June days. I stopped by her house and told her our locksmith friend said the key probably belonged to a large toolbox. I invited her to Millie's for lunch hoping she might be ready to visit Cliff's.

In the car she wondered out loud, "What did Don own that he needed locked up?"

We ate homemade chicken pot pies and drank strong black coffee. Della talked about her flowers and love of feeding the birds glad we shared these two interests.

"Cliff's is down the block. Do you want to go ask if he or one of the guys can drop Don's toolbox off at your house?" I asked.

"We might as well. Maybe it'll fit in your trunk. How big can it be?"

Cliff wiped his hands off on a rag but still refrained from shaking our hands. We stepped into the back room and got our first glimpse of Don's toolbox.

"That's big," we said in unison.

"Yep. The guys buy a lot of tools. They're expensive, so we each own a toolbox like this one to keep our investment safe."

I reached into my purse, drew out the key, and offered it to Della.

"Please, Jonica, you do it. I'm shaking too much."

The key unlocked the master and we heard all the drawers unclick.

"Don kept some personal things in the bottom drawer, Della. Things most mechanics don't. I'll leave you ladies alone to look through them."

Cliff closed the door, muffling the sounds of hydraulics, men's voices, and revving engines from the shop.

Della stood still staring at the drawer. I bent down. The bottom drawer was lined with clean towels. There rested an old Bible, a stack of envelopes and a ledger.

"Please take them out," she said.

She took the Bible in her hands. "This was his father's. I gave it to him at the gravesite. I didn't know if he'd keep it or not. What are those?" she asked, pointing to the rest.

The envelopes were addressed to her and his kids. The ledger was a handwritten journal.

"Let's go, Jonica."

I made arrangements for Cliff to deliver the almost-five-foot tall tool locker to Della's. She held on to the Bible with all her fragile might.

Back at her house, she sat and stared at the envelope with her name on it. Then she reached for the letter opener.

"Do you want me to leave?"

"No. I need you here. Could you call Bernice and ask her to come over too? Her number is on the list by the phone in the kitchen."

"I'll be right over," Bernice assured me.

As I hung up, Della hollered, "Praise the Lord!"

I hurried around the corner and saw her standing with her hands clasping the letter to her heart. "Thank You, Father!" she shouted.

"Della?"

"Jonica! He found Christ! My son is with the Father and Marty. I will see him again. He wrote in his letter to me that the ledger is a detailed account of his journey to God."

We hugged.

I helped her fix tea and put cookies on a plate. Bernice walked in through the kitchen door.

Della shuffled over to her friend and I saw she had Marty's slippers on again and now his Bible in her arms. "Bernice, our prayers were answered. Don came to Christ and is in heaven. You know how quiet he was and always keeping some kind of journal or telling me things in letters. He left us a gold mine. A letter to each of us sharing his faith and this ledger records his journey."

Bernice held Della as tears slipped silently down their crinkled cheeks. Their quiet rejoicing mingled with their deep sorrow.

We sat at the dining room table and sipped sweetened tea from bone china teacups with lilacs on them. The conversation eventually turned to me.

"Are you going to adopt?" Bernice asked.

For the first time, the question didn't push any buttons.

"No. Ben and I are committed to the children God is sending into our lives. We hope to pray for, share our faith with, and love these kids."

"That's good," Bernice said before taking another sip of tea.

"You'll be a blessing to them." Della said.

In the small silence that followed, they granted me a precious gift-acceptance.

The old friends held hands. "Let's pray," Della said and held out a hand for me. Bernice did the same. I joined their sweet circle of friendship. Later, I left them to a second pot of tea, Don's letter, and the ledger.

At home, I walked out to my garden with an iced grape juice, my journal, and our cordless phone. The breeze carried the soft scent of rose, and the sun warmed me. Cheeps, chirps, and song filled the air.

My thoughts turned to Stacie. I glanced at my watch. An urgency to pray sprang up from the center of my being. *Please be with her as she confronts her dad. Give her wisdom and understanding.*

I smiled at a bumblebee working his way in and out the petals. I set my juice on the arm of my bench and picked up my journal, never taking my eyes off the bee as he hovered in the flower next to me. Translucent wings hummed as he worked the pollen-laden stamens. With a full load, he emerged from the blossom slowly, turned around, and buzzed off. A verse I memorized long ago, came to mind, "Pleasant words are like a honeycomb, sweetness to the soul and health to the bones".

Lord, give me encouraging words when Stacie calls. Help me to lift her up. Be with her as only You can. Help the truth set this family free.

I jumped as the phone beside me jangled. Stacie's cell phone showed on the ID.

"Can I come over?" Stacie asked.

"Sure. Where are you?"

"In your driveway."

Stacie

For weeks I avoided my dad.

After her surgery, he spent extra time with Eve as she completed a regimen of radiation and chemotherapy treatments. She wanted total privacy. I knew she didn't want me to see her sick. I used busy and tired as my reasons for not talking to either parent. Mike saw them as excuses.

"Talk to him, Stacie. He'll be honest. Besides, you need to know how Eve is doing."

Instead, I reorganized my files and cleaned drawers and closets. Jonica planned a rummage sale so I cleaned out my stuff and left a message for Eve, just in case she had some good junk she wanted to get rid of. Her housekeeper dropped off Eve's donations. I also whined, cried, and threw hissy fits resembling the tantrums I'd seen toddlers attempt in Target. I saw everything as justified.

"He lied to me," I stated as I dumped a box of coats from Eve on the bed. "I trusted him with everything-my whole life-and he lied to me."

"He didn't lie. He just didn't tell you. Who did you ask about the mystery photo?"

"No one."

"Don't you think he'd have told you if you'd asked him?"

"Not anymore."

"When has he ever given you reason to doubt him?"

"Now. Big time."

"Come on Stacie. You haven't given him a chance to explain."

"Right," I mumbled, reaching deep into old pockets. On the bed lay a pair of Eve's dress pearl earrings, a single key, and a pile of old receipts.

"Why'd she send this? It's Dad's favorite coat."

The inside pocket bulged partly open as I lifted it up.

"What's this?" I looked across the bed at him as I pulled out a picture wallet. Sinking down on the pile of wool and cashmere, I made an executive decision.

"Stacie, what are you thinking?"

"I'm going to look at this. After all, Eve meant this all to go to the sale. I'm just making sure nothing of value goes with it." I explained.

Opening the soft, faded calfskin, I caught a scent of Dad's after-shave mixed with leather. Eve and Dad's faces beamed at me from the first photo. On the white edge in Dad's handwriting it read, "Our honeymoon."

"Mike, look."

"She's beautiful. You look like her in our wedding pictures. Even your dresses are similar. Did you notice that before?"

"No. I asked to see her photos several times but the opportunity never arose. When she saw my dress, she didn't mention it. I was relieved when she didn't disapprove of my choice."

The next two pages held photos of Dad and his children. In one, Dad held a tiny pink bundle. "Stacie and Daddy" was printed on the photo edge in Eve's handwriting. Dad's eyes shimmered into the camera and his smile reached from cheek to cheek. In the other, he held me on his knee and clutched the blue-blanketed bundle close to his chest. "My Kids" this one read in Dad's writing. My hand rested on the baby's blanket and I smiled at the camera. Dad looked down at his son.

Then came two pictures of me. One showed me curled up asleep on the couch surrounded by coloring books, popcorn kernels, and my teddy bear named Honey. "Date night with Dad" it read again in Eve's handwriting.

"She knew about our messes and didn't say a word."

"Honey, I know your dad let your Eve do the work she wanted to do, but I don't think he ever let her decide what he did with you."

"So, you don't think she was the pants in the family?'

"No. They have a partnership not all that different from my folks."

"You think?"

"I'd bet on it."

"You don't gamble"

"With your parents, it would be a sure deal."

Then came a wedding picture of Mike and I smiling at each other like no one else existed. For that moment, they hadn't.

I turned the page. Two photos of a boy. One, of a baby in Dad's arms, was titled, "Stephen Dunbar, Jr." In the other, more recent, a stocky blond boy stood holding dad's hand and a kite. Dad's smile warmed my heart like sunshine on a chilly morning run.

The last photo was more recent. Eve stood next to Dad in an elegant black velvet gown, her arm tucked into Dad's.

"Mike, look!" Dad and Eve smiled at each other. "Off her guard" was written on the edge in Dad's writing. "They love each other!"

"We knew that already honey."

"I know but I don't get to see her this way."

In the pocket, I found a piece of paper.

"You're not going to read that are you?" Mike asked.

"It could be a grocery list - something I can toss."

It wasn't.

Dear Stephen,

When we said "for better or worse," who'd have thought it would include breast cancer?"

I stopped reading but did glance to the end.

You are the love of my life, Darling.

Eve

The doorbell rang. Mike moved toward the living room. "I'll get it." I heard him greet someone then call, "Stacie, it's your dad."

"Be right there."

I got off the pile of coats in a series of not-so-smooth grunts and moves. I stuck the small album into my back pocket and walked into our living room.

"I'll make us some coffee," Mike said as he escaped to the kitchen.

"Stacie! You look beautiful."

"Hi, Dad. How's Eve?"

I sat on the couch careful not to harm the album.

"The radiation was rough and she reacted pretty strongly to the chemo. It's been a rough few weeks. I left her at her office drafting her farewell speech."

"She's not running again?" I should have been shocked and even worried but I was just plain mad.

"No."

"Is she dying?" It was a mean question and intended to inflict pain. *Like Mother, like daughter.*

"I hope not."

"So who does she recommend to fill her shoes?"

"She's leaving that up to the party."

"Huh."

"How are you?" "Honey, what's wrong? Is it the baby?"

"No Dad. It's this."

I saw him glance at the wallet in my hands. "Where did you get that?"

"In the pocket of a coat Eve sent over for Jonica's rummage sale."

"I see."

"I knew before I found this." I held him the album.

He sat beside me and took it in his hands. I noticed his slender fingers as they closed around his secret treasure. He kept his head bowed.

"How?"

I explained that the mystery photo and blanket were in a box Eve sent over. Then I told him about my visit to Peggy's house. "One of the kids in her house is my client. I saw the mailboxes and then I spied on you."

He seemed to sink into himself.

"Dad, why did you lie to me?"

"I wondered if I would ever be able to share this with you. Please don't think badly of your mother as I tell you these things. She loves you very much. Promise?"

I gave him my word as I watched him rub the leather rectangle in his hand.

"I met Eve when we both taught college. When she first entered the lecture hall on teacher orientation day, like every other man in the room, I was drawn to her beauty. Then she spoke and her voice seemed to beckon me. She smiled all the way to her eyes-not like now-and I know it sounds cliché but I felt myself get lost in them. I didn't hear the dean introduce me, although he used a microphone. Then she laughed, and it reminded me of water bubbling in a small brook I fished in as a boy. The orientation dragged on. I didn't retain a thing I heard. All I could think about was finding her later and asking her out. When she said yes, I started plotting how to get her to give the same answer to a marriage proposal. I knew I was in love for the first time in my life - with a stranger.

"Imagine my delight when after a year of courtship, I found out she loved me too. Our wedding, honeymoon, and first baby were perfect. Eve's second pregnancy was different. Morning sickness plagued her the full nine months. The delivery took hours and the doctor feared for the baby. Like with you, your mother insisted I stay with her in the delivery room. It was unusual in those days but, when Eve wanted something she usually got it. I watched his birth. His blue skin startled me and they rushed to get him breathing. You came out with a wail loud enough to be heard in the next county. He barely sputtered. I knew something was terribly wrong with our boy.

"Nurses helped Eve clean up. They avoided her questions about the newborn. About an hour later, the doctor returned. He told us our son had Down syndrome. Turned out it wasn't the difficult pregnancy or delivery. You know Eve and I married later in life-we're older than most of your friends' parents. She gave birth to you at thirty-five and Stevie two years later. His heart was weak and he struggled to breathe. They didn't think he'd live long and if he did, the doctor insisted, the only way he could get the right care would be in an institution. We begged to see him. The doctor offered to call social services to take over-they wanted us to make the baby a ward of the state. I demanded to see our son. Eve reached for him, hoping they were wrong. She cradled him in her arms and then looked up at me.

"Her eyes went empty and it cut me to the core of my being. She handed the boy back to me and curled up, sobbing. I looked into the face of my son and saw powdery blond hair, a smashed nose, tiny square hands, and oval eyes. Just like when I saw his mother and sister, I fell in love. I insisted we take him home and figure out a better solution. Eve refused to name him or care for him.

"The combination of her total rejection of our son and a severe post-partum depression, robbed me of any joy I might have had over his birth.

"My first book did well, and with my teaching, our finances stabilized. Then Eve's parents were killed. It was the last straw. I was terrified she'd do something to herself but the fortune they left her provided her with the freedom to pursue her dreams. I encouraged her, hoping for the spark to return to her eyes. I saw a fire there but very little true life.

"I named the boy Stephen Dunbar, Jr., wanting him to have a connection to his family. Your mother insisted on a separate nanny for Stevie to protect you from getting to know him and instructed me to find someone to take him. You only saw him once.

"Through a friend, I found Peggy and her husband. They had just moved into the house. Stevie was about a year old when they became his guardians. For weeks they visited him at the mansion daily, and he adjusted to his change of address with no anxiety.

"I visit him every week and take him out for breakfast on his birthday. We go to the zoo and to the art supply store. He enjoys water color painting and drawing. He's really very talented. When he succeeds at learning something new, we go out for ice cream sundaes. Chandler Daniels is also a special friend of his and his Sunday school teacher.

"Stevie's happy with Peggy and John. I'm still his dad, but they are his family too. He knows about you and Eve. His room is full of pictures of you. He prays every day that you will come and see him."

"Why didn't you tell me?" I heard the accusation in my voice and shuddered. I'd never talked to my dad that way.

"I promised Eve I wouldn't. I believed she would get her life on track and come back to Stevie. I bargained with her. I promised not to tell you, but I vowed to visit and know my son."

"And Eve's response?"

"She agreed."

"Are you ashamed of him?" I asked.

"No. Never. He is my son-a living, breathing blessing, and a beautiful human being. Although Eve can't see it, our son is a special reflection of our love just like you are."

"Is Eve ashamed of him?"

"She resists him because she believes she failed. She birthed a less than perfect child. Your mother does flawless better than anyone I know and never forgives herself for less."

"You love him."

"I do."

"Can I meet him?"

"I don't know how to deal with this. I want to keep my word to Eve. I love her and very often express that by respecting her whenever I can."

"Dad, we can't keep living this lie. I'll call and tell her the truth. Then it should be my choice to see him or not."

"I want to be on the line when you tell her."

I dialed the number with cold, shaking hands. I paced the room while her line rang. Then I wiped my cold hands on my jeans and tried to swallow the tension building in my throat.

"Senator Dunbar's office."

"Hi, Emily, it's Stacie. Can I talk to Eve please?"

"Sure. I'll put you right through."

"Stacie-are you all right?" Eve asked.

"Not really. I know you're feeling lousy and in the middle of an important letter, but we have something to tell you."

"We?"

"Dad is on the line too."

She listened in silence as I told her how I learned about Stevie.

Finally, I heard myself say, "I want to meet him."

"That's up to you."

"Stacie, I need to talk to Eve alone." Dad's voice said into the line.

"See you, Eve."

"Good-bye, Stacie."

Dad walked in from the kitchen, rubbing his face with both hands.

"How'd it go?" I asked.

"She isn't happy but she knows I didn't betray her trust."

"How are you?"

"Exhausted. But I feel freer. Chandler was right-living a lie is hard work."

"How do you know Mr. Daniels so well?"

"We grew up together. We lived about a mile apart on farms. We fished together, climbed trees, and made forts in the woods. He took a lot of teasing because of his fancy name. He was so handsome at birth his mother was sure he'd be a movie star one day and named him accordingly.

I came from a family of God-fearing people. Chandler was raised in a family that caused fear through rough talk and even rougher living.

In college I turned away from my religious upbringing. After hearing Billy Graham preach on TV, Chandler turned to Christ. He's been praying for me and us for years. I called and asked him to pray for us today-I knew something was wrong and hoped it wasn't anything with the baby."

"I asked Jonica to pray too."

"Good."

"Don't you think it's weird we're so willing to ask them to pray to a God we don't think exists?"

"It beats consulting the stars I guess."

"But aren't we sort of consulting the One who made the stars?"

Dad's eyebrows rose in unison higher than I'd ever seen them go.

"I mean, aren't we sort of using their faith?"

"Sure but it's always good to hedge your bets."

"When can I meet Stevie?"

"I'll call Peggy and see what his schedule is. He needs a certain amount of structure and some advance notice. I'll call you tonight."

"Sure. Let's make this easy for him and us."

"You cannot know how happy this is going to make Stevie." Dad smiled almost as big as the boy I'd seen in the album. "Sweet daughter, you have a brother." he proclaimed.

A tingle of joy rippled through my body. "I'm a big sister."

"I hate leaving you right now but I have a meeting in an hour. I need to head out."

"It's all right, Dad. Mike's here and I think I'll drive over and see Jonica anyway."

CHAPTER 21

Jonica

As Stacie prepared to meet her brother, I decided to have a prayer retreat. I knew of other women who set aside a day to pray and spend time fellowshipping with God in His Word. They'd shared testimonies of refreshment and new insights from the Bible. I needed both, so, I decided to go to the zoo. I packed my Bible, prayer list, notebook, favorite pen, and highlighter in my backpack. Others might have chosen a more secluded spot, but I wanted to talk with God and walk among the animals of His creation.

I pulled on Ben's black NASCAR cap, rubbed sunscreen on my face and left off the makeup. In old black jeans, walking shoes, a white T-shirt, and my sunglasses, I smiled at my reflection.

"I will be praying in secret for all the people there, Lord. So today, I am Your undercover agent."

First, I stopped at the coffee stand and bought a mocha latte - large. Settling on a bench under a maple tree near the polar bears, I read Psalm 103, sipping the sweet chocolate brew.

As sunshine filtered through the leaves, I was drawn deeper into His Word. I highlighted special passages and continued to read favorite verses. After awhile, the urge to move whispered through my legs.

I threw my empty cup in the trash, and moved to the primate exhibit. The male silverback gorilla paced his domain while the females and young sunned themselves. One little gorilla rushed toward his father in play. He climbed the mighty beast, only to be plucked off and put back on the ground, then nudged back toward his mother. In the orangutan area, the red primates glided through the air, their long arms reaching from rope to rope. One half-grown male hung on a branch and watched me. When I giggled at him, his mouth opened into a big O. For a moment, we enjoyed each other's attention.

I walked to a nearby picnic table and sat down. Taking out a prayer list, I wrote my requests in my journal. The scent of hotdogs and popcorn hit my nose at the same time my stomach growled. After a brief lunch of popcorn and lemonade, I found a bench in the conservatory and continued my prayer time. I asked specifically for someone to share my faith with.

Later, washing my hands in the ladies room, a woman in a zoo uniform approached.

"I saw you writing away in your book. Are you a journalist?"

"Not today. I'm enjoying a day of prayer and Bible reading," I responded.

Standing with her legs slightly apart and her hands on her hips, she kind of snorted. It was the sound of disapproval - my least favorite thing.

"I love being near the animals, the Lord, His Word, and spending time with Him in prayer."

"Interesting," she replied, watching me in the mirror.

"Do you have any spiritual beliefs?" I asked, turning to face her.

"No."

Reaching into my backpack, I pulled out my hand lotion and saw her step back.

"What's wrong?" I asked.

"I thought you were going to pull out one of those pamphlets. Sometimes people litter the park with them hoping we'll pick one up and read it out of curiosity and find God."

"Well, I have a book in here I'd love to give you, but won't if you aren't interested."

"A book?"

"By my favorite nonfiction Christian author. He helps me see Jesus vividly and what He did on the cross."

"Is it a church book?"

"He's a pastor but it's not about a denomination. It's about Jesus and what He did for us. I need to warn you, though, if you decide to read it, you might find yourself amazed by God's love for you."

Steel- blue eyes stared into mine. "Why give a total stranger you know nothing about a book? Why do you care?" she demanded.

"Because Jesus does."

"How do you know?"

"The Bible tells me so."

"And you believe the Bible?"

"Yes."

"I need to get back to the animals. It's almost time to feed the lions."

"Would you like the book?"

"Maybe. I don't know."

I pulled He Chose the Nails by Max Lucado out of my bag and handed it to her. She held it in her hands away from her body.

"This is a hardcover-I can't take this."

"Sure you can. When I bought it, I prayed God would send someone into my life to give it to. Looks like you're His answer to my prayer."

"I've been called a lot of things in life-but never that."

"Today you are. My name and phone number are inside the cover. If you have any questions please call me. Otherwise, I'm planning to spend more quiet mornings here from time to time."

"Well, maybe I'll see you then."

"I'll be praying for you, Maggie."

"How'd you know my name?"

"It's on your badge."

A lion roared in the distance.

"I better get back to work."

"Thank You, Lord," I whispered watching her walk away. "Please use Max's book to lead her to Yourself." I took a few moments to express thanksgiving for His love for me, and a wonderful day at the zoo.

Later, at the big cat exhibit, I watched the golden lions sleep off their lunch, their only movement the flick of the tip of a tail now and then. I listened to their purrs rumble their contentment with envy. If only a meal and a nap in the sunshine could give me the same comfort. I switched from a prayer retreat to poor-me-mode in under a second. The NASCAR guys would have been impressed with my speed shifting.

The story of Anna meeting baby Jesus in the temple came to my mind. She'd waited so long for the promise of God-to see the Messiah. Her faithfulness inspired me. The way she looked daily for the coming King and wasn't at all surprised when He came as an infant in His mother's arms amazed me.

Lord, help me to wait on You for everything and to recognize that You are always at work in my life - even infertility. Thank You for the peace that is beyond all understanding. Thank you for salvation - without You, I'd be hopeless.

Oh Jesus...you are the Hero of my soul.

Stacie

"I don't know what to wear," I grumbled at Mike.

"Your dad said to dress for McDonald's-how hard is that?"

Tugging on elastic-front jeans and a purple maternity T-shirt I realized my body was starting to look very pregnant. The bulge looked more like a basketball every day. My once chiseled cheek-bones were slightly rounded, and tying my shoes had become an uncomfortable task.

"I'm going to get some of those slip-on tennis shoes soon," I muttered just as the doorbell rang.

"Stacie, you look beautiful."

"Dad, I look pregnant. I can barely tie my own shoes anymore."

"I still think you're beautiful."

"Will Stevie understand I'm not just fat?"

"Yes." Dad grinned. "I explained it to him. Want to impress your kid brother?"

"That obvious huh?"

"He already loves you."

"How can he?"

"It is just his way."

That's what Jonica says about God.

Peggy welcomed us. "He's is waiting for you in his room. He wants to meet you there so the other kids don't interrupt."

Dad reached for my cold, sweaty hand. "Relax. Stevie won't notice details or make judgments. He'll simply be glad to meet you and experience an answered prayer."

"Sometimes do you believe in a God who answers prayer?" I asked.

"No. But your brother does."

Upstairs Stevie sat on the edge of his bed with his head bowed, hands folded, and eyes closed. "Amen!" he said as we entered.

"Hi, Dad." He stood up and opened his arms for a hug.

"Hello, Son." Dad reached for my hand again and said, "This is Stacie."

"Hi." Blue eyes shone love at me, and he held out his right hand.

I wiped my hand on my jeans and shook his. "Hi, Stevie."

He picked up a hand-drawn picture from his desk. "I drew this for you."

On the thick ivory paper were four figures. "You're the one in purple. Dad said it's your favorite color. I hope you like it."

We were in the same boat. We wanted to be liked by each other. "Thank you. You did a nice job on this. I'll frame this and put it in my office."

"Good."

While he and Dad caught up on his school work, athletics, and friendships, I looked around his room. Framed photos of Stevie and Dad covered one wall. Other photos displayed Eve and me through the years. Two empty frames hung among them.

Stevie came beside me and said, "I always knew you. Now you know me too."

"What are the empty frames for?"

"For our pictures when we're all a family again."

My mouth opened, but no words came out.

He looked at my tummy and asked, "When will it come out?"

"Soon. And when he does, you will be an uncle." The truth hit me as I said the words.

He smiled and said, "Yep. I want to give him a red ball. We can play catch when he gets bigger like me."

"I think he'll like that a lot."

"Are you two ready for lunch?" Dad asked.

"I am. Let's go," Stevie answered.

We ate cheeseburgers and fries. My brother and I discovered we both liked root beer, our fries drenched in catsup, and twist cones for dessert. We had a blast feeding the geese and telling silly knock-knock jokes. We laughed a lot.

I cried all the way home. I was so glad to meet him, but grieving I'd missed so much of his life. I'd never held him, hugged him, or argued with him. We'd never shared birthdays or holidays. I didn't know his favorite color, food, song, or TV show.

Neither did Eve.

"How are you, honey?" Dad asked, handing me his handkerchief.

"I'm so happy for me and sad for Eve. She is missing so much by not knowing him.

"Dad ...you're my hero more than ever!"

"Because I love my son?"

"Yes."

CHAPTER 22

Jonica

Stacie's delivery date approached and we often reviewed "the plan."

"Mike will call you."

"I'll get dressed and meet you at the curb."

"Your house is on the way. Don't worry. There will be plenty of time."

I had no idea how these things went and could only hope they were right.

One morning a flower delivery man rang our doorbell. He handed me a bouquet of wildflowers and a package. Inside the box was a white T-shirt with ASST. COACH printed in black letters. Then the doorbell rang again. This time Stacie stood there with a silly smirk on her face, holding her new nightshirt. It read, MOM.

"Mike did these for us. His says COACH."

We drank ice water with lemon and laughed out loud as we remembered the breathing lessons Mike had given me over the phone.

"As Assistant Coach, you will need to know this breathing stuff too. Ready?" he had asked and without further warning he started our practice session.

I barely held back the chuckles I knew would immediately be out of control whoops if I so much as let out a whimper.

"I'm serious, Jonica. Stacie is going to need our help."

"I agree." I swallowed a giggle that nearly escaped.

He then began to tell me how many long and short breaths Stacie would need as the contractions increased in frequency and intensity.

"You only need to be able to count to ten. She won't push until the doctor gives her the go ahead."

Then he demonstrated the breathing technique. I did fine until I heard Stacie on the other end, laughing out of control.

"If you don't quit it, Mike, I'm going to push this baby out now!" she had threatened. He gave her the phone.

Stacie took her glass to the kitchen for a refill, rubbing her back. I followed her and heard a small gasp.

"Uh-oh. I'd better go to the bathroom."

I heard her groan. Then she said, "I think something's going on."

"Stacie?"

"This might be it. My back hurts, I'm dripping water, and I just had a giant cramp. Maybe you'd better put that T-shirt on now."

"Did you look at your watch?"

"I did just in case we need to start monitoring them. Even if this is a false alarm, we'd better call Mike. He can pick us both up."

I made the call and Stacie came out of the bathroom. Her eyes looked like dark emeralds set into fine ivory porcelain. I changed into my new shirt.

"Mike's on his way."

"I'll call my doctor. This may be nothing, but I need to be sure."

"I think you'd better sit down."

She dialed and I heard her say, "My back hurt all night and I couldn't rest. I had some tightening and what might have been spasms too." After a pause she continued. "The cramps were about twenty minutes apart and didn't get worse or closer together. I haven't had any pain since about three o'clock. Now, they're back along with this fluid." She listened for a moment then said, "When Mike gets here, we'll come. We're bringing our assistant coach. I'm with her now. No, she's never been through this either."

Mike screeched up to the curb and I helped my friend to the car. "Dr. Steele will have someone waiting for us in the emergency room. There is special parking for maternity patients, remember, Mike? Shoot! This really hurts." Stacie chattered as the car picked up speed. "Whose idea was this again?"

"It was mutual," Mike answered.

"So you say," she bantered back smiling when the contraction eased.

On the way, I called Ben to let him know we were putting the plan into action.

The nurse told us the doctor was waiting for us upstairs and reminded Stacie that she would go through labor, delivery, and recovery in the same room.

In the birthing room, the doctor examined her, and said, "I think you're going to be staying a while. I don't expect this baby for several hours yet."

"This is it?" Mike asked in a soft voice.

"Looks like it. But like I said, it's going to take a few hours. Try to relax."

"By the way, it is good to see you, Jonica," Dr. Steele commented.

"You two know each other?" Stacie asked.

"Dr. Steele was our infertility specialist. Read any good books lately Doctor?" I asked with a grin.

"As a matter of fact, I'm reading one loaned to me by a patient. I'll be back to check on your progress, Stacie."

As he exited gladness washed over my heart a second before I heard my friend exhale. "It's building again."

A nurse hooked Stacie up to a monitor and we heard two hearts beating. Then Stacie muttered, "Here it comes." The monitor needle recorded the intensity and length of the contraction.

"Are they getting worse?" I asked.

"Oh yeah. Lots worse than I expected."

"Honey, you are just getting started. You're going to do a lot more work and that needle will go off the graph before we're through," the nurse commented.

I swallowed hard. "Off the graph?"

"When the contractions get stronger. Stacie, let me know if you change your mind and want something for the pain." The door closed behind her.

Three first-timers looked at each other with raised eyebrows.

Mike turned on the TV and we watched an old John Wayne movie. We laughed and breathed our way through *McClintock*.

The nurse came back and asked if we needed anything.

"I'm thirsty," Stacie said.

"You can have some ice chips."

I jumped up. "I can be in charge of ice chips."

The nurse showed me where they were in the hall and handed me a plastic cup and spoon.

Stacie savored ice chips, and we started watching game shows. I kept a close eye on her little finger. Resting on the sheet next to her, when a contraction hit, Stacie's pinky raised a bit. As the contractions got worse the finger went a higher. So did the needle on the graph.

Mike breathed and puffed through each pain with Stacie, while keeping an eye on the monitor.

Her hair clung to her face as the pain worsened. The nurse checked in again.

"I'm really working up a sweat here," Stacie commented.

"That's normal as things progress. You're doing great. You can have a cool cloth on your forehead. Keep breathing. You can holler if you want to-the walls are sound-proofed."

Another sweeping pain hit, the couple breathed and I got a cool cloth.

As I wiped her forehead after the pain passed she smiled and said, "Breathe, Jonica."

I did feel a bit light headed-I'd been holding my breath through each contraction.

A few minutes later, she whimpered, "Mike, something feels like it's happening. Oh boy-I want to push." This time, her pinky stood straight up.

He pressed the call button and asked the nurse to come in.

I wondered why my friend didn't cry out. My menstrual cramps usually made me whine, and her pain was heading off the chart.

She seemed to hold back and retreat into herself.

As she entered the nurse said, "We still have a long wait ahead of us. First babies take their time."

"This is different than before."

"How many minutes apart are your contractions?"

"Two," Mike said.

"Since when?" the nurse demanded and did a quick check under the sheet.

"The last three or four. You didn't say we needed to tell you," Mike answered.

"I want to push!" Stacie ground out through clenched teeth.

"Don't push. Breathe. I'll get the doctor. Swallow a few more ice chips. You're going to be doing some hard work very soon."

This time I spooned the chips into her mouth while she clutched the sheets.

Dr. Steele strode in, not unlike John Wayne in the movie, pulling on surgical gloves. "So you think this baby is ready to come, huh?"

Mike joined the doctor behind the sheet. He instructed the nurse to get ready. "The baby's head is crowning, Stacie. When I tell you to, push."

Sweat rolled off my friend's brow as she breathed with me and held back the desire to bear down.

Finally, the doctor said, "Push now, Stacie."

She pushed and I prayed.

"Good work! The head is out. Get ready to push harder than before. We need to get these shoulders out."

The needle left the graph, Stacie gripped the sheets, strained forward, and groaned. At least I thought it was her and not me.

The doctor said, "Now, Stacie. Bear down harder-harder. Jonica, if you want to see this child born, you can step down here."

As I watched the baby's shoulders release from its mother's body, it sounded like a big suction cup coming off glass. In the same instant, Stacie stopped pushing, the needle on the monitor dropped back, and the doctor held him for Mike to cut the cord.

"Congratulations, Stacie and Mike, you have a son!" the doctor declared over the cries of the newborn.

The nurse measured, weighed, and cleaned up the infant, and finally handed him, wrapped in a soft blanket, to his mother."

While the baby's parents greeted and quieted him, I applauded myself in my mind. *No tears Jonica-way to go.*

I had done better than I'd expected as my friend's cramps turned to crushing pain. I even did fine when I saw the baby born amid a flow of blood and fluid. I didn't flinch as I watched Mike cut the cord. Seeing him in his mother's arms brought unexplainable joy.

"What's his name?" the nurse asked.

"Jonathan," his parents said in unison.

"After his Aunt Jonica," Stacie announced as she handed her son to his dad.

I looked at them both and did what I do so well. I cried.

"Do you want to hold him?" Mike asked.

"I do."

Handing me his son, I heard Stacie say, "Jonathan, meet your Aunt Jonica. She is going to teach you Bible verses and all about God. She will make you laugh and you will be surprised at the ways she makes friends. You are going to love her very much."

The afterbirth came and Stacie's clean up happened quickly. Dr. Steele said a quiet good-bye and complimented us all on a job well done.

Mike mentioned going to call their parents and I asked him to call Ben too.

"Please tell him it's time to come and get me."

"Here you go, sweet boy, back to your mommy so I can blow my nose.

Admiring Stacie as she held Jonathan, I muttered, "I'm tired and you did all the work."

"This wasn't as bad as the abortion," Stacie said her eyes focused on the little boy in her arms.

"The abortion hurt?"

"More than I expected physically. But my heart shattered. Physical pain is bearable after that."

Now tears rolled down both our faces as we gazed in awe at Jonathan.

"I don't deserve him after what I did. He should be yours."

"No. Stacie, your son comes to you as a special gift from God."

"Why don't you get to have kids? I can hardly stand it."

"I don't know why. I do know that whatever God wills is His very best for me. I choose to believe and trust."

"I'm so overwhelmed. Every molecule in my body loves this baby and misses the other one."

"God understands. He saw His Son born and crucified. He knows your joy and grief."

"Can you do me a favor before Mike gets back? In my bag is the Bible you gave me. Would you get it out and put it here under my covers? I'll read it later."

I noticed how worn the book looked as I slid it under the sheet.

Mike came back with Ben right behind him.

As I handed the newborn to my smiling husband, Mike said, "Jonathan, meet your Uncle Ben."

Ben's eyes met Mike's. "Stacie and I want to adopt you two as our family, making you his honorary aunt and uncle."

The nurse came back and Jonathan decided it was time for a drink.

I stood beside Stacie and we took a long look together as her son pressed his mouth to her nourishment.

"Wow," I whispered. He's beautiful."

"I love you, Jonica." Stacie said.

"I love you too."

Stacie

I figured the baby's arrival would fall on the day set by the professionals.

A week before my official due date, a backache and cramps bothered me for a few hours then eased off in the middle of the night. I woke up strangely refreshed and energetic. I called my parents, stopped by the office, dropped of a new baseball cap for Stevie, and talked to Hope. I ordered some flowers and had the florist deliver the T-shirt Mike had had made up for Jonica. Restless, I went over to see her.

As we visited, a pull and pressure across my abdomen made it feel good to stand up. I thought my body was stretching again to give my growing boy more room. Then the first big one hit and I noticed some moisture.

At the hospital, everyone did their thing as my body prepared to deliver the child. As the pain increased I heard Mike encouraging me to breathe, appreciated the ice chips Jonica slid into my mouth, and was grateful for the coolness of a cloth pressed gently on my forehead. As I breathed and willed myself to make it through each contraction, the sounds, sights, and feelings were all there, but the pain blurred them and I retreated into myself. I didn't deserve to cry out-I'd stilled my first baby's cries so I wouldn't allow myself the privilege. I was determined to bear the pain in silence.

I continued to think about my children. The one I aborted- my first but not born and the one struggling to get out of my body-my firstborn. One my sorrow - the other my joy. One my shame - the other my pride. Eventually, the pains were no longer separate spasms but one long crashing wave. *You earned this*, I chided myself internally.

Then, in a push he arrived. The doctor held the baby while Mike cut the cord. An enormous love washed over me. My vision cleared, my skin tingled with life, and tears of gladness ran unchecked and cool on my warm cheeks. My womb emptied and my heart filled.

I saw Mike's joy, Jonica's response to his name, and the baby's contentment in my arms. As suddenly as the happiness came, it went. My arms and heart, so full of a little boy named Jonathan, ached for another. Would nothing fill the void?

Looking into the sweet face of our son, I also wondered how the God Jonica believed in could give me a child after what I'd done. Then I watched her holding Jonathan and felt a searing loss for her. *If this God of hers is love, what is going on here? Why me and not her?*

As this inner battle raged, I knew it was time to review what I now called my Jesus Case. Jonica lived as though He was real, someone she knew and who knew her and loved her.

Later, I would read the chapters again.

Then I told Jonica I loved her. It was that kind of moment.

After she and Ben left, Jonathan nursed then slept in his Isolette. Ben made all the calls then fell asleep on the cot next to my bed. His gentle snores comforted me, as did Jonathan's little breaths. With the reading light on, I took the leather book from under my covers. Pulling on the ribbon marker, I read about Jesus again. I let the writer re-introduce me to the women who interacted with Him. He treated each one with respect and dignity. Where had I gotten the idea He hadn't? I read about being born again because of God's love.

My heart beat a wild unsteady rhythm when I got to where they crucified Him. His mother watched. I ached for her. Her son! My sweet boy sucked in his sleep. Hers gave her to another to be cared for before His anguished cry, "It is finished."

I turned back to chapter three and reread Jesus' words to Nicodemus: "For God so loved the world that he gave his one and only Son, that whoever believes in him shall not perish but have eternal life. For God did not send his Son into the world to condemn the world, but to save the world through him."

I understood the man of the law asking tough questions. I was impressed that he sought out the source of the local trouble. I knew Nicodemus didn't show up in the story again until it was time to bury the Rabbi he'd cross-examined.

I also couldn't get the experience of the lawyer Paul out of my mind. From persecutor to preacher. Maybe the leap wasn't as far as I'd once imagined.

I again considered Jonica's challenge. As His lawyer, how would I have pleaded his case before Pontius Pilate and Herod? I found them both unethical politicians listening to the fervor of the crowd not the wisdom of the law. Their weakness resulted in the death penalty for Jesus.

I knew beyond a reasonable doubt Jesus was innocent of all the charges. No matter how I looked at it, the trial was a travesty of justice.

Turning back to the cross, I read about the disciple Jesus loved; the one who had earlier rested his head on Jesus. I wondered what it felt like to have God love you in person like that. And then the truth crashed into my mind. I not only believed what the Bible said about Jesus- I believed in Him.

"God, I put Your Word to the test. I came to You like Nicodemus-having full confidence in the law. Somehow I believe You love me in every way there is and some I don't know about yet."

Tears flowed as I hugged the book to my chest.

"I want to be born again, God-the way Jesus instructed Nicodemus. I don't know all the right words, but do know I've sinned. I don't understand, but it's true-You can and do love a woman who chose abortion. I need and want your forgiveness. Oh God, I believe in You. You sent Your Son to die for me, long before I was born. Thank You. Help me know You. Help me live for You the way Jonica does. Help me represent you to my husband and son."

When I opened my eyes, the soft light in the room seemed to shine not brighter but clearer. My husband's snores were like sweet music. My tiny son's face was more beautiful. The baby lotion smelled rich and fragrant.

The gapping hole that had plagued me for so long had been filled.

A love even bigger than the one I'd felt overtake me at Jonathan's birth swept into my heart.

I love You, Jesus.

CHAPTER 23

Jonica

The next morning I walked into Stacie's room and found her holding Jonathan and whispering secrets to him.

"Motherhood agrees with you," I commented. She was radiant.

"Hi, Jonica. I need to move. Can you hold the him for a minute?"

"Sure."

I snuggled the sleeping baby into me and kissed his downy head.

"Welcome to the world, sleepy one," I said.

Each time a baby came into my life I wondered how I could possibly love so much, or if there'd be room in my heart for the next one.

Then sure enough-it happened again. I fell in love with someone else's child.

I sat and rocked while Stacie paced. "So, what's up?" I asked.

"Do you see it?" She asked standing in front of me.

"You look great." My answer didn't satisfy my persistent friend.

"But do I look different? Changed?"

"Your skin and eyes are glowing. You are more beautiful than I've ever seen you and your tummy is a lot smaller." Still not the right answer. I'd never been given a pop quiz like this one and I was failing big time.

"I feel changed. Different. Recharged. Energized. Can you see it?" she insisted.

"Is this a natural part of giving birth? Like the opposite of the baby blues-maybe the baby highs?"

"No. This is bigger. I made a new Friend last night."

"Someone came to visit you?"

"I invited Someone to come in . . ."

I watched her in silence. I wanted to ask but the words would not come.

"I considered the Jesus Case from every angle. I gave the leaders from all sides the benefit of the doubt. He was convicted and sentenced without a fair trial. Politics, fear and jealousy ruled over law and evidence. Over time, I've come to believe with all my heart and soul in His innocence. Even more important, I believed in Him. I had a Nicodemus kind of encounter. I told God I wanted to be born again. I'm forgiven, Joni, and I'm sure it shows. Please look again."

Her words washed over me like a warm summer rain. I got up from the rocker with care, put Jonathan in his crib, and turned to my friend. We joined hands and I looked deep into her eyes. Sparkles danced where shadows once lingered.

"There. I see it."

"You do? What does it look like?"

"Like a woman in love with her Lord."

We celebrated with a long hug, a few tears of joy, our first prayer together, and ice water in plastic cups.

Stephen Dunbar brought Stevie to visit and Stacie introduced us. The big boy had eyes only for the little one sleeping in the blue blanket. I watched him settle into the rocker, arms out stretched, as Stacie handed him Jonathan.

"Can I kiss him, Stacie? I'll be careful. I'm going to be a really good Uncle. I love him a lot."

As I left them to this private moment, the door whispered shut behind me.

Back home, the phone rang.

Eve's voice asked, "Jonica, does your church have a prayer chain?"

"We do."

"My mother was the head of the one at our church for years. I hoped they still did this kind of thing today. Can you ask them to pray for me?"

"Eve, I have to confess something. You've been in their prayers for weeks now. I only gave your first name, but when you announced your cancer, some of them realized they were praying for you. I hope you aren't offended."

"I'm not. Do they take updates?"

"Yes. What's up?"

"I finished the treatments and although the doctors are expecting a good result, I'm exhausted and I'm pretty sure that can't be a good sign."

"You sound scared."

"I am. The waiting to know if I'm in remission is terrible. I want to live."

"I'll get the calls started right away."

"I'm leaving to see Stacie and Jonathan now. Stephen is taking me to see our son later."

"He's beautiful Eve. You're going to fall in love."

"With which one?"

"Both. And they are going to love you back."

"How can you be so sure?"

"You're worth their love."

"I'd never go that far." With that she hung up.

I clicked the phone off and then back on. I notified the prayer leader and then got on my knees.

I stood up amazed. A daughter had met God and mother moved toward Him. Could be another miracle in the making.

Stacie

After everyone left, I nursed Jonathan and settled into bed for a nap. When I woke up I thought I was dreaming. In the corner Eve sat in the rocker, holding Jonathan, tears staining the front of her silk blouse. I rubbed my sleepy eyes and she was still there.

"Eve?"

"Hi," she whispered.

"Isn't your grandson beautiful?"

"He is. I like his name. It's strong. I seem to remember a story about a man named Jonathan. A good friend of a king."

"I'm glad you like it." Her memory of a Bible story shook me, but her saying it out loud shocked me. I was surprised she knew anything about the Word. I didn't know where she'd learned it and I didn't know her well enough to probe.

I swung my feet over the side of the bed and slid into my slippers. "I'm thirsty and need something besides water to drink. Would you like anything?"

"I can get it."

"No. You and Jonathan need time to get acquainted. I'll be right back. Besides moving only hurts for a moment, then it feels better."

I walked down the hall with a tray holding two glasses of ice and two cans of 7Up. I chatted with a couple nurses, looked in on the babies in the nursery, and finally made it back to my room.

"You look so natural holding him."

"It feels good but I haven't held a boy-baby in a very long time. Not since I handed your brother to your dad all those years ago."

"That's sad Eve."

"Oh Stacie, you have no idea how absolutely wretched it is."

Pouring the bubbling liquid over the ice, I glanced at my mother waiting for her to say more. When she didn't I asked, "How are you feeling?"

"I see the doctor later today. We'll know more then." For the first time she smiled.

"I think Jonathan looks like Mike." I didn't miss her kind reference about my husband but made no comment. Our sarcastic banter and competition seemed a thing of the past - at least for today. In its place we spoke with quiet respect.

"What do you want him to call you?"

"Grandma sounds good. Why?"

"Since you want me to call you Eve, I just wondered."

"Does it bother you to call me by my name?"

"To be honest, yes. I just wanted you to be my mom."

"Is it too late?"

"No, it's not."

Her words embraced me, and I decided to try it out right away.

"Mom, I need to tell you some things." The old flinch in her shoulders was gone and I caught a glimpse of a twinkle in her eye.

"Let me put this little guy back in his bed and we'll talk."

As I walked back to the chair, I noticed that her slacks hung funny. She hadn't just lost weight; she was gaunt. Fear shimmied up my spine.

Sitting back in the rocker, she took a sip of her cold drink and said, "I'm ready."

"Stevie came up to meet Jonathan earlier."

"I know. Your dad called me when they left."

"Are you going to see him?" It came out sounding pushy when all I wanted was to see my family reunited. Before I could apologize Eve smiled. Amazed, I just sat there.

"Your dad is taking me today."

"Does Stevie know?"

"He does. I understand he has a celebration planned for me." She sighed. "I don't know how to do this, Stacie. For years I met with the president, other senators, faced opponents and handled the press. Total strangers called , wrote, and scheduled meetings. None of it intimidated me. Yet seeing my own son scares me.

"My palms sweat and my stomach flutters just thinking about him. Today I will come face to face with the child I abandoned. The last time I saw him he was a baby, and now I'm told he's almost as tall as I am. Your dad says the boy loves me and somehow understands that I couldn't see him yet because he is different. No one told him that, he just figured it out. His compassion for me is staggering."

"In his innocence and faith he can't imagine not loving you."

"I shunned him and made your father take him away. How can he love me?"

As she got up and paced, I saw her feet slip inside her pumps. Even her shoes were too big for her. My stomach clenched.

"We've never talked like this before, Eve. Why?" Okay, the mom-thing was going to take some time.

She sat back down, exhausted. "Probably because I never let my defenses down with anyone after Stevie's birth. It was too much. My son was defective, and imperfect. Everything I did before he was born was without flaw. Everything after, I made my battleground. I didn't let you in. Or anyone except your father, and I held him at arm's length. I stopped holding you altogether. I believed if I kept you a safe distance from me it would hurt us both less. I was wrong."

"So, what's different now?"

"Cancer changes everything. So does being a grandma."

"It's not too late. We still have time. Right?" A fear bigger than any

I'd ever faced rise up in me. Her frail body, her shaking hands, and the dark circles under her eyes indicated her serious illness. *Oh God, I just got my mother back-please don't take her from me. I want her to live.*

Before I could tell her about my newfound faith, someone brought my lunch, the nurse came to check on Jonathan, and Mike walked in.

In spite of the sudden interruption, Eve and I looked deep into each other's eyes for the first time as mothers. Nothing between us would ever be the same.

She took my hand and smiled-not for a camera-for me and me alone.

"We can use whatever time we have to tear down the walls. It should be quite a journey," she said. It felt like a promise.

I began to believe in miracles.

CHAPTER 24

Jonica

A week after Jonathan's birth, the publisher released my new children's book. I did a read-a-loud signing at our local bookstore. The store manager set up a cozy corner for us, including a rocking chair for me, and pillows on the floor for the kids. There were cookies and milk for everyone. She and another employee watched the kids, meeting little needs as they arose.

Looking into the faces, I rejoiced. They not only liked the story, they asked questions about God and His Word. Natalie stood nearby with Ben as Jeremy and Kevin listened, inching closer to my lap by the minute.

In Natalie's womb we now knew God was knitting together a little girl. Amanda. I loved her already. Contentment washed over me like a warm rain.

One little girl in the group resented the boys' crowding forward. "What are you doing?" she asked, standing, hands on her little hips.

"I want to sit on my Aunt Jonica's lap. She always holds us when she reads us stories," Jeremy declared.

"You know her?" she asked, taken aback.

"Yep. She's my family."

The loudspeaker announced the end of story time. Ben kissed me good-by before returning to the office. Moms gathered up their children and lined up to have their books signed. One woman asked if the boys who looked like my husband were my sons. When I told her no, that I couldn't have children, she asked, "So what gives you the experience to write for them?"

"I was one."

She smiled, and the tense moment passed.

Several women told me their children had asked questions after having my books read to them. Sometimes their discussions led to their sons and daughters inviting Jesus to come into their hearts. I silently thanked God for using me in their lives. I hugged lots of kids and their moms.

Eve came and bought a signed copy for Jonathan. She walked around for awhile as if shopping. She spoke with the manager, but I lost track of her as I visited with other customers.

As the little girl got ready to leave the store, she turned to Jeremy and said, "You're lucky."

"Yep, pretty lucky," he answered.

I mattered to these kids. A warm, fuzzy, feel-good emotion rose in my spirit at the same time humility hit home. They trusted and believed what I wrote about Jesus. Their parents used the stories God placed in my heart and mind to lead little their ones to Himself. The responsibility of representing God and His Word was a privilege I accepted enthusiastically and earnestly.

Father, I thank You for it all. Even the infertility. I don't understand, but I accept Your ways. Help me to always tell the children the Truth, the whole Truth, and nothing but the Truth.

I looked at the two little boys waiting to take me to lunch. Because I liked Chinese and we were celebrating my book, we'd go to Wong's. Then we wanted to feed the geese. Later the boys were coming to our house to spend the night.

I looked into Natalie's eyes. The ugliness and misunderstanding were long gone, lovingly replaced with acceptance. We acknowledged God had done the work in both of us. For the first time we were sisters in Him and in our hearts.

Through the door stepped my friend Stacie.

"Sorry I'm late. Jonathan had a fussy morning."

After I introduced my friend and my sister-in-law, Natalie asked if she could hold Jonathan. While the store manager and I compared notes, they compared baby stories.

Natalie introduced Jonathan to her boys and explained this was the one who would be visiting them at their house sometimes.

Stacie bent down to meet them face to face and shook their hands.

Kevin didn't let go. Jeremy asked if she liked Chinese, and Natalie invited her to join us.

"It looks like I'm having lunch with my three boys then," I said, grinning at a few of my favorite people. "This is my kind of party!"

I could hardly wait to get home and thank God for all the good He was doing in my life.

Stacie

The week following Jonathan's birth amazed me. The fall election went to the other party, but Eve didn't seem disappointed. "The people spoke and I trust them," was her only comment.

She called every day to talk to her grandson. "I want him to recognize my voice," she said.

When I told her what a good baby he was she responded, "So were you."

I hung on to those precious words. My body adjusted faster than I expected. Mike and I walked the mall in the evenings pushing Jonathan in the fancy stroller Dad and Mom had dropped off, dreaming of spring and jogging again.

On Saturday Jonathan woke up fussy. I realized that my rush to get to Jonica's book signing wasn't helping. He preferred a slow morning feeding, a bath, and a nap in his own bed. He reminded me of Mike. His morning routine set the tone for his day.

"Like father, like son," I said to my sleepy boy.

I was more than a little amazed when I drove into the bookstore parking lot and saw my mother walking toward her car.

"Oh Jonathan, Grandma just bought you a new book," she gushed.

My mother gushing? *Will wonders never cease,* I thought. *Oh, I hope not.*

When she opened the bag to get the book out, I saw a Bible box. Hope danced across my spirit.

"I didn't expect you back from Washington until this evening. Did you get all your stuff packed up?"

"The boxes and furniture are in storage for now. I flew home late last night. I wanted to be with your dad. Then I read about the book signing in one of last week's papers and decided to come. I've never been in one of these stores. It's very interesting. Full of pretty things," she rambled.

She noticed me starring and turned rosy. The woman who took any podium to talk about sexual freedom, birth control, and repro-ductive rights blushed about being in a Christian bookstore and liking it.

"Mom, you look good. Are you feeling better?"

"I am. Letting go of all the stress is a huge relief. And knowing I'm in remission at least for now helps. I don't know what I'm going to do with my time, but I hope to fill some of it with my family."

"Good. We're starting with supper tonight, right?"

"We invited the Daniels too. Madeline is a photographer and we're going to have our first official family portrait taken." Her eyes filled with tears. She touched her wig.

"It looks like your real hair, Mom. Don't worry. I like the salt and pepper look on you."

"I am a grandmother now," she said with a smile.

"You are."

"It's not the wig so much as the cancer. It could come back at any second. And then there's Stevie. You know he hung a bare frame on his wall waiting for this picture. I just can't get over his patience of his confidence. Well, I'd better let you go celebrate your friend's accomplishment and I need to get going myself."

I couldn't hold the words back. "I love you, Mom."

"I love you too."

Two pairs of emerald eyes looked at each other in wonder. She patted my cheek. "See you later."

Inside the store, my friend glowed. I'd prayed this day might give her a sense of worth and help her see the value in her work. She had expressed her concern that kids might find the book boring, that maybe it was a good story idea but she hadn't written it as well as it could be.

While she wound up her signing, I got to know Natalie and her boys. Jeremy bent down to say hi to Jonathan, and Kevin quietly touched the baby's cheek.

"He's soft," he said, and smiled. I knew I wanted my son to grow up knowing these kids. I wondered about the little girl Natalie carried in her womb. Would she play an important role in Jonathan's life? *Good grief. I'm a matchmaking mother.*

Jonica's crew invited me to lunch and I accepted.

At supper I enjoyed the feeling of family as we gathered around the table. We ate pot roast with all the trimmings. My dad asked Chandler to give thanks for the meal. Stevie concluded it with a hearty, "Amen!"

We ate the platters clean then Mom carried a homemade apple pie into the dining room. "I haven't made one of these since Stacie was a baby. I hope it tastes good."

Eve in the kitchen? Sometimes I still fumbled with the name thing. All the changes in our lives were staggering.

"Stevie, you told me this is your favorite, so I made it for you."

"Thanks Mom!" he grinned and rubbed his hands together as he waited to get them around his spoon and into the pie.

Madeline took several photos during the evening. We posed for the official family portrait but my favorite turned out to be the one of Stevie and Mom in profile. They were face to face, noses almost touching, connected in a long look as if memorizing each other.

Mom and I sat on the couch later while our husbands took my brother home.

"I wish I was strong enough for Stevie to move in here. But I guess it's more than a health issue. I'm old. He needs his younger 'parents' to care for him in ways I just can't. I regret my choices." Tears filled her eyes.

"Mom . . ."

"Please let me finish. I know I accomplished some good things. But Stacie, all the memories I sacrificed. I can't have them back. I also kept him from myself and from you. I'm so sorry!"

"I forgive you."

"I don't know how you can. I robbed you of your little brother."

I chose to hold her hand in silence. I had no words.

"Tonight was the most wonderful night I've experienced since I turned my back on my son and made your dad take him away." She took a few deep breaths then cried out, "Oh, God, how harsh will You judge me?"

I gently lifted her chin. "Mom?"

Looking into her eyes was like seeing my own reflection a few months earlier, when I first grieved for my aborted baby. "God is fearfully just and wonderfully fair. He is the inventor of love and forgiveness."

"You found Him?"

"I think it's more like He found me."

"Your grandparents' prayers have finally been answered."

Before I could share more, Mike and Dad returned, and it was time to go home. I hugged my mother and whispered, "When you decide to start reading the Bible I saw in your bag, begin with the New Testament. Pretend you're teaching a group of would-be politicians about the legal ethics of Pontias Pilate and Herod."

Hey, it worked for me.

In the car, Mike asked, "Do you want to go to church tomorrow with Ben and Jonica?"

Yes was all I said. I didn't want him turned off by the mixture of fear and giddy excitement zigzagging in my stomach.

It was almost too much good stuff for one day.

CHAPTER 25

Jonica

The doorbell rang and there stood Stacie, holding Jonathan, a bouquet of roses, and a diaper bag.

"Happy Anniversary, Jonica."

"Anniversary?" I asked, taking the bouquet she held toward me.

"Yep. One year ago today, I stood outside this same door for the first time."

"Oh my."

I put the roses in water while she unwrapped the baby. Together we watched as he yawned, stretched, then rubbed his eye with a tiny fist. Each movement held our undivided attention as if he'd accomplished something worthy of a CNN broadcast.

"Just rest, sleepy boy," his mother said rocking the car seat.

"He looks a little scrunched in there. Doesn't he sleep better in a bed?"

"This will work."

"So will the crib upstairs."

"Joni, are you sure?"

"Come on up."

I'd aired out and dusted the little room, looking forward to visits with the children who would fill it with life, and sleep there. Stacie handed me her son, and I put him in the crib, covering him with a soft cotton blanket, and turned on the music box. He stretched, yawned again, and opened his eyes for a second. Then they fluttered shut. I switched on the baby intercom, and we took one more peek before going downstairs.

While fresh coffee brewed, Stacie hunted for her favorite mug in the cupboard. As she stood on her tiptoes, I noticed her bare feet.

"Need another pair of socks?" I couldn't hold back a smirk.

"No. The ones you gave me last year are in the diaper bag. At least I came prepared."

"I'm so glad you're here, Stacie."

"Me too."

We hugged as the pot gurgled to a finish.

"So, how are you?" Stacie asked.

"Good most days. Every now and then a comment catches me off guard. I realize some people are simply ignorant; others are uncomfortable, but still want to be kind. A few are just mean. People always ask if we have a family, meaning children."

"How do you respond to that?"

"I don't want to offend anyone or say anything to make them feel sorry for us, but it's a challenge. I say, 'Yes, and here he is-my husband, Ben.'"

"Does it stop there?"

"Not always. Sometimes thinking I didn't understand, they ask how many children we have."

"And you say?"

"None. We enjoy our three lively nephews, and we're looking forward to a new niece in a few months."

Stacie smiled and took a sip of coffee.

"How's Mike?"

She told me how he enjoyed being back in church, although the upbeat music was different from what he remembered. "He is amazed at the number of people he knows though. He had no idea until our first Sunday that you went to the same church as his parents, the Daniels, and Stevie. Mike's parents sure are enjoying getting to know yours. I guess God had a purpose for us all being together in one place that week."

We settled into a comfortable silence, remembering the reunion in the narthex on what we now called Homecoming Sunday. Stacie had shared her conversion with her in-laws and Chandler Daniels. Stevie hugged his sister and headed to his class singing "Jesus Loves Me," shouting the "This I know" part. Della greeted Stacie at the nursery door and sweetly appreciated Jonathan's beauty.

Stacie said, "What a nice Grandma."

I thought, *what a difference a year makes.*

"How is your mom?"

"Oh, Jonica, I'm so scared. Even with her cancer in remission it's like there's a time bomb inside her that could explode at any moment. And then there are the risks I face."

So many things to pray for.

Stacie

I rang Jonica's doorbell, caught up in the memory of the first time I'd stood there. I looked back at my car parked neatly at the curb. The anger was long gone and I anticipated a sweet visit with my friend.

When she offered to let Jonathan rest in the crib upstairs, I didn't want to put her through that. She covered it well, but I knew there were still comments and criticisms. I hadn't faced that yet, but knew I might.

Our pastor had asked me to give my testimony before my upcoming baptism. I warned him it could cause a stir because it involved an abortion. He agreed I'd probably endure misunderstanding, but encouraged me to share the full extent of God's amazing grace. I knew that people on both sides of the issue prefer to see only the political aspects. Everyone, except a rare few like Jonica, seemed to forget that in every abortion there are two-sometimes three victims: the baby who dies, the woman who survives, and often the man who longs to be a daddy and grieves the lost child deeply.

A few days before, Mike and I had visited the cemetery. We'd purchased a small stone and plot. The stone reads, *Baby Cutter, we will come to you. 2 Samuel 12:23. Love, Mom and Dad.*

With some of the inheritance from my grandparents, we bought a small section of the cemetery for people like us. Parents who wanted to honor the memory of the little ones they'd aborted. They put the stone into the ground, on the anniversary of the abortion. As much as it hurt, it was also part of the healing.

Jonica and I giggled over my bare feet and the socks stuffed in the diaper bag. I'd never returned them because I kept needing them.

They were my only "borrowed" pair and my favorites.

A comfortable quiet enveloped us. It's so nice to be with a person who is at ease in a still moment. We were both remembering when Mike and I first went to church. God gave us a bunch of blessings that morning. First of all, Jonathan woke up earlier, making his morning routine easy because there was time to get ready. Then, when we pulled up in front of the church, Mike said, "Are you sure this is the right place?"

"Yes. Why?"

"This is where my mom and dad go."

That's when I saw Stevie and the Daniels going in.

"Hurry, Mike. There's my brother."

Stevie's voice reverberated off the hallway walls as he sang his joy to Jesus.

When I shared my newfound faith with Mike's parents they hugged me.

His mom told me, "Stacie, I'm sorry I wasn't kinder to you when you married Mike. You've always been the right woman for our son. You are the answers to this mother's prayers."

"I love him," I whispered.

"It shows."

Then Jonica's parents, Rose and Carl, stopped for a hug. They didn't say much, but their eyes spoke volumes. We sat between Mike's parents and Jonica. Ben joined us when he finished ushering. The music lifted my spirit even higher, and the honest response of the congregation, prepared me for the message. During the closing prayer, I heard my husband sniff. I peeked and saw his lips moving in prayer. I knew we'd both come home in our hearts.

Jonica's next question jolted me out of reminiscing. She only asked about my mom and couldn't know she'd entered my newest battle-ground.

"I'm so scared."

She set down her coffee cup and leaned forward. I told her about my fears.

How this insidious disease had attacked my grandmother and now my mother.

"Mom e-mailed me this." I reached into the diaper bag and handed her the information. It was a study proving the increased risk of breast cancer in women who'd chosen abortions.

"I have two strikes against me."

My friend's eyes filled with concern. Instead of offering empty words of comfort, she knelt down on the floor in front of me and took my hands.

And she prayed.

CHAPTER 26

Jonica

Della called and invited me over to meet her grandchildren. Since I was involved a little with the teens at church, she hoped we'd connect and the three younger ones would come to the teen group at church.

I'm not what kids today consider 'cool', Della."

"They don't need cool. They need a mentor, and Alisha needs a friend. Don shared his faith with each of them in the letters we found. These kids need a Christian connection besides me."

"I'd love to meet them. What if I come over early and we pray together for them?"

Della sat in her rocker and I settled on the footstool in front of her. We held hands and lifted Alisha, Eric, Evan, and Ashley to the Lord. As we said amen, a car pulled up, its bass booming out into the quiet neighborhood.

"They're here." Della hurried to the door as they tromped onto the porch.

"Hi, Gram," Alisha said, hugging her grandma close. Then she stood back and looked into Della's eyes.

"How are you?" she asked. Della patted her cheek.

"I'm fine, dear girl." The lovely blond stepped out of the way.

"Hey," seventeen year old Eric greeted her, bending to kiss her cheek. He was thin, but muscles rippled in his arms, and I knew one day he'd fill out his Jeff Gordon T-shirt. I noticed that his short fingernails had car grease under them. A boy after his dad's own heart. He ran a nervous hand through his short blond hair, leaving it standing on end.

Della gathered two fourteen year olds in one big embrace, and I heard their muffled hellos. Blond heads, green eyes, and freckled noses peeked over her shoulder at me.

I shook their hands as we were introduced. Della went to get a snack, and we all stood around looking at each other.

"Can I ask you a favor?"

Shoulders shrugged and somebody mumbled, "Sure."

I handed them each a CD. "I bought these and I need some people who know nothing about the artists to listen to them and give me their feedback. I'm writing an article about this kind of music and what kids think of it. Have you ever heard of any of these groups?"

Negative all around.

"Good. My phone number is on the back. You can call me with your thoughts. If I don't hear from you in a week or so I'll call you, if that's all right?"

Heads bobbed.

"Come and get it," Della called from the dining room.

We filed in, and instead of the cookies and milk we all expected, there were bowls of chips, dips, and M&M's, and ice cold cans of pop. "Fill up a plate and go watch the video I rented for you."

"What did you rent, Gram?" Ashley asked with raised eyebrows.

"*A Walk to Remember*. Have you seen it?"

Four puzzled faces looked at each other before Alisha said, "Yeah, it was great."

Evan said, "Gram, there might be what you'd consider some bad words and stuff in it."

"I know. I watched it last night."

"Huh?" Sixteen eyes grew wide.

"Go on now," she shooed them with her hands to the other room. We heard the TV come on and cans popping open.

She must have noticed my raised eyebrows too.

"The movie has good content. I'm sure most kids experiment with foul words. I hope they get the message in spite of the real life language and 'stuff'. I'm sure they've seen and heard worse."

"Della, you are the coolest."

"Of course," she replied and sat down with a sigh. "I just can't get used to drinking out of a can."

I got her a glass and ice.

Before I left, Alisha and I decided to meet for a late lunch on her next day off.

On my way home, I stopped in at my mom and dad's. A forest green Lexus sat out front. Stepping inside, I heard the familiar laugh of my friend and then my mother's voice saying, "More coffee, Eve?"

"Hello," I called out.

"Come in, Jonica. You're just in time. The coffee is fresh." Mom hugged me, and I greeted Stacie and Eve.

"I just got the new update from the shelter Jonica. Your article generated several record-breaking donations. Thank you."

"I'm glad. Maybe I can do a follow-up to let the public know their efforts matter."

"That's a great idea. Let me know how I can help," Eve said.

"We stopped by your house with this pie, but you weren't home so we brought it here." Stacie pointed to the center of the table where a French silk pie topped with pecans sat.

"Shoot," I said under my breath. The chips and now this. I'd need to power walk twice as far in the morning.

"We're celebrating."

"What?" I asked pulling out a chair.

"Prepare yourself Jonica, God has been up to some big stuff," my friend said.

Stacie

I answered the ringing phone.

"Stacie, can you come over to Stevie's?" Eve asked.

"Sure. Are you all right?"

"Can't a mother want to be with both her kids?"

Yeah but usually not mine. I wasn't used to Eve mothering me or needing me. I had no idea what to expect - just that she wanted me to come.

God, is it the cancer? I packed up Jonathan and we went. Outside Peggy's house sat Mom's Lexus and Dad's Catera. A chill ran up my spine, and I hurried toward the house.

"Can I take Jonathan while you visit with your family, Stacie?" Peggy offered.

"Sure. Are they all right?"

"Everyone looks and sounds fine. They're in the living room." She smiled and looked a little sly. At the very least, knowing.

I walked into the other room and found mother and Stevie holding hands and singing some chorus about God's love which was too weird to be believed.

"Hi?" I heard the question in my voice.

"Stacie," my brother hurried over to me. "Sit here."

I sat by my dad on the couch. He looked as confused as I felt. It was good to be on the same level as one other human being in this house.

Stevie looked at Mom and said, "Tell them." He wiggled and tried not to smile, pushing his glasses up his nose.

I compared my square-built brother to our tall and slender mother. So different and yet something similar shone out of their eyes.

"Today I came to visit Stevie and we talked. He told me about Jesus and quoted a familiar verse."

Stevie interrupted and said, "For God so loved the world, He gave His only Son and whosoever believes in Him will be saved. John 3:16. Mr. Daniels taught me it." He smiled, satisfied that he got the whole thing out, including the reference.

"His joy in Jesus was contagious and I caught it."

"She kneeled by my bed,"

"Kneeled?" Dad asked.

"Yes. Stevie thought that would be best. And then I asked Jesus into my heart."

"I made sure she was on the rug so she didn't get a sliver," my brother comforted our dad.

Stevie hugged Mom, then pointed at Dad and said, "You're next."

Dad looked stunned as he walked quietly into the other room. The three of us joined hands and Stevie said, "Let's pray."

His prayer was short and to the point. He said, "Thank You, Jesus. Amen."

We looked up and there Dad stood, holding his grandson.

"We weren't praying behind your back Stephen," Mom said.

"I know what you were doing," Dad replied, smiling. "Jonathan, I think we're outnumbered."

Peggy called us to coffee and when we entered the dining room I knew. "Mom. This dining room set is Grandma's, isn't it? And Stevie's bed upstairs came from their house too. That's why I feel so at home in these two rooms."

"Stevie's bed, dresser, and nightstand were once my own. And your Aunt Jen made his quilt."

"You knelt beside your own bed and asked Jesus into your heart?"

"The same bed my parents knelt beside every night and prayed for me."

"You're the benefactor-the one who paid for this house."

She just smiled and shrugged her shoulders.

"Eve?" Dad asked.

"Our son needed a home." Dad stood amazed. He handed the baby to me and silently took his wife in his arms.

"This is a God thing," I declared as my sweet brother planted a kiss on Jonathan's cheek.

"I'm beginning to believe it always was," my mother whispered.

CHAPTER 27

Jonica

It seemed impossible as I hung white baptismal gowns and put folded towels in the dressing rooms. Just outside the door to the women's room, I heard Stacie and Mike praying quietly. I stepped away from the door and washed my hands, the rushing water providing them with a little extra privacy.

My friend bounded through the door and declared, "This is the day the Lord has made! I will rejoice and be glad in it. That's the verse on my calendar today. It's perfect isn't it?"

Instead of the strength I wanted to feel, I burst into tears.

"Joni! You're not going to blubber today are you?"

I nodded.

"This is a day to celebrate."

"Yes. And I am," I replied, glad I hadn't bothered putting on mascara.

"You'll be out there front and center right?"

"Of course."

"Then everything will be fine."

Mike knocked on the door. "Hey you two, it's almost time for the service to begin. Jonathan is ready for his part in the dedication. Are you?"

Stacie opened the door and pulled me through with her. Our group filled up our normal pew-right in front of Della and Bernice. The pastor began with the announcements and prayer.

"As you can see from the service schedule, we are having a baby dedication and a baptism today. We normally do them at separate times but this is a special occasion. The parents who are dedicating themselves to raising their son in a Christian home are the ones being baptized. It is fitting we do them on the same day. We invite Mike and Stacie Cutter to come forward with their son Jonathan."

Stevie sat between Eve and me, leaning forward, his hands clasped together, smiling. As a congregation and his family members, we agreed to pray and live in such a way before Jonathan that he would see Christ in us.

We celebrated with praise songs and heard a sermon on living our lives with the faith of little children. God used the man-child beside me as a living testimony of this Scripture. His incredible faith and unwavering prayers led us to this day.

"Now we invite Mike and Stacie to identify themselves with our Lord Jesus Christ in believer's baptism," the pastor said as he stepped into the water tank.

Mike came first, declaring to the congregation his intent to lead his family in the ways of the Lord. He asked us to pray for wisdom as he sought to do this with all diligence and gentleness. Mike came out of the waters and the microphone picked up his voice as he prayed, "Lord, I am Your servant. May You always be well-pleased."

Mike helped Stacie down the steps into the water. My friend's face shone with peace. She stood before the congregation and shared her testimony.

"With a pre-planned agenda that only considered my dreams, I made an appointment with my doctor for a referral for an abortion. I met a woman in the waiting room who could not have children. I blatantly announced my intent, knowing deep inside me that it hurt her. Nothing mattered except my single-minded determination to succeed.

I didn't know that legally terminating the life of my unborn baby would hurl me into a pit of loss and devastation. God did. He put Jonica Johnson in the waiting room on that day for His purpose because He knew I'd need her. And Jonica did what she does best. She loved me when I was full of hate. She withheld judgment when I rained it down on her. She never preached, although I provoked her. I let her share Jesus with me to get it over with-but He was just getting started.

"When I got pregnant again, this time on purpose, she rejoiced, although I knew inside she wept for the child she'd never have. She wiped my brow in the delivery room when my son was born, and forgave me for what I thought was surely unforgivable. And then she loved me some more. She asked me to consider how I would have defended Jesus at His trial. After considering all the evidence, I knew He was innocent and I knew He was telling the truth. Belief took the place of unbelief."

Eve reached around Stevie and rubbed my shoulder with her fingers. Silent tears of joy ran down our faces. Two hankies floated from behind us and we accepted them.

My friend finished testifying and came out the water splashing drips all over as she raised her arms heavenward.

Thank You God for Your amazing grace!

Stacie

If anyone had told me I'd one day be in a church for any reason, other than a funeral, I'd have said that was impossible.

I watched Mike hold our son during the dedication and it hit me. This was big.

A celebration? Yes. But the depth of this commitment moved me. My bubbling confidence settled into quietness. I stood still before my God in front of a congregation I never in a million years thought I'd agree with. Yet here I was- living, breathing proof of God's love.

Mike walked into the baptismal tank calmly. He looked at his parents and nodded. His simple act spoke volumes to their faithful hearts. I remembered them accepting me as his choice with hesitance. They weren't sure I was the one God had for their son. Looking back, I can see why. They'd offered their mercy when we told them about the babe in heaven. Only God could take all our decisions and use them for His good.

As Mike came out of the water, his quiet prayer branded itself on my heart. Then he reached for my hand. I stepped into the warm water and Mike put my hand into our pastor's. It only took a moment as I looked into the eyes of my parents, my brother, Mike's parents, Jonica, and Ben. Dad held our son, who slept in peace snuggled in the arms of love.

Please, Lord, lead Daddy to Your peace one day.

I wanted the congregation to know how God had used a wounded woman to lead a lost one to Himself. And that He won me through her love.

I noticed some eyebrows go up at the mention of my abortion. A flesh-and-blood person put a face on the issue and made them uncomfortable. It was easier to handle if it stayed political. I saw two women look down, tears overflowing and wondered if they were like me- abortion survivors. *Use me in this church and anywhere there are women suffering this way, Lord.*

As I came out of the water, the organ began playing and congregation stood and sang the most wonderful song I'd ever heard. I'll never forget the words.

Amazing grace how sweet the sound, that saved a wretch like me . . .

CHAPTER 28

Jonica

I headed out for a late afternoon walk.

As I fidgeted on the curb waiting for the light to turn green, a small cloud passed over. It was so small that within a moment, I stood in the sunshine again. I watched the little sky puff move to the center of the park where it released its wet load then closed back up as a gentle wind moved it on.

I pondered the verse where the writer says that God releases the wind from His storehouses. When I looked up to thank Him for sending the breeze that rustled the leaves, I saw the evidence of God's promise. A rainbow shimmered in the heavens for a second then disappeared from my view.

I crossed the street praising God, knowing He always keeps His word-even when I can't see the radiant bands of color for the storm, or when I'm too caught up in life to notice.

As I walked into the center of the park I saw a mid-sized puddle shimmering in the sunlight. Not even thinking to restrain myself in a public place, I sprinted toward it and jumped into the center. A loud laugh rushed past my vocal cords and I watched as the ripples from my rain dance lapped up over my shoes.

I stood in a holy place surrounded by trees and birdsong, in the middle of the only puddle left by the little cloud.

Alone, or so I thought, I prayed out loud for His constant goodness to me. And I thanked Him for the sweet song of victory He placed in my soul.

Then I heard someone say my name.

Stacie

Mike came home early that afternoon. I was full of pent-up energy and he suggested I take a short run while he played with Jonathan.

I was in the center of the park when a small gray cloud rolled in overhead, then burst all over me. I stopped in amazement. All around me the sun shone except for where I stood. The drops were warm and comforting as if they came to me-as if just for me-from the Father Himself. And in the time it took to think it, I knew they did.

I stood dazzled by the shimmer of the raindrops. I raised my face into the crystal liquid, lifted my arms, and opened my hands as if to catch yet more of the clean water sent from heaven.

I said, "Thank You, Father, for Your forgiveness. It is fully mine." As I took ownership of what He'd already given me, I twirled in His presence, and danced in His rain.

As the words left my mouth, the rain stopped. I opened my eyes and caught a glimpse of a fleeting rainbow. God's promise to Noah extended to me.

I looked down at the pavement around me. Everything was dry except the circle around me where the water now swirled over the tops of my shoes. I stepped out of the puddle and walked to a bench under a giant old oak tree. It looked like the perfect place to contemplate the joy of my salvation and the vastness of God's forgiveness.

As the blessing of the moment started to sink in someone came around the corner and stood on the other side of my puddle. I watched as Jonica jumped into the center sending sprinkles dancing through the air and onto the dry pavement.

I walked toward my friend and whispered her name. Together we stood in the circle of fresh water sent by God...for us.

EPILOGUE

Release from the Associated Press/Sonya Bard, Freelance Journalist:

Former Senator Eve Dunbar shocked her party and former constituents today by not only attending but participating in a pro-life conference titled Truth and Consequences. She teamed up with her daughter, Stacie Cutter, a self-proclaimed "abortion survivor." The two other speakers were Rose Patterson and her daughter, Jonica Johnson. The mother/daughter teams want women to fully understand the impact that choosing an abortion can have on women and the people who love them.

Cutter chose abortion a little over two years ago and, according to her, ended one life and almost ruined her own. She stated, "God literally pulled me out of the lies and drew me to the truth- His Son Jesus Christ. It was in Him I found hope and healing. "

She also brought another topic to the session. She urged post-abortive women feeling despair to get help. "P.A.S.S. is real and can be diagnosed by its symptoms. Many distinguished doctors are no longer denying its existence."

Rose Patterson is a crisis pregnancy center volunteer who works with women who come looking for support after they've had abortions. She worked anonymously until recently when her daughter, Johnson, became involved with Cutter. Now she is calling on pro-life women to make it safe for post-abortive women to step forward without shame and tell their stories.

When asked if she knew of her mother's work, Johnson replied, "I knew Mom volunteered at Oasis but I didn't know she worked directly with post-abortive women. She wanted to keep the work secret so no one would ask her about the women whose stories were so deeply private. As Stacie confided her pain to my mother and me, Mom asked the women she counseled what they wanted her to do with what she knew.

They told her, 'Tell them.'"

Due to her daughter's experience and the other women who've expressed their regret with her, retired Senator Dunbar has changed her once staunch pro-choice position. She also wants women to understand the connection between abortion and breast cancer. She announced that she is in remission after having a radical mastectomy, radiation, and chemotherapy. Her mother was suffering from this form of cancer when she died in a car accident.

"My greatest concern is for my daughter," said Dunbar. "Stacie has two strikes against her. We are genetically predisposed to breast cancer, and she chose an abortion without full knowledge of what it might cost her later. Women must know the facts and understand the risks."

Dunbar apologized to her daughter and to all the women in the audience who have chosen abortion and are, as she put it, "suffering the consequences." She told the silent audience of approximately one thousand women, "If any of you have chosen abortion because it was legal and easy, I am partly responsible for the deaths of your children. I am sorry."

Behind the former senator, they'd put up a picture of a young man with Down syndrome. Dunbar said, "Ladies, I'd like to introduce you to my son Stephen. Twenty-three years ago, I gave birth to him and turned away from what I saw as his imperfections. I considered him a mistake. I was wrong. Because of his diligent and faithful prayers, I am at peace with God."

Johnson closed the conference with a challenge to pro-lie women everywhere. She said, "It is right to stand strong against abortion as a political issue and vital that we stand for the women who are suffering its destructive consequences. I can't change a mind, but if I dare to love another woman even when I disagree with the choice she made, God can change a heart."

This is an editorial and so far, I've kept myself to reporting only what I heard and saw. I'm still one who believes in a woman's right to choose. But I admit, these women-a housewife, a former senator, an attorney, and a writer-seem to share an uncommon bond. And they may well be a power to be reckoned with.

AUTHOR'S NOTE

Dear Reader,

Although Rain Dance is fiction, it is also based on my life. I'm childless. The name Jonica mattered to me-it was the name I longed to give our little girl. (I wanted to name her after her daddy-my husband Jonathan-known to most people as Jon.) God had other plans for us and the name.

While I was cleaning house one day the idea for this book came to me. My first response was less than positive. I wanted to write children's books-not put my very personal pain on the paper for everyone to read. Even though I resisted, the story came together in my mind.

When I began putting the story on the paper, I took what I considered the biggest risk of all; I put myself in the story. I thought writing Jonica's part would be a breeze-I'd lived it, so what could be so hard? Letting you see my hurt, anger, pity parties, and grief was rough. As the writing continued, I admitted to myself that one of my greatest fears was that if you don't like Jonica, you won't like me. Then God gently reminded me: although He let me live this and write about it-it is not about you liking or agreeing with me. It has always been about telling His story.

I wondered if I'd be able to write about Stacie, whose life I had not lived and whose decision I couldn't understand. By the time I wrote the fourth chapter I was deeply in love with Stacie and reliving my hurt through Jonica.

I started praying right away that anyone who read this book would fall in love with Stacie. When I asked writer friends to read the manuscript before it went to print, I was delighted when they told me how much they cared for her and that she quickly became their favorite character. Readers now tell me the same thing. I can't tell you how that pleases me.

If you are a Jonica, please know your sorrow is real. You are grieving the death of a dream and it hurts. You are not being punished; you are being trusted. God loves you. Please read John 9 and let Him show you how to bring Him honor and glory through this trial. I want you to know I'm praying for you.

If you are a Stacie, God loves you . Taking a public stand is not expected or required but it should be safe for you. If you feel led to share this experience with the world you live in, you can literally give the pro-life movement in our nation a face. You will probably encounter misunderstanding and perhaps harsh judgment from some, but nothing can replace the firsthand account of your abortion experience. Heaven only knows how many babies you can save or how much suffering you can prevent other women from carrying by telling your story. Also please know some of us out here love you, are praying for you, and will stand beside you.

If you are neither of these women, please consider praying for women like Jonica and Stacie. Ask God to give you a heart of love and acceptance for people different from yourself. We are hurting and often suffer alone. You don't need to understand us-we want you to know that we long for your acceptance just as we are.

To all pro-life women, I'm praying that you will help bring new breath to the pro-life movement. Usually, in churches across this great land, it is safe for people to admit to struggles with alcohol, drug addiction, adultery, or divorce - all painful things. But the post-abortive woman cannot admit the pain of her choice. The risk of human condemnation is too hard. It is up to you and me to make it safe for them in our lives and in our congregations. How would Jesus treat these women who are among the walking wounded in our society?

Will they find sanctuary in our sanctuaries?

Please don't think post-abortive women don't sit in the pews of your church. According to the Alan Guttmacher Institute statistics (www.agi-usa.org), one in six women who have chosen abortion are evangelical Christians. Based on these statistics, 5.6 million women in our churches have chosen abortion as a way out of a crisis pregnancy. If 1.5 million women choose abortion this year that means it is possible 250,000 evangelical Christian women may be among them.

I know dozens of post-abortive women. How many do you know without realizing it?

Please ask yourself this: If I knew that one of my close friends had had an abortion in her past, would I still love her? The post-abortive women in my life all had to consider my response to that question carefully. Because of God, I truly love them with a passion that surprises me and them. It doesn't have to make sense. It is from God and that is enough for us.

The women I know who chose abortion are serving life sentences for their decisions. Some have experienced the healing forgiveness of Christ but they cannot forget what they did. My heart breaks for the ones who believe they cannot be forgiven by God.

For those of you who have come to Christ and still hold on to the guilt, please ask God to help you take ownership of His forgiveness. Let Him rebuild your soul the way He promises to rebuild Jerusalem (Ezek. 36:25-37). And, as in Stacie's rain dance, ask Him to send you a moment of spiritual "fresh water" and let any and all sin you hold on to be washed away. You are forgiven!

Think your sin is too big for God to forgive? Read His words in 1 John 1:9: "If we confess our sins, He is faithful and just to forgive us our sins and to cleanse us from all unrighteousness." Notice, there are no exclusions.

If you are seeking God, please consider these verses found in Romans 3:23, "For all have sinned and fall short of the glory of God."

The tiny word all includes me. What about you?

And later He says in Romans 6:23 "For the wages of sin is death, but the gift of God is eternal life in Christ Jesus our Lord."

He doesn't say, "Except for people who have committed specific sins." Have you received this most precious gift of God?

Are you asking, "What has God ever given to me?" Stacie found the answer when she read John 3:16. Remember Jesus' answer to Nicodemus?

Do me a favor. Put your name in the following blanks and read it out loud:

For God so loved _____ that He gave His only Son, that when _____ believes in Him she will not perish but have everlasting life.

God also said in Acts 2:21, "And it shall come to pass that whoever calls on the name of the LORD Shall be saved."

Have you called on Him for the forgiveness of sins and asked Him to be your Lord and Savior? Salvation is only a prayer away.

I'd enjoy hearing your thoughts on Rain Dance. If you need prayer, please feel free to contact me. Maybe you're a Jonica and just need a friend. Or a Stacie and want to tell someone. I'm an e-mail away. Or perhaps you came to Christ recently (maybe reading this book) and you want to share. I'm here.

Contact me:
Joy DeKok PO Box 7542 Rochester, MN 55903
Email: joydekok@charter.net
Or visit my web site at www.raindancebook.com

Links

Post-abortion support:

Healing Hearts Web site: www.healinghearts.org Address:
P.O. Box 7890 Bonney Lake, WA 98390 phone: 360-897-2711
Email: htohhdqs@integrityol.com

Ramah International Web site: ramahinternational.org Address:
1776 Hudson St Englewood, FL 34223 Phone: 941-473-2188 Email:
Sydna@aol.com

Safe Haven Web site: www.safehavenministries.com
Rachel's Vineyard Ministries Phone: 1-877-HOPE-4-ME Email:
rachel@rachelsvineyard.org

Victims Of Choice, Inc. Web site: www.victomsofchoice.com
Address: PO Box 815 Naperville, IL 60566-0815 Phone: 888-267-3998
Email: VictimsOfChoice@covad.net

Operation Outcry Web site: www.txjf.org Address: 8122 Data-
point, Suite 812 San Antonio, Texas 78229 Phone: 210-614-7157 Fax
number: 210-614-6656 Email: info@txjf.org

Infertility support:

Hannah's Prayer Ministries Address: PO Box 168 Hanford, California 93232-0168 Phone/fax: 775-852-9202 Email: Hannahs@Hannah.org

Stepping Stones Web site: www.bethany.org/step Address: c/o Bethany Christian Services PO Box 294 901 Eastern Ave NE Grand Rapids, MI 49501-0294. phone: 1-800-BETHANY

Printed in the United States
67911LVS00003B/136-207